PUFFIN BOOKS

Editor: K

THE LOTH

It was the year 1736, and in
Sandy Maxwell, working ou
Edinburgh lawyer, was bored to death. He didn't know
what he *did* want to do for a living, and it never occurred to him that his special knowledge of smuggling
on the notorious 'Lothian run' would help him find
his true vocation.

Then he met Deryck Gilmour, an officer of the
Special Investigations branch of the Customs service,
and he became involved in a life filled with action, yet
requiring brainpower and reasoning, for the apparently
simple task of tracking down the smuggler Robertson
presented more difficulties and dangers every day, since
the treason-mongering Jacobites and the Edinburgh mob
became involved as well.

Mollie Hunter really knows Edinburgh and the surrounding countryside, and her feeling for time and
place makes this an unusually convincing and exciting
historical story. Her other books in Puffins are *The
Kelpie's Pearls, The Spanish Letters* and one for younger
readers, *Patrick Kentigern Keenan.*

For readers of eleven and over.

The Lothian Run

Mollie Hunter

Puffin Books
in association with Hamish Hamilton

Puffin Books: a Division of Penguin Books Ltd
Harmondsworth, Middlesex, England
Penguin Books Australia Ltd, Ringwood, Victoria, Australia

—

First published in the U.S.A. 1970
Published in Great Britain by Hamish Hamilton 1971
Published in Puffin Books 1974

—

—

Made and printed in Great Britain by
C. Nicholls & Company Ltd
Set in Linotype Granjon

To

JOHN DRUMMOND NESS

Dominie of Innerwick School

and to

MABLE NESS

Scriptwriters Extraordinary!

Contents

1. The Case of George Robertson

FROM a window high up in one of the tall tenement buildings of Edinburgh's High Street, Sandy Maxwell looked out on to the bright sunshine of an August day. Behind him, like a small dusty prison-cell, lay the deed-room of Lawyer Wishart's office. Before him in a brawling panorama of activity was spread the freedom of the city. And Sandy, that morning, was keenly aware of the contrast.

Hating the very sight of the black deed-boxes that hemmed him in, his gaze quested hungrily over the life and colour in the street below, and picked out a tall young man striding westward towards him. There was something unusual in his appearance, and Sandy could not place at first what this was, but presently he realized what had caught his notice.

The young man's coat of plain, dark-blue silk was cut to sit well on broad shoulders and there was a certain spare elegance in his appearance which declared him, undeniably, a gentleman, but despite this he walked with a long, lithe stride which was quite unlike the fashionable mincing walk of the times. Also, even from that distance it was possible to see that his face was bronzed to an equally unmodish degree.

Nevertheless, Sandy decided, there was a vastly dashing effect in the contrast between the bronze of the fellow's face and the white of his neat tie-wig – and was checked at this point in his thoughts by a sound coming from behind him. With a quick, guilty move away from the window he turned to see the opening of the door between the deed-room and Mr Wishart's personal office.

The man who appeared in the opened doorway had a

face rather like that of an elderly sheep, long and pale, and pouched over many wrinkles, but with much experience and a certain kindliness in it. A lawyer's gown drooped from his bony shoulders and with long hands he clutched the black folds of this, scarecrowlike, around himself. The gaze he bent on Sandy was stern, and he spoke in a voice that matched his look.

'Well, Sandy, you have had time to think over what I said to you. Are you still determined to be a fool?'

'I am not a fool, Mr Wishart,' Sandy protested. 'I know quite well what I am doing.'

'All laddies of sixteen are fools,' the elderly man said brusquely. 'It is just something that has to be beaten out of them, but you will be a bigger fool than most if you persist in this nonsensical idea of wanting to break the articles of your apprenticeship with me.'

'I do mean to persist, sir,' Sandy told him stubbornly. 'I have quite made up my mind that the law is not for me.'

Chin squared, defiance sparking from grey eyes deep-set under strong, jutting brows, he glowered at his employer, and with mounting impatience Wishart said,

'If you are not a fool, Sandy, you are at the very least an ungrateful puppy! You know very well that Bankton Farm gives your father only a lean living and that he has had to scrape every penny of income from it to pay for your education – an education, mark you, that your brother Archie never had!'

'Archie is content on the farm,' Sandy pointed out. 'He has never wanted anything but to continue working there.'

'And what do *you* want?' Wishart demanded. 'Tell me plainly if you can, Sandy Maxwell!'

'I want to be free to choose for myself what I will do.' Firmly Sandy stated his credo, but Wishart only stared uncomprehendingly and repeated,

'Choose for yourself! What rebellious rubbish is this?'

'It is not rubbish,' Sandy insisted. 'I am not the only son nowadays who feels he cannot blindly pursue a career chosen for him by his father. After all, Mr Wishart, this is the year 1736! The times are changing, and –'

'Changing indeed,' Wishart exploded, his frayed patience suddenly snapping, 'when a boy of your age questions his elders' decisions and turns up his nose at the chance to enter a gentleman's profession!'

'Sir!' As angry as the lawyer himself now, Sandy faced recklessly up to him. 'I do not care a fig whether I am a gentleman or a churl. There are better measures than rank for judging a man's worth!'

'*So!*' His breath coming hard through his nostrils and a kind of horrified dismay beginning to replace the anger in his face, Wishart looked Sandy over from his queue of untidy brown hair to his stout country shoes. 'This is the kind of revolutionary cant young people talk nowadays, is it!'

'I – I am sorry if my views have offended.' Abashed by the effect he had created, Sandy muttered an apology that Wishart acknowledged only by a curt little nod, and still groping for words, Sandy went on, 'You have told me often enough, sir, that I have a good brain. But I – I also have an active body and I want to – I want –'

A girl's voice calling, 'Father! Father, where are you?' broke into his stumbled explanation, and without waiting to hear the end of it, Wishart called back, 'Yes, Isobel. What is it?'

He turned away into his own office again, and through the connecting door Sandy glimpsed Isobel Wishart's flowered dress and the scarlet ribbons that trimmed the cap she wore perched on her fair curls. As Wishart advanced to meet her, she told him, 'There is a gentleman here asking urgently to see you, Father.'

The visitor appeared beside her as she spoke, and with surprised interest Sandy recognized the tall young man who had intrigued his curiosity a few moments before. Over his shoulder Wishart called, 'Close that door, Sandy!' And affably to his visitor he said, 'Pray do me the honour to introduce yourself, Mr – Mr –'

'Gilmour,' the visitor said, 'Deryck Gilmour, Special Investigations officer in the service of His Majesty's Customs.'

He extended a paper held ready in his hand and Sandy closed the door on the words, 'My credentials to the Lothian run, sir.'

'*The Lothian run.*' Sandy leaned against the closed door, thinking of the words. He knew them well. Everyone who lived in Fife or the Lothians knew the name the Customs men gave to the smuggling routes that ended in the little ports on the north and south shores of the Firth of Forth. But what had happened on the Lothian run to bring a Special Investigations officer to see Wishart in Edinburgh? For that matter, what was a Special Investigations officer? He had never heard of *that* branch of Customs before.

Soundlessly he opened the door the slightest crack again, and with amusement heard Gilmour say – as if in answer to the same sort of remarks from Wishart, 'Few people have, sir, since our work is by its nature, secret. And in any case, we are a comparitively new breed in the Service.'

His voice was an extremely cool and assured one, Sandy thought, and decided that his intonation placed him as being a Scot – although possibly one who had spent some considerable time away from his native home.

Wishart said something that he could not catch, and of Gilmour's reply to this he heard only, '. . . in the case of the smuggler, George Robertson. And it is now suspected by our Head Office that he could not have carried out the robbery in the first place without the co-operation of some corrupt official in the local Customs service.'

Quietly Sandy closed the door. Mr Wishart had a habit of

striding about as he talked, and if he noticed that the deed-room door was not properly closed –!

It was, of course, a highly reprehensible matter to eavesdrop on a conversation between his employer and a client – but it was satisfactory, all the same, to have proved he was right in thinking there was something unusual about this enviably dashing Mr Gilmour! Smiling at the thought, he pushed the dispute between himself and Wishart temporarily into the back of his mind, and walking over to the window again, began to piece together his own knowledge of '. . . the case of the smuggler, George Robertson.'

With his back strategically placed against the light from the window of his own office, Wishart studied the face of his visitor and decided it was not one which revealed much of its owner's thoughts. There was shrewd intelligence in the greenish eyes, and the lean, aquiline features were strong. The long mouth had humour in it, but this human emotion apart, the face had a schooled stillness which, to a man of his volatile nature, was disconcerting. To cover this feeling he said in his most precise, legalistic voice,

'I think, sir, we should first verify that we have the same set of facts about Robertson. Agreed?'

'Agreed.' Gilmour nodded.

'To summarize briefly then,' Wishart continued. 'In January this year he and another smuggler by the name of Andrew Wilson robbed the Collector of Customs on the Lothian run of a large sum in notes and gold. They were arrested for this crime and condemned to death. They attempted to escape from the Tolbooth prison in company with a horse-thief – a fellow called Rattray. Rattray was successful in this, but the other two were caught in the act. Shortly afterwards, however, Robertson did manage to escape from the church of St Giles, to which he and Wilson had been taken to hear their execution sermon preached. Wilson was duly hung a few days after that, but Robertson is still free.'

'And to complete your summary,' Gilmour took him up, 'I have now been assigned to recapture him. And that, sir, is the whole purpose of my visit to you, for I have been told that there is no one in Edinburgh better fitted to give me the kind of help I require at this stage in my assignment.'

Wishart laughed, with unconvincing modesty. 'You flatter me, Mr Gilmour,' he protested.

'Perhaps my informant was the flatterer,' Gilmour returned coolly. 'His recommendation was based on the opinion that you have a longer nose, a sharper eye, and a wider ear for gossip than anyone else in Edinburgh!'

For a moment Wishart looked as if he did not know whether to be pleased or annoyed at this description of himself. He gave himself time to think by walking over to his desk and seating himself behind it, then warily he asked,

'Who was your informant, Mr Gilmour?'

'A very eminent personage,' Gilmour told him, 'and as well as thinking you would be able to give me the kind of assistance I need, Mr Wishart, he inclined to think you would be willing to do so. You are, he told me, a very loyal adherent of the House of Hanover, and consequently a staunch and valued supporter of Government.'

'A Very Eminent Personage, eh?' Wishart repeated, a gratified expression replacing his wariness and his tone giving capital letters to the words. 'Eh – would that be – would that be, by any chance, Mr Gilmour –'

'His Grace, the Duke of Argyll,' Gilmour supplied gravely, not by a twitch of a muscle revealing his amusement at the smugness of the smile growing on Wishart's face.

'You move in high circles, Mr Gilmour,' the lawyer said reverently. 'Aye, high circles!' The beam of pleasure on his face widened, and complacently he added, 'One does one's poor best of course, sir, and maybe gains a little reputation thereby. And it is true that one has been able to render a small political service to the Government every now and then . . . His Grace of Argyll, you say? Well, well!'

He sat in smiling silence for a moment and then said slowly, 'Well, I shall certainly do all I can to help you, Mr Gilmour, but Geordie Robertson has been gone to earth these past four months and I fear you'll not find him now.'

A little wearily, as if he had heard this kind of statement too often, Gilmour said, 'No man can disappear utterly, Mr Wishart, for every life leaves traces of some kind behind it and it is by these traces that a fugitive can be tracked down. This much I have learned in my work. Furthermore, I have also learned that the official record is only the bare bones of a case. The meat of it is in the small detail, the observation of some odd little circumstance that may have become the subject of gossip although it has escaped official notice. And that, sir, is the kind of thing I hope to discover from you!'

'The odd circumstance, eh?' Wishart mused. He offered his snuff-box to Gilmour and when the latter declined, dosed himself liberally from it. Recovering from the sneeze this produced he said thoughtfully, 'Well, d'ye know, sir, there *was* an odd sort of thing about Robertson's first attempt to escape – the one that failed.'

'Yes?' Suddenly alert, Gilmour invited, 'Tell me about it, sir.'

Wishart leaned back in his chair. 'First of all,' he said slowly, 'it was not Robertson who arranged that escape. It was Rattray, the horse-thief. Did you know that?'

'No.' Gilmour shook his head. 'There was only the briefest account of it supplied to us by the prison authorities.'

'Then listen to this,' Wishart told him. 'It was Rattray who managed to have the tools needed for the escape smuggled into the prison, *but he did not use them to break a way*

15

out from his own cell! Instead, he cut his way through the
floor of his cell into the one beneath, where Robertson and
Wilson were kept, and the three of them used the tools to
break a hole in the outer wall of that cell. Rattray was first
out through this hole and Robertson tried to follow him, but
Wilson insisted on going next. However, Wilson was a big
man – an extraordinar' big man, Mr Gilmour – and the gap
was too small to allow him through. He stuck fast in it, and
it was the noise he made trying to free himself that brought
the turnkeys down on him and Robertson.'

'How did you come by all these details?' Gilmour asked
curiously.

'Ach, they are common knowledge now.' Wishart shrugged. 'But they were not hard to discover in the first place for
anyone who inclines to be a wee thing curious by nature, as
I am. It so happens, you see, that I have a young articled
clerk – a country lad by the name of Maxwell – who has
some slight acquaintance with both Rattray and Robertson.
All I had to do was to invent an excuse for him to visit a
client of mine in the prison the next day, and he soon fer-
reted out the story for me.'

'And Rattray did not try to break out through the wall of
his own cell,' Gilmour remarked. 'Is that your odd circumstance?'

'It is!' Wishart assured him. 'Very odd! It put both time
and danger on Rattray's escape to cut through into the
smugglers' cell and break out from there, yet Jim Rattray is
the meanest-minded man alive and a vicious coward into
the bargain. Why should he have taken that extra danger on
himself when he could have escaped just as easily from his
own cell?'

'Could it be a case of "honour among thieves"?' Gilmour asked doubtfully. 'These people have their own
strange codes of behaviour, Mr Wishart.'

'Aye, but Rattray has no honour even to his own kind,'

Wishart said derisively. 'He'd sell his mother for tallow, that one – although, mind you, there was a queer kind of honour between the two smuggler fellows. I saw it at work for myself on the day that Robertson finally did escape – and man, I can tell you it was a moving sort of thing in its own way!'

'So you were in St Giles that day,' Gilmour commented.

'I was.' Wishart nodded. 'With my wife and my daughter Isobel, and all my clerks, and all of us in our best Sabbath black, fearing the Lord and expecting no evil. Then in comes Robertson and Wilson between their guards, and of course we all took a good look at them to see if it was true what they were saying in the town about Wilson.'

'What were they saying?' Gilmour asked quickly. 'Leave out no detail, Mr Wishart.'

'Why, just that Wilson blamed himself for the failure of the jail-break,' Wishart told him. 'Robertson could easily have got through the gap after Rattray that night, you see, and it was being said in the town that Wilson had moped ever since over spoiling Robertson's chance of escape.'

Understanding had been dawning on Gilmour's face as the lawyer spoke, and now he said, 'I confess I had wondered why Wilson gave up his own opportunity to escape from the church in order to pin down Robertson's guards that day!'

'Well, now you know,' Wishart commented. 'They were friends, these two, you see – great friends, and Wilson was a man of fearful strength. He had a debt to pay back to Geordie Robertson – a life for a life, as you might say – and that was how he paid it.

'He just seized hold of his own two guards suddenly and yelled, *"Run, Geordie! Run!"* Then he pinned down a third man with his teeth – with his teeth, Mr Gilmour! My wife fainted at that point, but Isobel and my clerks were standing up on their seats yelling with excitement, and I did a wee bit of yelling myself, I confess! Geordie took a swing at the fourth guard and knocked him down, and then he was running away out of the church as fast as the hammers of hell – if you'll excuse the expression – and half the congregation tripping up the guards when they tried to run after him!'

He paused for breath, grinning a little at his recollections of the scene, but Gilmour's face remained serious. 'So,' he observed, 'the mob is on the side of the smugglers!'

'The smugglers are heroes to them – heroes!' Wishart declared. 'You will have no one on your side at all except the Customs men of the Lothian run!'

'And even these I cannot count on,' Gilmour said wryly, 'until I have discovered which is the corrupt one who gave Robertson the information that enabled him to waylay the Collector on his rounds.'

Frowning, he paced a few turns of the room, and presently he went on, 'I think your "odd circumstance" about Rattray can be dismissed, Mr Wishart. The proceeds of the robbery were never recovered, and it seems likely that Robertson bribed his way into the Tolbooth escape plan by promising Rattray a share in that money.'

'Greed as a motive would certainly be more consistent with Rattray's character than *noblesse oblige*,' Wishart admitted dryly.

'And that being so,' Gilmour told him, 'I must look for my first lead in Robertson himself. I will need a description of him, of course, and if you can oblige me in that . . .'

'Indeed I can,' Wishart said, 'for I observed him closely at his trial.' With a resumption of his precise, legal tones he continued, 'Robertson is a small man, about five foot five inches in height, and of a wiry strength in build. His skin is a sun-burned sallow, and he has sharp, thin features marked with a scar running from his right temple to his lower right jaw.'

'An excellent description,' Gilmour approved. 'And now, as to his nature – how would you estimate that?'

'He is a violent man,' Wishart said promptly. 'Also, he is very cunning – though I judge his intelligence to be a shallow one.'

With another nod of approval Gilmour asked, 'And his habits?'

'There,' Wishart admitted, 'I am not so sure. I know that he was born and bred in Fife and that he commonly berthed his boat in the port of Anstruther in that county, although he also frequented the ports on the Lothian side of the Firth of Forth.'

As if thinking aloud, Gilmour muttered, 'There is a Customs post at Anstruther . . .'

He stood silent for several moments with his head bent in thought, then looking up again he said decisively, 'From what you say, Mr Wishart, it seems that I am most likely to find the traitor to the Service in one of the Customs Houses in Fife, and since I cannot mount a really effective search for Robertson until I have uncovered this man, I think that my next move must be to proceed there immediately.'

'Not immediately, sir,' Wishart protested. 'You must take dinner with us before you go.'

'I could not dream of imposing myself –' Gilmore began, but firmly Wishart over-ruled him. 'Mistress Wishart will be delighted to entertain you – delighted,' he declared. 'And if there is anything more I can do for you, you must not hesitate to mention it.'

'There *is* a further service I was about to ask you,' Gilmour admitted. 'Would you consider, sir, acting as a sort of listening-post for me here in Edinburgh while I am on this assignment? It would be a service, I assure you, that those in authority would have certain reasons to appreciate.'

'Certain reasons?' Wishart grasped quickly at the words. 'Political ones, Mr Gilmour?'

'No, no.' Gilmour shook his head, smiling with good-natured mockery. 'You veteran Hanoverians, I am afraid, see a Jacobite behind every bush!'

'Oh, I grant you, I grant you,' Wishart returned shrewdly. 'But it does seem strange to me that your Head Office should have thought it worthwhile to assign someone of your authority to deal with a common criminal like Robertson!'

Gilmour's smile vanished on the instant, and with his face once more schooled into stillness he said in a curt voice, 'There are reasons for that which cannot be spoken of outside the Service at present.'

'Just as you say.' Wishart nodded, apparently not at all put out by this rebuff. 'Nevertheless, I assure you that you can still rely on me to gather any news that may be going. There's a few folk I can ask, you know – Andrew Monro, the Governor of the Tolbooth, for instance. I could have a crack with him about the gossip he hears from the rogues in his charge. And Jock Dalgleish, the Doomster of the High Court, is a terrible man to gossip. I'll speer a few questions at him. And –'

He stopped abruptly, a sudden light of inspiration dawning on his long sheep-face. 'Here's a thing, Mr Gilmour,' he said slowly. 'That clerk I mentioned to you – Sandy Maxwell – Before you came in I was considering sending him home for a few days' furlough, and it so happens that his home is at Prestonpans, a coastal village about nine miles from Edinburgh where they do a large trade in dredging for oysters.'

He glanced quickly at Gilmour. 'I suppose you know what an important link these inshore fishermen are with the smugglers?'

'Of course.' Gilmour nodded.

'Well,' Wishart continued, 'Prestonpans used to be a great haunt of Robertson's – may still be, for all I know, and young Sandy Maxwell knows every soul in the place. Moreover, he is on friendly terms with the fisher-folk there, and he is a lad that has a very good head on his shoulders. D'ye think . . .'

He hesitated, leaving his questions hanging in the air, and with considerable doubt in his voice Gilmour asked, 'Is he the kind that can keep his own counsel?'

'He has learned discretion in this office – trust me for that!' Wishart said energetically. 'You could rely on him to ask the right kind of questions about Robertson – and to keep the answers he gets to himself.'

'Then I think it might be as well for me to have a look at him,' Gilmour decided. 'I would like, if you do not mind, to form my own estimate of him.'

'A very fair suggestion,' Wishart agreed. 'But hold hard while I write a short note to his father about some private business between us.'

Drawing paper towards himself he bent to the writing of his letter. For several minutes after that the scratch of his quill was the only sound in the room, then lifting his head again he lit a candle preparatory to sealing his letter.

'*Sandy!*' he bellowed in the direction of the deed-room. Then glancing at Gilmour as he picked up his sealing wax, 'You'll find this lad has character, Mr Gilmour,' he promised. 'Maybe more than you bargain for, at that!'

The visitor had gone, Sandy thought, as Wishart's shout brought him jumping up from where he sat in the deed-room. Now he would be able to have it out with Mr Wishart about releasing him from his articles! Unaccountably, for all his eagerness to take up the cudgels again, his heart began to pound at the thought, but nervousness vanished again as he stepped through the door of the deed-room and found Gilmour still in Wishart's office.

With some surprise, he met the cool, appraising look the other turned on him, and then advanced obediently at Wishart's command to stand in front of his desk. He had time to note that the lawyer held a letter in his hand before the words hit him like a blow between the eyes.

'I am sending you home on furlough for a few days, Sandy, while I think over what action to take about you. Here is a letter to your father to explain the situation to him.'

He made no move to take the letter and he did not speak – he could not, or he would have choked on the outraged pride surging up into his throat. He felt himself flush and then go pale again while all the muscles of his face grew tight with anger. When the moment passed he managed to bring out stiffly,

'I am not a bairn to be sent home with a note, sir. I am old enough to speak for myself and I am quite capable of doing so.' Not looking at Gilmour, he added, 'And if you please, I do not care to discuss my personal affairs in front of a stranger.'

He waited for the explosion, but for some reason he could not fathom, Wishart did not seem angry. It almost seemed, in fact, as if he were pleased with the answer he had been given for he half-smiled as he retorted,

'Then we will not discuss them further, Sandy. You will just do as I say!'

There was steel beneath the softness of the tone he used. Sandy, who had had cause to recognize this tone in the past, recognized it now again and called a temporary but still hostile truce. Holding out his hand for the letter, he said coldly,

'Very well, sir, I defer to your authority – but I pray you take notice that I do not yield my opinions also.'

He turned away, not giving Wishart time to reply, and so, missed the look that passed between him and Gilmour and the nod the latter gave.

'Sandy!' Wishart's voice brought him up short in his tracks. 'Mr Gilmour here has no interest in your personal affairs, but he does have something of importance to say to you. Kindly oblige me by giving him your attention for a moment.'

Dourly obedient, Sandy did as he was commanded, and with a grim, inward amusement noted how quickly Gilmour leapt in to bridge the gap of his silence.

'Mr Wishart assures me,' Gilmour began pleasantly 'that you are both discreet and intelligent, and he thinks you might be able to help me with some confidential inquiries I am making about a certain person. Would you like to try?'

Geordie Robertson! He is after Geordie Robertson! The thought flashed into Sandy's mind, but he kept it under control and asked cautiously, 'What person is this, sir?'

'I think you know.' Calmly Gilmour walked towards the deed-room. He pushed the door of it open by a fraction of an inch and immediately a thin ray of light fell across the shadow of a bookcase standing against the wall between the window of Wishart's office and the slightly opened door. With an expressionless face glancing back over his shoulder, Gilmour said,

'Shadows are important, Sandy. Remember that the next time you eavesdrop.'

It was a bad moment, Sandy admitted ruefully to himself. Unable to control the flush of embarrassment rising to his face, he looked away from Gilmour and found Wishart watching him with a mixture of reproof and amusement in his expression. The lawyer's glance met his own and he said dryly,

'You are fairly caught now, Sandy. Best come down off your high horse and do what you're told for a change, eh?'

'Yes, sir.' Shamefaced, Sandy muttered agreement, and turning back to Gilmour asked in the same subdued voice, 'T'is Geordie Robertson, the smuggler, you are interested in, is it not, sir?'

'It is,' Gilmour confirmed. 'I want to find him and your

inquiries might help me to do so – but you must be as secret as the grave about your reason for making them. Can you promise me that?'

There it was again, Sandy thought resentfully – that suggestion that he was no more to be trusted than an unbreeched bairn! The shamefaced feeling dropped away from him, and with all his accustomed spirit he answered,

'Certainly I can promise, sir, and will do so if you wish. But there is no need for oaths when I am already bound by professional secrecy.'

There was a sudden approving chuckle from Wishart at this, and Gilmour also smiled, as if well pleased by his reply.

'Very well, then,' Gilmour said. 'Here is what you must do.'

2. A Spy, and a Hanging

MISTRESS WISHART presided over dinner, her large figure straining after elegance in a half-hooped gown of grey silk. In deference to the guest, Isobel also had changed her flowered morning-gown for a silk one which matched the quite startling blue of her eyes, and both ladies smiled as Gilmour took complimentary note of their attire.

'We follow the Paris fashions here, sir,' Mistress Wishart explained complacently. 'The London modes seem dull and rather ugly to us.'

'Indeed, the London ladies are not noted for their taste in dress,' Gilmour acknowledged. 'Also, they paint too much.'

His eyes rested briefly on the glowing fairness of Isobel Wishart's complexion, and with amusement, Sandy noted the direction of his glance. As a boarder in the Wishart household he had shared many meals at which young men had been smitten by the charm of Isobel's beauty, and this

Gilmour, he thought, was not going to be an exception to the rule.

'Our tastes in wine are French also, you will note,' Wishart remarked, pouring claret with a liberal hand.

'Then I give you an appropriate toast,' Gilmour responded. *'Aux belles Écossaises!'* He bowed, glass in hand to Mistress Wishart and Isobel.

'Certes, sir, you are gallant!' Mistress Wishart preened herself on the compliment, smoothing the ample folds of her grey silk, but Gilmour's eyes were now resting too long on Isobel for comfort, and with a blush rising to her face she remarked tartly, 'Perhaps "forward" would be a better description of Mr Gilmour!'

Sandy was not sure, but at that point he thought he saw a movement of the grey silk which indicated that Mistress Wishart had kicked her daughter under the table. Nor would it be for the first time, he thought, stifling a laugh at the idea. Mistress Wishart tried hard, but her match-making plans were always being spoiled by Isobel's independent attitude. Still, she was expert at drawing young men out to talk about themselves. He continued listening intently to the conversation, curious to learn as much as he could about anyone who followed such an odd pursuit as 'Special Investigator', but to his disappointment Gilmour made no mention of this occupation.

Instead, at Mistress Wishart's prompting, he talked of the fashionable amusements of London, and with Mr Wishart he discussed the University of St Andrews where, apparently, he had been educated. Briefly also he mentioned later studies in Leyden and Paris, but not a word was said about Customs, or smuggling, or the pursuit of criminals.

Boredom crept in on Sandy. His mind wandered from the conversation and he was about to write it off as entirely unprofitable when something happened to alter his opinion.

Dinner was almost over when the incident took place.

Mistress Wishart and Isobel were retiring to carry out the ritual of teamaking, and as they swished away from the table, Wishart said in a low voice,

'A point we have not discussed, sir. Robertson is a violent man, yet you appear to go unarmed.'

'A point I have not mentioned,' Gilmour said as quietly. 'My boyhood's home was in the little town of Doune, in Perthshire, and the most skilful gunsmiths in Europe practice their craft there.'

He slipped a hand inside the left breast of his well-cut coat and quickly withdrew it again. On his palm rested the smallest pistol Sandy had ever seen – a toy, he would have called it, with a total length from butt to barrel-point of less than six inches. It was double-barrelled also – another marvel, Sandy thought, and watched in fascination as Gilmour snapped one of its tiny hammers back and then delicately uncocked it again.

'A pistol does not have to be large to be effective,' he commented, still preserving his quiet voice. 'Thus my old gunsmith friends in Doune have enabled me to remain presentable in the drawing-rooms I sometimes have to frequent, without depriving myself of the armour my occupation requires.'

With a nod that acknowledged Wishart's appreciative comment, he slipped the pistol back inside his coat where it rested, Sandy noticed, without the least indication of a bulge in the material. Looking up, Gilmour went on,

'A good riding-horse is my only requirement now, Mr Wishart. Can you direct me to a suitable stable?'

'Hoseah Eastgate – the man who runs the Edinburgh to London stagecoach service – he will supply you,' Wishart told him. He turned to Sandy. 'Your road out of the city matches the one Mr Gilmour must take. Guide him to Hoseah's place, and remind them there that only the best will do for a client of mine.'

Gilmour rose from the table. 'If you will make my excuses to the ladies, then . . .'

'Certainly, certainly!' Wishart rose with him. They walked to the outer door of the house, talking in low voices that were evidently not intended for Sandy's hearing, and following at a respectful distance, he caught a snatch of a different conversation through the half-opened door of the drawing-room.

'. . . *and if you act coldly to young men of such good estate as he appears to be, you will be left on the shelf, miss, I warn you.*' That was Mistress Wishart's voice, low and complaining, but Isobel's reply came as clear and decisive as iron striking iron. '*I will marry a man for his worth to me, ma'am, and not for his credit at the bank!*'

And that, Sandy thought with a sudden rush of fellow-feeling for Isobel, was exactly the right reply for a modern young miss of spirit!

Chuckling inwardly he followed Gilmour down the dim winding stairway that served all the floors of the tenement in common, and as they emerged, blinking, into the sun-lit bustle of the High Street, pointed eastward down its cobbled slope.

'This way, sir,' he announced, and continued in his role of guide as they moved off together. 'That is the Lawnmarket, where the country people come to sell their produce.' A sweep of his arm indicated the higgledy-piggledy collection of booths set up in the part of the thoroughfare just ahead. 'And that building just beyond is the Tolbooth jail.'

'A monstrous-looking creation!' Gilmour's gaze shifted from the bustle in the Lawnmarket to the Tolbooth towering above it, and he slowed his pace the better to examine the structure of the jail.

As black and grim-looking as any building of its purpose could be, it stood right in the path of the High Street's traffic, which had to divide to flow through a narrow alley on one side of it and a rather broader one on the other. A row of ramshackle buildings several stories high leaned crazily against its western wall, with shops of various kinds occupying their ground floors. Ribbons, gloves, and other trifles were the kind of goods on display there, and with amusement Gilmour noted the brisk trade being done by the vendors of these gew-gaws.

'A strange place to come for the purchase of folderols,' he said, smiling.

''Tis not all rubbish that sells there,' Sandy objected. 'Look, there is Allan Ramsay's bookshop – you have heard of Allan Ramsay, the Jacobite poet, surely, Mr Gilmour?'

'I believe I have – *The Tea-Table Miscellany*, *The Gentle Shepherd* – are these not his works?'

'Aye, but I like *The Gentle Shepherd* best. I have seen it bravely performed at –'

'Have you, now!' Gilmour's voice interrupted him, with cool disinterest in his comment. He halted abruptly, a hand on Sandy's arm checking his progress also, his eyes on the figure of a man idly leafing through a trayful of second-hand books outside Ramsay's shop.

'St Clair!' he said softly. 'The Colonel himself! Well, of all the –'

He checked in mid-sentence, and in one swift motion drew Sandy with him into a narrow alley opening off their side of the High Street. From there he continued to stare at the man outside the bookshop and Sandy stared also, slightly resenting Gilmour's high-handed ordering of his movements but curiosity keeping him quiet.

They were some fifteen feet from the object of their stares, with the traffic of the street forming a shifting screen between them, and there was nothing remarkable about him that Sandy could see. He was of medium height and slightly built, with a full dark wig falling luxuriantly down on either side of a thin-featured face. There was a French style to the cut of his coat but, Sandy decided, with Paris fashions so popular for men as well as women in Edinburgh, there was nothing odd in that. He was about to say so to Gilmour when the other forestalled his comment by asking quietly:

'Sandy, what's the easiest way you know of passing a message unnoticed?'

Sandy's mind flashed back to school-days and the surreptitious passing of notes between the leaves of Latin grammars. 'Between·the pages of a book,' he said promptly.

The slight smile lifting the corners of Gilmour's mouth became deeper. Softly, as if speaking to himself, he murmured, 'The answer any competent spymaster might have given!'

'Sir?' Sandy glanced at him, doubting whether he had heard correctly, and still smiling his enigmatic smile Gilmour answered, 'In other words, the simple method is always preferable to the complicated one – there is less to go wrong with it!'

The question, *'Is this man a spy?'* rose briefly to Sandy's mind, but he could not seriously entertain the idea of encountering a spy ouside the pages of a romance and so he changed the question to ask,

'What is it that's worth noting about this man, sir?'

'Well, for one thing,' Gilmour told him slowly, 'he is thought to be in France at this moment. And for another, his presence usually spells trouble for certain people.'

'What people?' Sandy demanded.

Gilmour flicked him a glance of half-veiled greenish eyes. 'That,' he said blandly, 'is not a question that is in my province to answer.'

Brief as his glance had been, there was an authority in it that set up a barrier to further questions, and wryly acknowledging this to himself, Sandy turned his attention back to the dark-wigged man. Gilmour did not offer to speak again and a few minutes later the man turned from the book-tray and sauntered off westwards up the High Street.

Almost immediately, the place he had occupied was taken by an elderly clergyman, and Sandy turned to Gilmour to see if he would make any remark about this. Gilmour continued silent, however. For a moment or two longer he remained motionless, his eyes on the clergyman leafing through the books the dark-wigged man had handled, and then suddenly he broke the spell of his concentration.

'We will go on now,' he announced, and motioning Sandy out of the alley with him, he set off again down the High Street. Sandy fell in alongside him, matching his steps to those of Gilmour's long, easy stride. Like this they walked for a short distance without further speech, and then abruptly Gilmour said,

'You were present at the hanging of the smuggler, Andrew Wilson.'

It was a statement, not a question, and thoroughly taken aback by it, Sandy could think of nothing to say except a rather lame-sounding, 'How do *you* know I was there?'

'Boys like you always take French leave for events like that.'

It was such an obvious piece of reasoning, Sandy realized, that the need to explain it merited the scorn Gilmour put into his voice. Wincing under this, he waited for the next remark, and Gilmour went on,

'That was the last occasion on which Robertson was seen in public. I want you to describe it for me.'

Sandy hesitated, frowning a little as he tried to assess what was in the other's mind now. It was strange, he thought, that Gilmour should want to hear his account of this rather than Mr Wishart's, and with some caution he asked,

'Would you not rather speak to Mr Wishart about that, sir? He is much better at describing things than I am.'

'Not this sort of thing.' Gilmour met his doubtful look

with one of ironic amusement. 'Mr Wishart would most certainly have found himself a safe point for observing the rioting which took place that day, but you would just as certainly have been in the forefront of the action! Besides which –' his ironic smile deepened, '– you have as much relish for gory scenes as any other of your age, have you not? You will enjoy describing this one!'

That was not strictly true, Sandy thought, suddenly haunted again by the memory of Wilson's face as he climbed the execution ladder – poor, stupid Drew Wilson with all his great strength bound down, and all of a sudden looking pathetically like a big, tethered ox stumbling into the slaughter-house! Involuntarily he shivered at the memory, and as if guessing at the reason for this Gilmour asked,

'Did you know the man well?'

'Quite well,' Sandy admitted. 'He and Geordie Robertson often used to put in at Prestonpans to buy Pandores. Drew Wilson had a perfect passion for them.'

'Pandores?'

'That's the name of the kind of oyster they dredge for there,' Sandy explained.

The movement of the crowded street jostled them apart momentarily, and as he struggled to regain his place beside Gilmour, Sandy wondered why he had bothered to mention such an irrelevant detail as Drew Wilson's liking for Pandores. The oyster-fishing season ended in April of each year, of course, and it was on an April day that Wilson had been hung. He wondered if the two things had become linked in his mind, and shivered again to recall how incongruously the thin, sweet sunshine of that April had fallen on the face of the hanging man.

Gilmour's eyes were resting on him in question and he began hesitantly, 'They brought him down to the place of execution in the Grassmarket at four o'clock in the afternoon, and the crowd – the crowd was very silent, and pitiful for him. But they were excited under their silence for there was a rumour that Robertson intended to rescue him from the scaffold.'

'Was that,' demanded Gilmour, 'because Wilson had sacrificed his own chance of escape by holding on to Robertson's guards in St Giles's church?'

Sandy turned a curious face to him. 'Did Mr Wishart tell you about that?'

'I will ask the questions,' Gilmour told him curtly.

The barrier was there in his eyes again, that same barrier of authority which had blocked Sandy's curiosity over the mysterious St Clair, and reluctantly deferring to it once again, he answered,

'Yes, sir, it was. Everyone knew of the friendship between them and they could not believe that Geordie would let his friend die after what had happened in St Giles. The rumour was so strong, in fact, that the Captain of the City Guard – Captain John Porteous – got special permission from the Magistrates to turn his men out in force for the execution, and the crowd grew very restless when he came marching down to the scaffold with the soldiers.'

He checked himself here to explain, 'Captain Porteous is a most brutal man, sir, and the mob has always hated him.'

Gilmour merely nodded to this and Sandy went on, 'Well, sir, Robertson did have a rescue planned, but he delayed it till the very last moment – hoping, I suppose, to have the element of surprise on his side. He sprang on to the scaffold at the head of a band of men armed with cutlasses, just after Wilson was turned off the ladder, and tried to cut him down off the rope. The soldiers fought him off and that made the crowd angry. They began pelting the soldiers with stones, and one of these hit Captain Porteous on the temple. He lost his temper and ordered the soldiers to fire a volley at the crowd, and then –'

'Were you afraid when that happened?' Gilmour interrupted.

Sandy stared at him. 'Man, I was at the front of the crowd,' he exclaimed. 'Right under the muzzles of their muskets. Who would not have been afraid? There were people falling and bleeding and dying all round me – all over the Grassmarket. I could hear bairns and women screaming, and people howling over their dead as they tried to drag them away. But after that, there was a great, bloody stramash of a fight, with the soldiers trying to break away back to their barracks, firing volley after volley at the crowd as they went, and the crowd itself going mad pelting at them with more and more stones, and I was not afraid then, I can tell you! I brought down a Guardsman myself with a stone *and* knocked the musket out of the hand of another!'

'But I suppose you lost sight of Robertson in this "stramash".' Gilmour's tone was disappointed and slightly sarcastic, and with a feeling of triumph at being able to contradict him, Sandy said,

'I did not! I saw him running through the West Port into Portsburgh before I –'

'Wait, wait!' Gilmour told him. 'I do not know the city. You will have to make these terms clear to me.'

Sandy considered this instruction and then explained, 'The wall that encloses the city, sir, forms a boundary to the west side of the Grassmarket, and the West Port is the gate that is set into this part of the wall. Portsburgh is a city suburb which is a most notorious haunt of thieves and other rogues, and it lies just beyond the West Port.'

'Did you tell anyone you saw Robertson headed for it?' Gilmour asked.

'I was about to mention that when you interrupted me,' Sandy pointed out. 'I told Mr Wishart of it when we were discussing the riot afterwards in the office.'

'Good!' Gilmour exclaimed. 'Very good!' He saw the

questioning look Sandy gave him and explained briefly.
'That will link up with an arrangement I have with Mr
Wishart.'

'It will take a very good arrangement indeed to catch
Geordie Robertson,' Sandy told him. 'He is cunning, and
he has a vicious streak in him, too.'

He was feeling pleased over having managed eventually
to hold his own in discussion with someone so self-assured
as Gilmour. The other caught the cheerful note in his voice
and asked sharply,

'Is that a cause for merriment?'

'No, sir – caution!' Sandy answered, and was forced to
postpone the rest of what he had to say as a water-carrier
laden with buckets jostled his way between them.

They had reached the far end of the High Street by this
time, and before them in the east wall of the city loomed
the massive towers supporting the arch of the gate called the
Netherbow Port. The busy traffic of the High Street had to
narrow its stream to pass beneath this arch, and in the tangle
of foot-passengers, sedan-chairs, and high-wheeled country
carts all jostling for precedence there, Sandy was pushed
even farther away from Gilmour.

In the street called Canongate on the further side of the
arch, they caught sight of one another again, and closing
up to Gilmour, Sandy spoke the friendly tail-piece of his
interrupted remark.

'I would watch out for him if I were you, Mr Gilmour.'

In the act of adjusting the tilt his wig had suffered in the
melée under the arch, Gilmour paused to look blankly at
him, then the link snapped into place in his mind. 'Would
you, indeed!' he remarked. His blank look had changed
to the familiar one of ironic amusement, and the sarcasm
also returning to his voice, he added, 'I will bear that in
mind.'

The rebuff intended was plain enough to make Sandy

regret his small, friendly overture and biting back the angry retort that threatened to break from him, he walked on down the Canongate with Gilmour towards the archway that led into Eastgate's stable-yard. As they approached it he could see old Bowdy Jock, the head ostler, leaning against the wall of the arch, and pointing him out to Gilmour, he broke silence at last to say,

'There is Hoseah Eastgate's place, and that old man is his head ostler.'

He turned to the old man then, and in a much warmer tone than he had used to Gilmour, greeted him, 'Aye, Bowdy!'

The old man gaped a toothless grin at him. 'Aye, yourself, Sandy. D'ye bring us business?'

'This gentleman wants a riding horse,' Sandy told him, 'and you are to see it is a good bit of flesh, Bowdy, or Mr Wishart will have something to say about it!'

'Lord save us, ye have me feared!' the old man retorted sarcastically. 'If his money is good, the horse will be good.'

With a jerk of his head and 'This way, sir,' to Gilmour he set off at a shambling trot into the stable-yard beyond the archway, and Sandy would have taken his leave then but Gilmour's hand on his arm checked his move away.

'A moment,' he said. 'Is there any other stagecoach service to London apart from the one provided by this man, Eastgate?'

'There is no one else with enough good horses to make it pay,' Sandy told him, wondering at the reason for the question. 'Hoseah's coaches take passengers, parcels, mails – everything.'

'And his timetables?'

Sandy gave consideration to an idea that had come suddenly to him, and answered absently, 'There is a coach leaves every week – but you could get a proper list of times from Hoseah's advertisement in the *Edinburgh Courant*.'

'That would be useful.' With a nod and a brief word of thanks Gilmour was about to turn away when Sandy decided to test the calculation he had made.

'So you will not be going back to London by sea, Mr Gilmour,' he commented.

Gilmour turned an expressionless face to him. 'You are assuming a great deal, are you not?' he asked, and with seeming innocence Sandy replied,

'No, sir – at least, not any more than you did when you guessed I had been at Wilson's execution.'

'Which means to say . . .?' Gilmour prompted.

'That I deduced you came from London because you wear a coat with a London cut to it and speak like someone well acquainted with the place. Also that you did not come to Edinburgh by coach, or you would have known that Hoseah's is the only service to London. And that leaves only the sea route which – you being a Customs man – you would naturally incline to make your first choice, in any case.'

Gilmour studied him in silence for a few moments before he replied slowly, 'If your reasoning continues as shrewd, your inquiries about Robertson may be of more use than I had anticipated.'

His voice was still expressionless enough to rob the words of the compliment they might have conveyed, but then suddenly and surprisingly he smiled, a wide friendly grin that demolished the barrier he had set up between them. 'All the same,' he added, 'you should remember that the master does not relish the pupil using his own methods against him.'

'You made it very clear that you thought me too young to be taken seriously,' Sandy defended himself. 'I was only trying to show you differently.'

'Eh? Oh, that!' Gilmour looked puzzled, then embarrassed as he recalled the rebuff he had dealt at the Netherbow Port. 'Touch!' he admitted. 'But you must realize that in my profession any new alliance must be subject to some degree of testing!' He held out a hand. 'Pax?'

'Aye, pax!' Sandy agreed. Vigorously he returned the proffered handshake, and immediately pressed home the advantages of peace by asking:

'But why did you want to know about Hoseah's time tables?'

'You are very tenacious!' Half-serious, half-smiling, Gilmour explained, 'This coach-service represents a quick and regular line of communication with my Head Office – and one, also, which is not subject to the uncertainties that bad weather inflicts on ships' sailing times. Therefore it might be important to me. Therefore I find out about it *now*, rather than later. And that, Sandy, is rule one in the profession of investigator. *Never let a piece of information that might be useful slip by you*. Remember that, and you will not go far wrong in the task you have been set.'

'I will remember it,' Sandy promised. They took smiling leave of one another, but as he strode on down the Canongate Sandy realized he could have taken the opportunity of Gilmour's new friendliness to ask further about the mysterious St Clair, and cursed himself heartily for having been so slow. Yet Gilmour had called him shrewd – with his tongue well in his cheek, no doubt!

It was not till he had passed the city limits and struck out into farmland that his thoughts reverted to his own affairs, and looking out over the wind-rippled gold of the oatfields that lined the homeward track, he fingered the letter in his pocket and tried to calculate the effect it would have at home.

Archie would stand by him, of course. He had always been able to count on an elder brother's support from Archie. But what about his mother – so proud of her young Sandy and all his previous book-learning? She would never understand why he wanted to give up the law. She would treat him like a little boy wanting to play truant in the sun instead of a young man striving to find himself in – in what?

As always, at this point in his thoughts, Sandy stopped short with a feeling very like despair in his mind. That was the trouble, he admitted gloomily. The law had become a trap to him, a dim dusty trap where he was slowly being smothered under the dry weight of torts, writs, deeds of conveyance, precognitions – but he had no idea what he wanted to do with himself once he did get free of the trap.

What would his father think about that? Would he call him fool or rogue for throwing up a safe, prosperous career with nothing else in view? Would he think it at all reasonable that a son should want to live independently of his father's plans for him?

He might, Sandy thought cautiously. His father was a forward-thinking man, and by no means so set in his ways as the rest of his generation. Why, he was even willing to try the new scientific methods of farming the Improvers Society had recommended recently, and surely that argued he would be willing to listen to reason!

The thing to do then, he decided, would be to hold on to Mr Wishart's letter until he had had a chance of explaining his views privately to his father. After that – no matter what the outcome of it – he would hand the letter over and do battle or not as the case might be.

The day seemed brighter and the road home to Bankton Farm shorter once he had come to this decision. He began to whistle as he stepped along, and to speculate what the trout-fishing had been like on the River Tyne that summer. If there was a good hatch of fly out, he thought, he would persuade Archie to cast a rod over the river with him that evening after supper. A holiday – even an enforced one with a task imposed on it – might as well be enjoyed!

3. The Honest Horse-Thief

'I was thinking,' Sandy announced through the last mouthful of his next day's dinner, 'of taking a walk down to the harbour this afternoon. Is there anything I can bring you from there, ma'am?'

Mistress Maxwell paused in the act of clearing away the dinner dishes. 'I am not needing anything particular from there just now,' she told him, 'unless you could happen to get me –' She looked quickly around to make sure her husband was not within earshot and finished wistfully, '– a drop of tea perhaps? I do not have much left in the caddy, and you know how much I like my dish of tea.'

Sandy glanced across the table at his brother Archie, and saw the grin that was spreading over his round, red face. He nodded, grinning in reply, and the hounds of mischief fairly loosed now, Archie rose to tower over the small figure of their mother.

'Aha, Mistress Maxwell!' he menaced her. 'Well may you look furtive, ma'am. You know what Mr Maxwell thinks of dealing with smugglers!'

'You know what he thinks of *tea*!' Sandy took up his share of the teasing. In a solemn voice that was a very bad imitation of his father's deep tones he declaimed,

'*Tea is a vile, pernicious drug, foreign to this land and to the stomachs of its inhabitants . . .*'

He rose to his feet, striking a pose that invited his brother to join in the sermon, and hastily composing his cheerful face into solemn lines also, Archie contributed,

'*It poisons the liver, weakens the action of the heart, and thoroughly undermines the constitution of all who indulge in it!*'

'*It is a craving . . .*'
  '*A habit . . .*'
  '*An addiction . . .*'
Shoulder to shoulder, with voices rising in antiphonal chant, they bore down on their mother:

'*Which if not checked by Government legislation,*' Archie droned, '*will eventually ruin the character of our people –*'

'– and present the Scots as a nation of weaklings to the world!'

Quietly from behind him, the sentence was finished by the genuine holder of these beliefs. At the sound of his voice both boys jerked like shot rabbits. They spun around to faced their father and hurriedly Sandy exclaimed,

'It was my fault, sir. I persuaded Archie to the jest.'

'No, sir, the fault is mine,' Archie contradicted, 'I spoke the first word of teasing.'

Mr Maxwell surveyed his sons with a hard and dangerous eye. 'I can never decide,' he remarked, 'whether you two boys sin your souls more by the things you do than by the lies you tell to shield one another from the consequences.'

He gave this comment time to sink in, eyeing each son in turn before his gaze came to rest finally on Archie. In a slightly softer tone then he said, 'Take a look at this, lad, I think we should be starting the oat-harvest tomorrow.'

Archie looked at the little cluster of fleecy white oat-grains lying clean-husked on his palm, and nodded, 'You are right, sir. I had better go and make ready for a sunrise start to the cutting.'

'Good lad!' With a satisfied nod as Archie strode away out of the kitchen, Mr Maxwell turned his attention to Sandy.

'Get you along to Wintonhill Farm,' he ordered. 'Present my compliments to Mr Fairbairn, and ask if I can have the usual loan of his second pair of horse for the oat-harvest to-morrow.'

'Willingly, sir,' Sandy agreed. 'I was thinking of fishing the Tyne up Wintonhill way, in any case.'

A glimmer of a smile crept over Mr Maxwell's stern face. He turned over the lapel of his coat and carefully unhooked two fishing-flies from the underside of the material. 'Try these,' he said, 'Grouse and Claret, and Partridge Hackle. They are the lures the trout are taking just now. Where is your line?'

'I have it here, sir.' Sandy patted the coat pocket holding the fishing line he had searched out as soon as he had reached home the previous day. ''Tis a little frayed, but it should serve a while yet.'

With a smile of thanks for the flies he went out to cut him-self a straight willow stick that would serve as a rod, think-ing as he did so that his plans for his vacation were falling into place very neatly indeed. His father's bark, after all, was really much worse than his bite! It would not be diffi-cult to talk to him when the right opportunity came. And his mother had just given him a perfect motive for asking the kind of question that would turn the conversation at the harbour to smuggling, and so possibly to Robertson!

Gaily swishing his willow stick he strode off on the south-easterly track that pointed to the Lammermuir Hills rising in green fold after green fold with the River Tyne coiling silver across the farmland at their feet, and the three miles to Win-tonhill Farm fell effortlessly away behind him. He would start fishing at the bend of the river enclosing the farm itself, he decided, and with a quick thrill of anticipation at the thought he turned in to the short length of rutted track leading to the farmhouse.

Voices coming from the stable-yard drew him in that direction, and reaching its entrance, he saw Mr Fairbairn

standing by a loose-box holding the halter of his black gelding, while another man moved round it bending double to
run a hand over each hock and lift each hoof. To Sandy's
eye, this other man was acting like a prospective buyer, and
not wishing to interrupt the transaction, he halted where he
was until Mr Fairbairn would be free to speak to him.

He wished he could see the other man's face. There was
something familiar about him although all that showed at
the moment was a bent back! Patiently he waited for the
man to straighten up, and eventually he did so, turning to
speak to Mr Fairbairn as he rose so that Sandy had a clear
view of his face.

It was a clown's face – large, and round in shape, with a
surface that showed a curious mixture of wrinkles and
knobbly, irregular swellings. A curved slit for a mouth,
triangular slits for eyes, and a broad, flat nose gave it the
total effect of a Hallowe'en lantern stuck on top of the
man's long, gangling body, and with surprised distaste,
Sandy realized that he was looking at Jim Rattray, the horse-
thief.

No one, he thought, had ever heard of Rattray buying a
horse! He must have been mistaken in presuming the sale
of the black – or had he? Staring in disbelief, he saw Rattray hand over money to Mr Fairbairn, and the two men
spit on their palms before they sealed the bargain with a
quick hand-clasp. Rattray took the gelding's halter and began to walk it towards the entrance to the stable-yard. A
dozen of his loose-jointed strides brought him to it, with
recognition touching his eyes as they travelled over Sandy
standing there. He nodded a casual greeting.

'A fine day, man.'

'Aye, indeed,' Sandy responded drily, 'but 'tis a strange
one too that sees *you* do an honest trade in horseflesh!'

The grotesque Hallowe'en face looking down at him
froze for an instant with its smile still fixed on the thin,

curving mouth. Then Rattray laughed, but there was no humour in the triangular slits of eyes winking from the bloated mask of his features.

'Ach,' he said easily, 'that last spell of time I spent in Edinburgh's Tolbooth brought the hangman's rope too near my neck for comfort. Live legal, live long, is my rule now!'

He gave a shake to the gelding's halter and continued on his way, and turning to Mr Fairbairn, Sandy saw him thoughtfully weighing in his hand the money he had just been paid. Their eyes met, and slipping the money into his pocket, Fairbairn came towards him.

'You look puzzled, Sandy,' he said. 'Has no one told you about Rattray turning honest trader?'

'I have not had much chance to hear the news of the county yet,' Sandy told him. 'My home leave only started yesterday.' He jerked a thumb in the direction of Rattray's retreating figure. 'But I find it hard to believe in *that* rascal turning honest!'

'So do I,' Fairbairn admitted. 'But the fact remains that he has been willing to pay cash, these three months past, for horses he would have stolen before.'

'And does he sell them as honestly?' Sandy asked curiously.

Fairbairn scratched his head while he thought of this. 'That,' he decided eventually, 'is something I would not like to answer, for he does not seem to be selling to people hereabouts. But he buys only good strong beasts, and for what it is worth, my belief is that he may be shipping them abroad – to the Low Countries, maybe, where there is always a good demand for cavalry mounts. Either that, or he is acting as a middle-man for some other party engaged in the same trade, for *he* certainly did not have two ha' pennies to rub together before his last spell in jail!'

Sandy looked his respect for this shrewd reasoning, and nodding to the willow stick in his hand, Fairbairn asked,

'But what brings you here, Sandy? You look all set for the fishing.'

'I am,' Sandy assured him. 'I am on my way down to Tyne water this very moment, but my father asked me to call and present his compliments to you, and to ask if he may have the usual loan of your second pair of horse for the oat-harvest tomorrow.'

'Indeed he may,' Fairbairn agreed. 'Tell him they will be down first thing tomorrow, with Alec Aitken at their head. I'll away and have a word with Alec now.'

With a smile and a wave that acknowledged Sandy's thanks, he turned towards the row of cottages lying beyond the stable-yard, and still thinking of the earlier part of their conversation, Sandy set off across the half-mile of moor and fields that separated him from the River Tyne at this point.

Rattray, he argued to himself as he went, belonged to the class of rogue that *never* changed its ways. '*Once a horse-thief, always a horse-thief.*' Many a time he had heard his father say that, and it was true, for no one could succeed at that trade unless he had been born and bred to the handling of horses and men like Rattray were proud of their special skills. What then, he wondered, had been the inducement for the fellow to take up honest trading?

He reached the Tyne with this question still very much in his mind, and setting up his rod beside a likely pool, decided that Mr Fairbairn's reasoning held the only possible answer to it. '*Money!*' he muttered aloud, casting a Grouse and Claret skilfully over the pool. Someone, for some reason, was paying Rattray to buy horses for him – and paying him well, too, otherwise he would never have been able to persuade the fellow to forgo the thrill of stealing horses!

Fishing downstream towards the village of Pencaitland, he speculated on the identity of this mysterious 'someone', but could think of no one he knew who would be prepared to take up a business venture with such a known bad character as Rattray. In any case, he reminded himself, it was about Robertson the smuggler he had been told to inquire, and not Rattray the horse-thief. And suddenly found that the two names coming so close together in his mind had recalled something that seemed to justify his curiosity.

Robertson, he remembered, had been involved in the jailbreak that had allowed Rattray to go free from the Tolbooth. Did that not argue a link of some kind between them? And if there was such a link, ought he not to try to trace it by following up this curious business of the horse-thief turned honest trader?

It was a feeble argument, of course. As soon as it took shape in his mind he realized that, and tried to bolster it up by recalling Gilmour's saying, '*Never let a piece of information that might be of use slip by you.*' Even that, however, did not serve to convince him that the supposition he was making had any truth in it, and he would have dismissed it from his mind altogether if he had not seen Rattray again.

It was at Pencaitland it happened. He had reached the bridge that carried the road over the river and through the village, and was fishing the pool under the bridge's arch when he heard the clop of horses' hoofs overhead. The hoofs passed over the bridge, going away from the village, and peering out from under the arch he saw Rattray mounted on Mr Fairbairn's black gelding with two other horses in tow.

Sandy acted on impulse then. Bending to his rod, he slipped the line free. Quickly he untied his cast of flies from the line and hooked them into the back of his lapel again, then throwing the willow aside he coiled the line and thrust it back into his pocket. By the time he had done this Rattray was almost hidden from view by a bend in the road. Seconds later, however, he had him in sight again from the cover of a stand of birch that lined the roadside at this point, and plunging deeper into the wood, he kept on his track with the steady clopping of the horses' hoofs to guide him.

A quarter of a mile farther on the birch wood ended in moorland, but still there was plenty of cover for the moor was ridged and hollowed and there was a thick scattering of gorse on it. Keeping low, Sandy veered away from the road, and from the cover the moor provided, he continued to keep Rattray in sight. It was an easy task, for the road he was following ran southeast in a more or less direct line. There were no side turnings off it, and on the other side of it stretched the same kind of moorland as on his own.

It was too easy a task, in fact. The only problem in it occurred when they reached the village of East Saltoun and the moor gave way to the flat and well-cultivated fields around this place, but by choosing barley fields for his cover and keeping down behind the waist-high grain, Sandy succeeded in remaining hidden from the road. On the far side of the village where the moor began again, he quickly picked up Rattray's trail, but now the first excitement of the impulse had worn off and as he dodged once more from hollow to gorse-clump to hollow, the uneasy feeling that he was making a fool of himself cropped up in his mind.

Should he give up now, he wondered, or should he follow Rattray at least for the two or three miles that remained of this road before it ended at its junction with the track connecting the hamlets of Newtonhall and Stobshiels?

He cast a quick glance over his right shoulder at the sun. It could not be much more than four o'clock in the afternoon, he decided. He could afford the time it would take to reach the road junction to see which way Rattray would turn from there. That would give him some clue as to where he was taking his new purchases, and perhaps some other day of his leave he would follow up that clue.

With this decision made he could feel that there was now a more definite aim in following Rattray, and some of the first excitement of the chase returned to him. He quickened his pace to draw ahead of his quarry, and from the cover of a boulder outcrop above the point where the road ended at its junction with the Newtonhall-Stobshiels track, he waited to see which way Rattray would turn once he had drawn level again.

Crouched in hiding there, it struck Sandy that the pursuit had led him farther into the hills than he had realized till that moment, for straight ahead of him now he could see the highest points in the Lammermuir range – the twin summits of Lammer Law and Priest Law, with Blinkbonny Water and Kidlaw Water scarring their faces and running down into valleys leading to the moorland around the road-junction.

It was a lonely place, he thought. The only sign of life in it was a scattering of sheep grazing the slopes of the valley ahead. The only sound it held was the mournful crying of a moor bird from somewhere far off, and the eeriness of the note it sent wailing over the silent moorland made a shiver run up Sandy's back. 'It's only a whaup crying!' he lectured himself, and diverted his mind into practical channels by thinking how well sounds carried in the clear quiet of the air. Moments later he heard the clopping of the horses quite distinctly on the road below, and edging around the boulder outcrop he looked down to see them advancing towards the road junction.

Rattray did not turn left to Newtonhall when he came to it, and neither did he turn right to Stobshiels. He bore straight on across the junction into the valley of the Kidlaw Water, and quite dumfounded by this, Sandy sat back on his heels to watch the little cavalcade plodding on. Then suddenly, light dawned on him.

There was no way – absolutely no way to get out of the Kidlaw Valley again except by climbing over the top of either Priest Law or Lammer Law, and no one in his senses would attempt to take horses over the loose slatey stone that covered their upper slopes. Rattray's destination therefore, he thought exultantly, must be in the valley. He had discovered where he was taking the horses!

Cautiously he scrambled to his feet and viewed the valley slopes rising up to Lammer Law on the left and Priest Law on the right. A quick dash across the road junction, he reckoned, and from a line along the higher ground on the Priest Law side of the moorland, he would be able to continue tracking Rattray's progress up the valley. He waited till a jutting shoulder of ground cut Rattray off from his view and then ran, low and swift, to the point he had marked out.

The bracken grew thickly there, as it did along the rest of the valley slope. The tough green fronds rose shoulder-high to him, and delighted at finding good cover again so easily, he pushed through it, parting the fronds with a sweeping movement of both hands and keeping his eyes fixed on the valley below in case Rattray should turn to look up in his direction.

He had a good view of the valley floor. Some distance ahead, on the left of the Kidlaw Water, he could see something dark on the green of the turf below the first of the ridges rising up towards Lammer Law. He pushed on, watching the dark blotch take shape until he saw that it was a hut of the kind he knew the Lammermuir shepherds built for use in the lambing and sheep-shearing seasons. Two smaller blotches, round in shape, came into view also and these, it seemed to him, could be tents of the kind used by the tinker people. They stood only a few yards from the hut, and some distance off, there were horses – quite a number of them – grazing the valley floor.

It was wonderful, he thought, how far it was possible to see in the clear air, and could have laughed aloud at finding everything made so easy for him.

He never felt the blow hit him. He was in line with the

hut below when it came, too suddenly for his mind to register any impression of pain before he was smothered by something being dropped over his head and pulled tight like a bag over it.

He crashed down among the bracken fronds kicking out wildly as he fell, and the toe of one heavy leather shoe struck against something that gave at the impact. A yell of pain cut through the grunts of effort from whoever was pulling the material tight around his head. The folds of it slackened. A weight landed on his chest, and he reached up frantically to grapple with it. His left hand closed around a flapping garment. He pulled on it and tried to swing his right fist up to meet the face above it. Hands with thumbs that pressed powerfully into his windpipe suddenly encircled his throat, and a blow brought his clenched fist jarring back to the ground.

He heaved upwards, with all his strength trying to dislodge the weight on his chest, and the slope of the ground aided him. The weight fell sideways on to his outstretched right hand, then he and another body were rolling over and over down the hill with the clasp of the hands around his throat and the thing around his head loosening at every turn.

Voices came muffled to him through the blindfold and the thudding of his head on the ground as he rolled, one in Lowland accents from the body intertwined with his own, and another shouting breathlessly in French from somewhere farther away.

The rolling came to a stop with a jar that shook his head free of the last fold of material around it, and he found himself scrabbling on the ground with a squat, red-haired fellow, freckle-faced and heavy-shouldered. From higher up the slope the owner of the French voice was pounding down to them, yelling as he came, '*Attendez! Je viens vous assister!*' But the red-haired man had no need of assistance.

He had the upper position in the struggle, and suddenly heaving himself on to his knees, he brought his right hand down in a sharp, chopping blow on Sandy's throat and then jerked him, choking and only half-conscious, to his feet.

Vaguely he was aware of the Frenchman skidding to a halt beside him and snatching up the blindfold from the ground. It was his coat which had been used for this purpose, to judge from the complaints he began making then, but his French speech was too rapid for Sandy to follow easily, and the red-haired man only shrugged as if not understanding any of it.

'Stand quietly, now!' he warned – unnecessarily, for Sandy was still too dazed to make any attempt at further resistance. The bracken farther down the slope was swaying as someone forced a way through it. Sandy waited, drooping in the grasp of the red-haired man, and the bracken parted sufficiently to let him see Rattray labouring towards them. The red-haired man greeted him angrily.

'Who is this callant? Eh? And what the devil d'ye mean by letting him follow you?'

Rattray halted just short of them, glaring up at Sandy. Breathless as much from anger as from the climb up the slope, he panted, 'Maxwell – that's who he is. Son of a farmer at Prestonpans – and what's more, he is the same meddling young fool that was asking questions in the Tolbooth about me and Geordie Robertson the day after I broke out from there!'

'Never mind Geordie and the Tolbooth,' the red-haired one said tartly. 'Why did he follow you here?'

'I was only trying –' Sandy began, but Rattray cut angrily across him.

'I'll tell you why, Jock Lumsden!' he shouted to the red-haired man. 'He works for James Wishart, the Edinburgh lawyer – and you know what *his* politics are!'

The red-haired man gave a long whistle of dismay. Rattray nodded. 'Aye,' he commented, 'and you know what the Colonel will have to say about *that*!'

Sandy gaped from one to the other. 'You are both daft!' he exclaimed. "It was only curiosity at seeing a thief turned honest man that made me follow Rattray here.'

'Liar!' Lumsden snapped out the word, twisting his hand chokingly tight in Sandy's collar again. 'Who knows you came here? Who saw you follow Rattray?'

'No one!' Sandy gasped, and immediately realized his mistake as Rattray flicked open one side of his coat and reached swiftly for the pistol thrust into his belt.

'Wait!' A quick, forward movement from Lumsden checked Rattray's action. 'We have no orders to kill, you fool! We will have to keep him here till we get instructions about him.'

'But the Colonel's next visit is not due for another three days,' Rattray protested.

'No matter,' Lumsden over-ruled him. 'The hut will hold this fellow secure enough till then,' and with a quick change of grip that forced Sandy's arm up behind his back, began marching him down to the hut on the valley floor.

4. The Ingenious Prisoner

IT was hard, suddenly, not to feel frightened. Crouched on the floor of the hut, Sandy fought the panic rising in him, grimly telling himself that he could not afford such a luxury now. Nor could he afford to waste time in speculations about his captors. He had to get out of this prison they had found for him.

Gradually, as his eyes adjusted from the daylight outside, he realized that it was not so dark as it had seemed at first. There were hairline cracks in the fitting of the wall timbers.

The door showed a good half-inch of clearance from the lintel at the top as well as from the ground beneath it, and there was enough daylight filtering through these spaces to make a twilight gloom of the hut's interior. Moving slowly, with exploring fingers to help him, Sandy took stock of it.

The floor, he discovered, was of earth, damp and hard-packed, with a few stones embedded in it. A pile of sheep-skins, mouldering from contact with this damp earth, lay in one corner. Door and walls were stoutly made of timbers placed vertically and strengthened with horizontal cross-pieces. There was a small window-space, but this had a heavy wooden board nailed across it. The dampness which had affected the sheepskins had also caused a slight rotting at the base of the wall-timbers, but there was no other apparent weakness in the hut's structure.

It seemed, in fact, escape-proof, yet he could not accept that this was so. Determinedly he snuffed out the small flame of panic that had sprung up again in his mind, and ignoring the stench that rose from the rotting sheepskins, sat down to think out a plan of escape.

They had left him with nothing he could use for such a purpose. Lumsden had searched him before he was pushed into the hut, and had divided the contents of his pockets between himself and Rattray. They had even taken his fishing-line from him, and tossed it down contemptuously when they saw how frayed it was! Yet there must be a way out, he told himself. There simply must! All he had to do was to think hard enough and he would see it.

Head on hands he concentrated his whole mind on the problem, and gradually he found the beginnings of an idea.

He let it grow, carefully working out each step of the difficulties it presented, and at the end of half an hour he was ready to act. Dropping to his knees then he began crawling over the floor, feeling among the stones embedded in it for one which would have a sharp enough cutting edge for his purpose.

He worked methodically, casting back and forward in a straight line from wall to wall, but he had only covered a small section of the floor when the sound of voices outside the hut brought his crawling to an abrupt stop. In a lightning-swift reflex, he jumped for the pile of skins, and dropped down on them to lie as if he had been resting there all the time he had been in the hut. The door swung open. Lumsden came in, followed by Rattray.

'Get up,' Lumsden ordered. He had a rope in his hand and Rattray had a pistol held ready. Sandy rose to his feet, his heart beating suddenly fast and raggedly again. His fear must have shown in his face for Rattray laughed and said, 'Make your choice, Maxwell. Would you rather be shot than hung?'

'Hold your noise, you fool!' Lumsden's tone was contemptuous, as if he were used to suppressing such violent talk from the other man. With swift, expert movements he tied Sandy's hands together behind his back, then thrusting him back on to the sheepskins again, brought the loose end of the rope down to tie round his ankles.

Sandy made no resistance. There were two of them, after all, and Rattray was holding his pistol as if the least provocation would cause him to fire. It was only as Lumsden tied the last knot that he ventured to ask,

'Why have you tied me? Are you not content to know you have me safely locked up?'

Lumsden stared down at him, his freckled face hard and calculating. 'Second thoughts,' he answered sombrely. 'I am in charge here, I have my own skin to think of, and I never knew the laddie yet that could not think up some ingenious way out of trouble. So now you can make up your mind to it that here you are and here you will stay until we get word what is to be done with you.'

He jerked his head towards Rattray. 'And there is a man who is only too anxious to use his pistol on you if you try to show us differently.'

Rattray nodded his misshapen head, smiling his carved-on clown's smile. 'Aye,' he agreed. 'Just give me one wee excuse, laddie, and I will put a proper period to your meddling!'

He turned to the door. Lumsden said, 'You will be bound every night like this, and in the morning your bonds will be untied. But do not deceive yourself about the day-time freedom, for there will always be one of us watching this place.'

He followed Rattray from the hut, and as the door thudded closed behind him, the panic Sandy had been holding at bay took command of him at last.

Struggling upright, he fought wildly to release himself from his bonds, but the more he pulled on the connecting rope between wrists and ankles, the tighter Lumsden's rope became. The pain of them cutting into his flesh added to his panic, clouding his brain until his struggles became nothing more than a meaningless tossing that sent him rolling off the sheepskins altogether.

The shock of impact with the floor brought him back to his senses again. With his face pressed to the dank coldness of the ground he lay for some minutes taking in the realization that he had achieved nothing but the tightening of his bonds and the loss of the only bed he was likely to have that night. Then, setting his teeth to the effort, he began the long, slow business of hauling himself back on to the pile of sheepskins. The ropes cutting into his flesh increased their toll of pain as he did so, and as an antidote to this, he set himself to calculate the prospects of outside help for his situation.

There was his father, and there was Archie. They would both search for him when he did not return home that night – but the snag in that, of course, was they had no reason to think he had ever left the valley of the River Tyne. Still, he could always hope that someone had noticed him tracking Rattray from Pencaitland – a shepherd, perhaps, or maybe some children off to the moors to pick blaeberries.

It was getting dark outside now, he guessed, pausing before the last heave that would bring him back on to the sheepskins. There was no longer any light filtering into the hut. A twist and a heave brought him to his feet, a jerk sent him sprawling face-down on to the sheepskins, and immediately he was assailed by a nightmare sensation of being suffocated by the overpowering stench that arose from them.

It was a final touch that almost brought him to despair again. He rolled over, face uppermost to the blanketing darkness of the hut, and regret at his own stupidity surged through his mind. It was all his own fault, he admitted bitterly. He had no one but himself to blame for his situation. If he had stuck to making inquiries about Robertson as he had been told to do, he would have been sitting safely at home just now instead of lying a bound prisoner at the mercy of such men as Rattray and Lumsden. But now that he had time to think of it – why *were* they holding him prisoner? There must surely be some political reason for it, otherwise Rattray would never have hinted that there was danger in a staunch Hanoverian like Mr Wishart getting to know of the cache of horses in the valley.

Then there was the man they had referred to as 'the Colonel' – from whom, it seemed, they took their orders. If his captors *were* involved in some sort of political plot, then 'the Colonel' must be of the rebellious faction of the Jacobites. That much was clear – but what could be the nature of their plotting?

Sandy sighed, wishing he knew more about the subject of politics. The country had been ruled by a king of the Hanoverian line for the whole of his short life, after all, and he had never taken any great interest in the claim that the exiled Jacobite monarchs laid to the throne. All that he really knew of the Jacobite party, he admitted wryly, was that they had raised a great rebellion to try to win back the throne. But that had been in 1715 – fully five years before he was born, and he had never dreamed there would come a day when he would be involved in their activities!

His thoughts flashed back to the man he and Gilmour had watched outside the bookshop of Allan Ramsay, the Jacobite poet – the man Gilmour had hinted was a spy or a secret agent of some kind. He had found *that* hard enough to believe at the time, Sandy remembered, but now here was an even stranger thought! '*St Clair,*' Gilmour had called the man – '*the Colonel himself.*' Was it possible then, that this St Clair was the same Colonel that Rattray had mentioned?

That, he decided, was something he was never likely to know, for he had absolutely no intention of remaining a prisoner long enough to find out! But one thing he did know now was that some kind of action would have to be taken on the situation into which he seemed to have stumbled, and Mr Wishart was obviously the person to decide what that action should be. And so, once he was free, the business of Robertson would have to wait while he posted as fast as he could to Edinburgh with his news.

The decision turned his mind back to the practical considerations of his escape. He would have less time to carry out his plan now, he thought, and he would also have to take the added risk of making his escape attempt in daylight. Also, his first step would now have to be directed towards finding out what sort of watch Lumsden was setting on the hut.

He thought round this last problem and settled eventually on a solution to it. Then with nothing else to occupy them, his thoughts drifted back into a confusion of questions, fears, regrets, and wild resolutions never, never again to stray from any brief he was given. From time to time he dozed, but this brought no relief to the turmoil in his mind, for every time he tipped over the edge into sleep he was haunted by a nightmare in which it seemed to him he was drowning in the River Tyne. He struggled to escape the suffocation of the water closing over his head but there was no hope for him, for Rattray was holding his hands and Robertson had a grip on his ankles and every time he tried to surface they pushed him under again.

Gasping, and sweating with terror, he woke each time to darkness and the determination not to sleep again, but somehow he did, and somehow eventually the night was over. He could see grey under the door, and after a while he heard faint sounds of voices as the camp outside stirred into life.

Patiently he schooled himself to wait for the opportunity the day would bring, watching the colourless light that seeped into the hut change gradually, as the sun rose higher, into spider's-line-thin threads of gold. He tried to guess who would come to untie his bonds, and awarded himself a mark when the door opened and Lumsden appeared with a dish of porridge in his hand.

Behind him came the Frenchman who had been on the fringe of Sandy's capture the previous day. Their eyes met. For the first time Sandy looked at him properly and saw him as a plump little man with dark eyes in a round, anxious face. Also, he noted, there was a distinct impression of pity in the look the man was casting at his bonds. Hope rose warmly in him at the thought, and remembering that Lumsden apparently could not speak the man's language, he ventured a tentative, '*Bonjour, m'sieu!*'

The Frenchman paused in the act of putting down the slop-bucket he carried and threw him a look that was half-startled and half-pleased at hearing a word in his own tongue.

'*Je m'appelle Alexandre,*' Sandy continued, a wary eye on Lumsden's face. '*Comment vous appelez-vous, m'sieu?*'

'*Je m'appelle Gérard, m'sieu,*' the little man said shyly, and with a gleam of pride in his brown eyes added, '*Je suis le valet du Colonel*'

'Enough!' Brusquely intervening, Lumsden snatched the bucket from Gérard's hand, and setting it down in a corner, motioned him outside. He scuttled away, and Lumsden began untying Sandy's bonds, muttering when he found how tight they had become.

'You have yourself to thank for that,' he remarked sourly, watching Sandy massaging the blood painfully back into his limbs. 'Maybe tonight you will have the sense not to struggle after you are tied.' He gestured to the porridge-dish. 'Ten minutes,' he added, and went out to wait beside the Frenchman.

Rapidly spooning down the porridge, Sandy calculated where he would need to stand to have a good view of the ground immediately outside the door, and was ready in position when it opened again. His glance raked the trampled grass beyond the threshold, and took in his fishing-line still lying where it had been tossed down a foot or so from the door.

Gérard passed him on his way to collect the slop-bucket, and still with the idea that he might be able to make an ally out of him Sandy searched quickly through his school French for the correct form of words to use. Speaking low and urgently, he said,

'*Aidez-moi, je vous prie, M'sieur Gérard: Mon père est un homme généreux, et il vous récompensera.*'

'I said, enough of that!' With real menace in his voice now, Lumsden thrust between them, and Gérard shrank back from him, fear making his plump face suddenly haggard.

'If you speak once more to Frenchie in that monkey talk

of his,' Lumsden threatened Sandy, 'I will tie you by day as well as by night. D'ye understand!'

There would be other opportunities to speak to Gérard, Sandy told himself, and the next time it happened he would be more circumspect about it. He faced Lumsden boldly.

'I understand you are very much on the wrong side of the law in keeping me here, and sooner or later you are going to have to face the consequences of that!'

'I do what I am paid to do,' Lumsden said, his voice taking on its even, indifferent tone again. 'You will be fed again this evening.'

Motioning Gérard ahead of him he strode out. The door-bar clunked into place in its socket, and immediately Sandy went down on hands and knees to resume his previous evening's search for a stone with a sharp, cutting edge.

As before, he quartered the floor carefully, using finger-nails and the heel of one shoe to dig up the first stone his hands encountered. An edge of this stone made a crude lever which helped to prise others out of the earth, but they were mostly quartz which was too smooth for his purpose, or sandstone which was too soft. It was a stone as hard and sharp as a wood-chisel he needed, and doggedly he pursued the search for it.

Fingernails ragged and bleeding, he found it at last – a narrow, fou-inch long piece of the local whinstone – and with a grunt of triumph scrambled over to the window with it clutched in his hand. Inch by inch he felt over the board that was nailed across the window-space. It was, as he remembered, a piece of rough, unplaned wood studded with knotholes. He chose a knot that measured about two inches across and began chiselling around it with his sharp piece of whinstone.

At first he worked hastily, impressed with the urgency of what he had to do, but as his makeshift chisel slipped, and slipped again under the hasty strokes, he settled down to a slow, methodical scoring of the wood around the knot.

His fingers became cramped. He paused to rest them, changed the stone to his other hand, and began again. The board, he reckoned, was just under an inch thick, and at the rate he was managing to score a channel around the knot, it would take him hours yet to work it loose enough to remove it entirely. He had no choice in the matter, however, and with the mindless energy of a mole tunnelling in the dark he continued chiselling away at the wood.

His breakfast of porridge was the only food he had eaten since his dinner of the previous day, and as time wore on hunger-cramps began to add their pain to that of his cramped and bleeding fingers – but the knot was coming loose! He could feel now that there was only a thin skin of wood holding it in position, and with infinite care he began using his stone as a lever instead of as a chisel. The knot *had* to fall inwards to him, so that he would have a spyhole which could be opened and closed at will and thus remain undetected by his captors!

A last gentle easing of the knot released it completely. There was no danger, of course, that the space it would leave could be seen from the tents since they were too far away for anyone there to detect such a small, lightless aperture, but there was the risk that one of his captors might be fairly close to the hut at that moment. Fraction by fraction, Sandy edged the knot out of its socket and peered cautiously through the spyhole that opened as it slid slowly into his waiting palm.

Lumsden was on guard. Squatting outside one of the tents he was polishing away at a saddle laid across his knees, and raising his head every few minutes to glance at the door of the hut. Gérard was crouched over a fireplace of stones a few yards away from Lumsden, and away beyond the tents, Rattray was moving back and forth among the horses grazing the valley floor. A scattering of sheep near at hand and a small flock grazing farther off were the only other things to be seen in the valley.

Sandy withdrew from the spyhole, contemplating his next action. The hole would give him a little extra light to work by, he thought, but if he left it open, it might well be discovered by one of his captors coming towards the hut while he was too absorbed in his escape plan to hear their footsteps on the grass. With rapid movements he smoothed down its rough edges, and then did the same for the knot of wood before he returned it to its socket. It slid smoothly and easily back into position and was as easy to take out again, but it was only when he was satisfied that he could repeat these actions at speed that he proceeded to the next step in his plan.

Dropping to his knees again beside the wall of the hut, he began scoring his sharp stone down the timbers at its base. The damp wood splintered freely under the heavy pressure he put on it, and hopefully he continued gouging away. To reach his fishing line, he had calculated, he would need a stick at least eighteen inches long, but he did not waste time in trying to break this off in one complete piece. When he had managed to get two splinters which could be spliced together to make the necessary length, he pocketed his stone. With the heel of his shoe he hacked up some of the damp earth from the floor and moulded this in his hands to make a paste with which to plaster over the fresh scars in the wood. This done, he turned to the task of splicing his two sticks.

He used a strand of wool from one of his stockings for this purpose, tearing with his teeth at the firm edge of the knitting until he found an end which unravelled neatly from the rest of the stitches. The splicing completed, he found himself with a short length of wool still in hand, and taking his fishing hooks from underneath his lapel, he used this wool to bind the hooks firmly to one end of his stick.

Then, quickly, he went over to the spyhole to check that there was no one near the hut.

The slant of the light outside startled him into realizing how long it had taken to make the crude tools of his escape. There was no sign of either Rattray or Lumsden, but Gérard was there and he was apparently combining his turn of guard duty with the cooking of the evening meal. A pot hung over the fire was sending savoury wafts through the air, and with hunger knotting his stomach more painfully than ever, Sandy closed the spyhole again.

Lying flat on the floor behind the door, he pushed his hooked stick slowly through the crack beneath it. He knew exactly where the line lay, although he could not see it, and all he needed now was a little luck to make his hooks catch on it! Gently, cautiously, he moved the stick around, praying for that one little stroke of luck, and then slowly drew the stick back in under the door.

A thin green coil of line came snaking in with it. Heart hammering with excitement, he detached the coil from the hooks which had caught it and carefully drew the rest of the line in under the door. He had a small flat stone in his pocket, saved from among those he had hacked up out of the floor. Quickly he doubled the line, and for further security, knotted it at intervals along its doubled strand. Then he tied the flat stone to one end of it and rose to his feet with the weighted line dangling from his fingers.

The last part of his plan, he reckoned, would be quick and easy; the work – literally – of a minute! But now that he was compelled to make his escape in daylight, he would have to be very careful to choose exactly the right minute. Hiding the line and stick under the sheepskins, he went back to the spyhole and looked out again.

All three of his jailers were now beside the tents, and with quick apprehension he saw that there was now a fourth man with them. Gérard moved to add fresh fuel to his cooking-fire, and the fourth man came more clearly into view. He was small and thinly-built, dressed in the loose trousers, short jacket, and knitted cap commonly worn by seamen, and on an indrawn breath of astonishment Sandy recognized him as George Robertson, the smuggler.

Triumph rose in him. He had been right! That wild guess at a continuing connection between Rattray and Robertson must have been right – or why should the man be here now? Eagerly he strained to make sense of the murmuring conversation that drifted to him from the group by the tents. Was there a quarrel of some kind going on? Robertson's gestures seemed to show that this was so, although he still could not make out what was being said. A shouted word broke out here and there from the murmur. Lumsden shook his fist at Robertson. The voices rose into loud, angry tones, and Sandy began to distinguish the general drift of the quarrel.

Robertson seemed to be trying to persuade Lumsden to some sort of action, for several times he caught phrases such as, '*You will not suffer for it, Jock, I promise you*' and '*I tell you there is no danger,*' but Lumsden seemed adamant in refusing, for twice Sandy heard him say vehemently, '*I will have no part in it*!'

Rattray interrupted at one point to tell Robertson, 'Geordie, the Colonel is not the sort of man to take this lying down!' But Robertson shrugged this off contemptuously and turned away as if he had had enough of the argument.

'I will do it myself then,' he shouted over his shoulder, 'and may Drew Wilson's ghost haunt both you *and* the Colonel!'

Rattray lounged with his hands in his pockets as Robertson made off, but Lumsden's posture was that of a man who seemed uncertain of his next move. Suddenly he made up his mind. Leaning towards Rattray, he snatched the pistol out of his belt and fired after Robertson.

The answering shot came so quickly that it seemed Robertson must have been ready for some such attack. Lumsden was equally prepared for his reply to it. He ducked, and rising from his crouched position by the fire at precisely that moment, Gérard took Robertson's shot full in the chest. Hands flung wide to clutch despairingly at the air, he crashed forward over the fire. Lumsden and Rattray dragged him clear. Over his body Lumsden yelled to Rattray to go after Robertson, and Rattray yelled in reply,

'And get myself killed, like Frenchie! What kind of a fool d'ye take me for, Jock Lumsden!'

Lumsden sprang to his feet as if he meant to go after Robertson himself. Then he swung to look at the hut and struck his fist into his palm in a gesture that said clearly he was cursing the responsibility of being tied to guarding his prisoner.

Sandy had seen enough. Perhaps Gérard had played some small part in his capture, but it could only have been out of fear of the other two for clearly he was a man of gentle nature. *'Je suis le valet du Colonel,'* he had said – '*I am the Colonel's valet.*' And he had spoken proudly, as if it were an honour to serve this mysterious Colonel who had left him alone with these violent men! Now he was dead.

Feeling sick and curiously weak at the knees, Sandy closed his spyhole and lay down on the sheepskins. Today Gérard, he thought dully. Tomorrow it might be his own turn. It was not an easy thought on which to face the night.

5. Fear on a Hot Afternoon

THERE were more visitors to the camp the next day – two men who sat their horses well and who, when dismounted, walked with the rolling, wide-legged gait of men accustomed to long hours in the saddle.

They came in the late afternoon, and with sharply quickened interest Sandy watched from his spyhole as they culled horses from the herd and then departed with a string of the best animals. Rattray went with them to make their selection, but Sandy noted that it was to Lumsden they spoke briefly on arrival, and then at greater length before they left again.

Seeking for a word to describe the visitors to himself he remembered Mr Fairbairn's guess that Rattray's purchases were intended as cavalry mounts, and the description he sought flashed into his mind. The men were well-dressed, and they had an air of authority about them as well as being skilled horsemen. They were neither farmers nor drovers, then – but, he decided, they could very well be cavalry officers out of uniform, and rapidly he revised the story he had to tell Mr Wishart to include an account of their visit to the camp.

Nothing further happened to attract his attention that day and he grew incredibly weary of his one-eyed peering from the spyhole. He could see the place where they had buried Gérard, and time and again his glance kept on returning to the cairn his captors had heaped over the grave. It lay on the right-hand bank of the Kidlaw Water, opposite the tents, but Lumsden and Rattray did not seem to be troubled by its proximity, and thinking of this, Sandy fell to wondering what sort of man Lumsden really was.

Certainly, he decided, the fellow was not a rogue of Rattray's low type – in spite of his rough manner. He looked more like a drover, of the footloose, hardy kind that was always to be found at the big horse fairs and cattle markets of the Border country – the kind that would drive stolen beasts as readily as any other, provided they were paid well enough for the risk.

'*I do what I am paid to do.*' His own words, Sandy thought, summed up the man – but that still did not answer the question of whether he included murder in his scale of charges! So far that day, there had been only one occasion when he had stood guard alone and he had been carrying Rattray's pistol then, but that did not necessarily mean he would shoot to kill if he saw his prisoner escaping. A wounding shot might be his limit, Sandy thought hopefully, and then wondered if he dared risk even that.

Lumsden had begun preparing the evening meal by this time. Watching him stir away at the pot that held it, Sandy felt the hunger that had plagued his captivity claw fiercely at his stomach again, and when the man eventually came with his share of it he bolted it in ravenous haste. Feeling slightly sick as a result, he submitted to being tied for the night, and huddling down on the sheepskins tried to sort out his impressions of the day that had passed.

Two things, he thought, stood out with the clarity of beacons charting his course. First, he could not endure to spend another day and night inactive in this stinking confinement, and second, there was only one time in the following day when he could risk making his break for freedom – the morning watch that left Lumsden alone on guard while Rattray attended to the horses.

Tomorrow then, he would wait for Lumsden's attention to wander briefly during the morning watch. He would have the last move in his escape-plan ready in preparation for that moment, and when it came he would slip quietly out to reach the cover of the bracken that grew right down to the back of the hut.

But what if Lumsden's attention did not wander? What then?

He would make his break all the same, Sandy decided. All other considerations apart, another day's waiting would bring him too near the day on which Lumsden and Rattray expected the arrival of 'the Colonel'. He would keep low as he ran for cover, making himself as twisting a target as possible for any shots Lumsden sent after him, and after that he would simply have to rely on his wits to save him from being recaptured, or killed.

Like Gérard, he thought, suddenly remembering the out-flung arms and the body toppling forward across the fire. Sick horror rose again in him at the memory, and recoiling from it, he sought refuge in other thoughts. Where had the search for him taken his father and Archie? Were they any-where near the Kidlaw Valley at that moment? So far, they had had two days to search the valley of the River Tyne. Had it occurred to them yet to strike out beyond it, towards some of the small, tributary streams flowing down from the Lammermuirs?

Archie knew he was keen on fishing these hill burns – but there were so many of them! Humbie Water, Binns Water, Kinchie Burn, Blinky Burn, Stobshiels Burn – even if Archie speculated that he had tired of the Tyne and gone off to fish its tributary streams, which valley would he choose to search?

There was no certain answer to the question, any more than there had been certain answers to any of the questions he had been asking himself since he first saw Rattray at Wintonhill Farm. Tiredly he accepted the fact, and after a long time, fell into what he hoped would be his last uneasy sleep as a prisoner.

It was Lumsden as usual who came with his breakfast the next morning and for once, it seemed to Sandy, there was some uncertainty in the man's manner. Almost apologetic-ally, as he collected the porridge-dish and the bucket again, he remarked,

'I'll say this for you, young Maxwell. You keep extra-ordinar' calm for one in your situation.'

'And I'll say this for *you*,' Sandy retorted swiftly. 'You are a fool to run your neck into a noose for anything Rattray says.'

'I have my orders,' Lumsden insisted, but he cast a doubt-ful glance, all the same, through the open door of the hut to where Rattray was walking off towards the horses.

'If you were to let me loose,' Sandy pressed home the slight advantage he thought he had gained, 'I would not prefer charges against you.'

'Charges!' Lumsden repeated ironically. 'D'ye think there is any Sheriff's officer with a writ would get within a mile of me!'

'At least let me out to wash in the burn, then,' Sandy persisted. 'I am stinking from the two days you have kept me locked up in this hole.'

'You can wash tomorrow, when the Colonel comes,' Lumsden told him. 'If I let you out now you might make a break for it, and then I would have to shoot you.'

He went out, dropping the latch of the door into its socket with its usual final-sounding thud, and Sandy moved over to the spyhole. He would give Lumsden an hour to settle down to his spell of guard duty, he thought, and then he would keep to his decision to make a break – regardless of whether or not anything happened to distract the man's at-tention. An hour would be long enough to bring the doubts in Lumsden's mind from a simmer to a boil, and a man un-sure of his purpose might well be unsure of his aim also. He settled himself at the spyhole, and silently counting, began to check the passage of the hour he had allowed himself.

Some forty minutes had passed by his reckoning before he shifted position, and then it was because his ear had caught a faint thudding noise that sounded like a horse's hoofbeats. Head cocked to the sound he stood listening intently, and then applied his eye to the spyhole again. The hoofbeats echoed past the wall of the hut, and a man rode into his line of vision. Lumsden, standing up to greet the visitor, called out 'Good morning, Colonel!' and caught the reins thrown forward as he dismounted beside the tents.

Dismounted, he showed himself a sparely built man of medium height, and with a shock of almost pleased surprise at finding he had guessed so accurately, Sandy realized that he was indeed the dark-wigged man he had watched outside Allan Ramsay's bookshop. A sharp awareness of the danger in which he stood followed instantly on this first reaction. This was the Colonel who would settle his fate. He had arrived a day earlier than Lumsden had expected, and that spelled disaster to his plans, unless –

With the wild idea that he might yet be able to make use of the tools of his escape he darted over to pull them out of their hiding place. Then, with his weighted line and stick in one hand and the plug of his spyhole in the other, he took up position by the window again.

Lumsden was talking rapidly to the Colonel, with gestures that made it clear he was telling of Sandy's capture. The Colonel swung round to look at the hut, but as the flow of explanation went on, he turned sharply back to Lumsden again. His voice rising in a shout of anger that carried the words clearly to Sandy, he exclaimed,

'Gérard! You say he shot Gérard?'

Lumsden nodded and went on talking, with a gesture to the cairn where Gérard lay buried, but the Colonel interrupted him with words that Sandy could not catch, and with a curt inclination of the head that commanded Lumsden to follow, began marching toward the hut. In a flash, Sandy replaced the plug of his spyhole, and with his ear pressed to the wall of the hut he listened to the growing sound of feet and voices approaching him. The Colonel's voice, harsh with anger, dominated that of Lumsden.

'. . . and as if the death of Gérard were not enough, coming on top of the trouble that rascal Robertson threatens to make for me,' he was storming, 'you have to present me with the problem of this stupid young clerk – this prying farm-lad, this –'

'I told you, sir,' Lumsden interrupted. 'Rattray says he works for lawyer Wishart in Edinburgh.'

'Rattray is a rogue and you are a blockhead,' the Colonel told him brusquely, 'and God knows why I left two such scum here with my poor Gérard instead of putting an intelligent gentleman in charge of the camp!'

The feet halted outside the door of the hut, and with a snarl in his voice now, Lumsden retorted, 'Perhaps it was because you know that the gentlemen who engaged you would not tolerate some of your methods, Colonel. You *have* to use men like Rattray and me!'

Colonel St Clair made no reply to this. He was moving from the door towards the window, and halting again beside this, he called out,

'You say this boy has been shut up securely all the time he has been here? That he has seen nothing of what has gone on in the camp?'

'That was what I said.' Lumsden's feet swished through the grass as he also moved to the window.

'What about this, then? Eh?' A solid thump against the shutter over the window-space sent the loosely placed plug of the spyhole flying from its position, and through the hole it left, the Colonel's muffled tones came clearly to Sandy.

'You fool, Lumsden, you fool! See how that plug of wood fell inwards! Look at the fresh markings round the space it left! That boy has fooled you neatly – he has seen everything there is to see in the camp! So *now* think of the story he has to report to his Hanoverian employer!'

In the brief silence that followed this outburst, Sandy could hear his own blood roaring in his ears as loudly as a cataract of water pouring over rocks. He made desperate attempts to steady his breathing, and through the pounding of his blood heard Lumsden ask,

'What d'ye want with him, sir?'

'Kill him,' the Colonel said flatly.

Another brief silence, and then Lumsden's voice, oddly uncertain now in tone, 'But – but, sir, he is only a laddie!'

'He is clerk to one of the wiliest supporters the Hanoverian government has in Scotland,' the Colonel replied coldly, 'and he knows too much for mercy now. Do as I tell you, Lumsden.'

'I will not!' Lumsden's voice had recovered its certainty, and with growing defiance in his tone he went on, 'You hired me to keep this camp secure and to frighten Rattray out of cheating you over the horses. I have done that, Colonel, and my contract does not call for more.'

As if astonished at this, the Colonel exclaimed, 'What is this squeamishness, Lumsden? Your hands are not clean of blood!'

'Aye, I have the death of some men to answer for,' Lumsden retorted, 'and I would have shot even so young a laddie as this if he had attempted to escape. But killing him in cold blood is another thing, and I am not for hire for such an order.'

There was another silence – a longer one; then the Colonel said curtly, 'Fetch Rattray. He will be happy to oblige!'

Feet moved away from the hut, the sound dying quickly into the muffling grass, and unaware that he had changed position at all, Sandy found himself looking out again through the spyhole. Hands clasped behind his back, head down-bent, the Colonel was moving to the cairn that marked Gérard's grave. Lumsden was walking away up the valley towards the horses. In a few minutes, Sandy knew, he would return with Rattray, and Rattray would kill him, but he felt nothing – not fear, excitement, or despair. Moving with lightning speed, as if some demon of cool intelligence had taken charge of him, he darted to the door and pushed the stone that weighted his fishing line through the crack at the top of it.

Down tumbled the stone to the grass outside the hut door,

dragging a length of line with it. Holding the rest of the line taut with the unweighted end of it gripped in his left hand, Sandy flopped down and thrust his hooked stick through the crack between the floor and the foot of the door. The hooks caught and held the line's weighted end. With careful speed he drew this back in under the door and stood up again with an end of the line held in either hand and the whole of it now forming a loop around the vertical aspect of the door.

Rapidly then Sandy eased this loop along towards the crack between the edge of the door and the door jamb, shortened the grip he held on it, and pulled. The line rasped down the edge of the door, and checked at the bar holding it shut. Once again he shortened his grip so that the line now made a small, tight loop around the door bar. Another pull – this time with a steady upward pressure, and he had lifted the bar out of its socket to let it swing soundlessly free.

The door was open, and the cool, calculating thing inside his brain told him that it had taken less than a minute to achieve this.

Darting back to the spyhole, he checked what had happened in this time. Lumsden was well on his way to the horses' grazing ground. The colonel was standing by Gérard's grave, his back to the hut and his head still downbent like that of a mourner at a funeral. Seeing him thus, Sandy's first impulse was to follow his original plan of making a silent bolt for the bracken behind the hut, but now he could no longer count on the time he needed to make a clear getaway by this means, and instantly he dismissed the idea again. His eye took in the usual small flock of sheep cropping near the hut, and in a flash, his next move became clear to him.

One bound carried him over to the sheepskins in the corner. He snatched one up and draped it over himself. It was large enough to cover him from his head to the calves of his legs. Holding it in place with both hands, he shouldered the door open a fraction and peered out. The Colonel was still standing motionless by the graveside. Twenty feet from the hut the forms of three sheep made a greyish-white blur on the grass. They would break and run for it, Sandy knew, if he approached them rapidly. Steeling himself to the action, he slipped around the door of the hut, closed and barred it behind himself and then walked with slow, noiseless steps towards the sheep.

They looked up at his approach and wandered a restless foot or two away, but there was no panic in their movements. He crouched low beside them, and began to crawl slowly towards the main flock some fifty yards away. The sheep, in the manner of their kind, followed blindly on.

They had almost reached the main flock when the Colonel moved. He turned from the grave and walked back to the hut. Sandy froze into stillness. The sheep halted when he did, and from the shelter of their forms bunched about him he watched the Colonel discover the loop of fishing-line trailing from the bar of the door, heard his exclamation at the find and the shout of anger that followed as he swung the door open and found the hut empty.

'*Lumsden! Rattray!*' Roaring the names and waving his arms in a signal towards the grazing-ground, the Colonel spun round from the door. Then as if to point the urgency of his summons, he drew a pistol and fired into the air. Reloading as the echoes of the shot died away, he ran for the bracken behind the hut and began thrashing through it. Sandy scuttered for the cover of the flock just ahead of him and wormed his way into its centre.

The sheep, bunching restlessly away from the noise of the shot, began a slow movement down the valley towards the grazing-ground. Towards Rattray and Lumsden, Sandy thought, and pinned all his faith on the knowledge that men in the panic of an emergency do not stop to stare at familiar things, and that the hunters do not except the hunted to come towards them. A minute later his faith was justified as the two men passed the flock, running hard and shouting breathlessly in reply to the Colonel's urging.

'Hurry, you fools!' he was yelling. 'The boy is loose somewhere here in the bracken. Hurry! He cannot have got far yet!'

The ruse had worked, they were intent on searching the most obvious place for him to seek cover after his escape. The directing force in Sandy's mind acknowledged the fact without self-congratulation, recognizing that he had still to solve the problem of getting out of the valley. He began to crawl faster, urging the sheep around him with nudges and sharp flicks at their hind-legs, and responding as they would have done to a collie's driving, they moved obediently forward.

A loop of the stream met their path. They splashed through it and straggled out on the other side. Ahead of them, Sandy saw the slope down which he had been marched into captivity two long days and nights before. Behind that slope rose fold after fold of the lower reaches of Priest Law's peak, and once hidden among these, he reckoned, he would be lost to pursuit. He risked raising himself for a backward glance.

The Colonel and the other two men were still beating the bracken on the lower reaches of Lammer Law's facing slope, their backs partly turned to him as they flailed the green of the cover there. He was far enough off from them now to take another risk, Sandy decided, and crawling rapidly free of the flock he headed off on his own up the slope in front of him.

The majority of the sheep stayed peacefully grazing on the lush pasture by the bank of the stream, but the few inquisitive ones to be found in every flock followed him, running warily alongside when he crawled, stopping when he stopped, staring with blank yellow eyes at him as he glanced furtively back towards the searchers on the other side of the valley.

He spoke to the beasts, muttering words of praise and thanks aloud to them as he worked his way upwards. They were his cover, his unwitting allies, his good-luck piece, and never in his life had he been so grateful for anything as he was for the continued sight of their long stupid faces. Yet he left them without a qualm as he met the bracken that marched down from the crest of the ridge to meet the grass of its lower slopes, though he did not drop the skin that had served him so well. Clutching it round himself he worked his way through the bracken until he was over the ridge, and it was only then, when speed was obviously going to serve him better than disguise, that he discarded it at last.

With the ending of the long, painful trickery that had brought him out of the valley, came also an end to his planning. He ran, and as he ran, panic surged in him, washing away the support of the directing intelligence that seemed to have guided his actions thus far.

He felt naked, vulnerable, small as a hare fleeing from large, pursuing hounds, but underneath his panic there was still working in him the countryman's instinct for direction, and it drew him westward over the long, swelling ridges of Priest Law's foothills – westward to where his instinct told him the hamlet of Stobshiels lay at the mountain's foot and the Binn's Water tributaried down to meet the River Tyne.

His course took him away from the bracken growth and over heather, tough-rooted and slippery-stemmed. Toes stubbing against the unyielding root-tangle, feet sliding over the purple-budded smoothness of the flower-stalks, he stumbled and blundered from one fall into another. Forcing his laboured lungs to greater effort his side contracted in a stitch of pain, and he ran on almost weeping with rage at his own weakness.

Up there on the exposed ridges of the hillside there was no escaping the heat of the August sun or the swarms of midges it brought clustering round his sweating face. His run falling away to a stumbling trudge, he tugged off his cravat and tied it over the lower part of his face as some sort of protection against their stinging attacks. After that he could not pick up his pace again, and he shambled on looking up only occasionally to check that he was still heading in the right direction.

The sight of Stobshiels Loch in the valley beginning to open out below him was what he prayed for during these glances, and wiping sweat from his eyes with the sleeve of his coat he saw it at last, glinting peacefully in the sun. He plunged towards it, careless of the risk of a turned ankle as he slid and skidded down the heather-slopes rising from the water.

From the far end of the loch ran the stream called the Stobshiels Burn and a mile down this water lay the farm of Stobshiels itself, but he would not stop there, he decided – tempting though he found the prospect of resting even for a few minutes. He would press on home by way of the valley of the Binn's Water, and he would beg Archie to lend him his horse, Gambler. Gambler was fast. He could be in Edinburgh telling his news to Mr Wishart that evening if he rode the beast hard enough !

They were bringing in the barley-crop at Stobshiels. Sandy waved to the harvesters but did not slacken his pace. He was bearing northeast now, into the valley of the broader stream of the Binn's Water, and away to his left he could see the great patch of green made by Saltoun Big Wood. He set his eyes on it as the next landmark to be gained and swung rapidly on.

Where the stream looped to pass the wood he heard voices

calling and a crashing sound like that of men beating the undergrowth. 'A shooting-party,' he thought, and went on ready to duck quickly if he found himself walking into the line of fire. Figures armed with long sticks appeared at the edge of the wood. A man mounted on a tall bay horse broke cover and whistled to the beaters, making sweeping gestures that waved them on up the valley. He rode forward, a broad purposeful figure clenched into his saddle, with the sun behind him gilding his head and making a shadowed mystery of his face.

Sandy halted to watch him, shielding his eyes from the sun's glare, and then suddenly broke into a clumsy run. '*Archi!*' he yelled as he ran. '*Archie!*' over and over again repeating the name in a voice that rose almost to a scream.

Archie slid down to catch him and hold him upright as he fell against Gambler's side. His voice babbling questions and exclamations went on and on in Sandy's ears, and slowly he came out of the daze that had made everything blur so strangely before him. With difficulty finding his voice again, he asked,

'What brought you here? What made you search *this* valley?'

'Why should we not?' Archie demanded. 'Good grief, Sandy, do you not realize the stir you have caused? We have the countryside fair blanketed with search-parties for you, and we have sent men as far –'

'Lend me Gambler, Archie,' Sandy cut hoarsely across his words. 'I must ride to Edinburgh – now – this minute!'

'Eh?' Checked in the full flood of his relief, Archie gaped at him. 'Have you gone daft? Why the devil should you want to ride to Edinburgh – now, of all times!'

The beaters were gathering in, curious-faced, around them. Sandy dropped his voice to a whisper. 'I cannot tell you with these others here. Trust me, Archie! It is secret and very urgent. Please trust me!'

'Of course I trust you – we have always trusted one another –' Archie began, and paused as if the true meaning of his words had just struck him. Slowly the uncertain look on his face gave way to one of decision, and with a leap of excitement Sandy heard him voice their old, familiar bargain.

'Right, then! I will cover for you at home, if you will cover for me.'

'Done!' he exclaimed and swung himself, in a single move, into Gambler's saddle.

6. Lines of Action

MR WISHART, on the evening of that same day, was feeling in extremely good humour, and demonstrated it with chuckling laughter and a rubbing-together of papery palms as he strode, storklike, back and forth in his office. Deryck Gilmour, watching from a seat where a full glass of claret stood by his elbow, smiled at the lawyer's good spirits while he enjoyed his own quiet sense of triumph.

Four days' hard probing through the Customs Houses of Fifeshire, he was thinking, had entitled him to a little relaxation. And now that he had the traitor to the Customs Service safely under lock and key in the Tolbooth, he could afford an evening's unbending from duty! In his mind's eye he pictured Isobel Wishart setting out the table for cards in the room next door, and smiling, reached out for his wineglass.

'Aye, drink up, drink up, sir, you deserve it!' Wishart agreed enthusiastically. 'You have had a marvellous success in tracking down your renegade.'

Gilmour looked modest. 'It was your mention of Robertson berthing his boat at Anstruther that led me to him in the first place. You must take credit for that.'

'I do, oh, I do!' Complacently Wishart accepted his due,

and stopped in his pacing to cock a curious eye at his visitor. 'But it needed more than that to ferret him out from among the honest officials of the Anstruther Customs post, heh? How did you do that?'

'There is a method to these things.' Gilmour was cautious, not wanting to reveal more than necessary of professional secrets. 'One relies on knowledge of Service procedure as a starting-point. From there it is easy to detect small things that do not fit the picture of an honest officer, and after that it is a case of how much skill one has as an interrogator. This case did not require much. The man had a very simple method of passing Customs information to Robertson – and, of course, to various other smugglers who had him in their pay.'

'What did you say his name was again?' Wishart frowned, trying to remember. 'Ah – Johnstone – yes, that was it – William Johnstone. I remember now. Well, here is a toast to him, the rascal!'

He picked up his own glass of wine from his desk. Gilmour waited expectantly. 'To a short trial,' Wishart said jovially, 'and a long sentence!'

'Amen!' Gilmour answered, smiling. They drank the toast, and lowering his glass, Gilmour said, 'Now I can start my search for Robertson in good earnest.'

'And I,' Wishart told him smiling yet more broadly, 'have news that may bear on that.'

He set his glass down with a small decisive thump on his desk. 'I have set my spies scouting in the suburb of Portsburgh, the place where Robertson was last seen,' he went on, 'and they have come back to me with a very curious story that concerns Captain John Porteous, the Town Guard officer who presided at the execution of Robertson's colleague, Andrew Wilson.'

'I know about that event.' Gilmour nodded. 'That young clerk of yours – Sandy Maxwell – gave me a description of it.'

Wishart looked slightly put out at being thus forestalled. 'And do you know,' he demanded, 'that Captain Porteous was arrested after the rioting which took place then, and brought to trial for the murder of the citizens who were killed when he ordered his troops to fire into the crowd? Do you know he was found guilty and condemned to death, and that he has petitioned Queen Caroline for a reprieve? That he lies in the Tolbooth now, awaiting an answer to that petition?'

'I knew about the trial and the sentence,' Gilmour admitted. 'That was included in the official information given to me, but I was not aware of his petition for reprieve. Is it likely to be granted.'

'I think it is,' Wishart said. 'Porteous has a good record of loyalty to the House of Hanover – in fact, it was on the strength of his showing against the Jacobites in the '15 rebellion that he was appointed an officer of the Town Guard.'

'And Robertson? Where does he fit into this information?'

'Robertson blames Porteous for the failure of his rescue attempt, and so for the death of his friend Wilson. If the reprieve is granted, he has sworn to kill Porteous himself.'

Gilmour considered the news in silence. 'You are sure of this?' he asked at length.

Wishart shrugged expressively. 'As sure as one can be of anything that comes out of the underworld of places like Portsburgh. But one thing I can say is that my acquaintances in the criminal fraternity know better than to try to deceive me with false stories.'

'To kill Porteous,' Gilmour said slowly, 'Robertson will have to come out of hiding.'

'Exactly!' Wishart shot a look of sly triumph at him. 'And so, if you do not succeed in unearthing him by other methods, you have a good chance of taking him by having a watch set on Porteous, once he is released.'

'This is good news and I am grateful to you for it, sir, very grateful.' Rising on the words, Gilmour set down his glass. 'And now, if you will excuse me, I must go to seek a lodging for myself before I join your ladies in that hand of cards I promised Mistress Wishart.'

'You will do no such thing,' Wishart told him firmly. 'The lodgings in Edinburgh are exceeding mean and dirty, and I have already told Mistress Wishart to prepare a guest-chamber for the rest of your stay here.'

He rose, good-humouredly silencing Gilmour's polite protests. 'Come, sir,' he commanded. 'The ladies will be impatient for their entertainment.'

They walked together to the drawing-room, and with his mind still on Robertson, Gilmour asked as they went,

'Have you heard any news yet from young Maxwell?'

'Give him time, give him time,' Wishart replied, and laughed in complimentary fashion. 'We do not all work so quickly as you, Mr Gilmour!'

In the drawing-room, Mistress Wishart and her daughter sat in conversation behind their fans, and in a bustling rush of grey silk at their entry, Mistress Wishart rose to flutter greetings at them. Isobel, in rose-coloured silk, remained seated on the couch, concealing her expression with her fan and saying nothing. Candlelight behind her formed a nimbus of misty gold around her fair hair, and rested in shifting pools of deep gold among the folds of her rose-coloured silk. Gilmour bowed over the hand she extended politely to him, and found that the glib compliment he had ready for her had died on his lips. Instead of speaking it, he said honestly,

'You are very beautiful, Mistress Isobel.'

'A flower! She is the flower of Scotland!' Wishart said, with great satisfaction and unexpected poetry, at which Isobel dismissed the conquetry of her fan and laughed heartily.

'The flower of Scotland, Father, is a thistle,' she reminded him, and with a challenging glance at Gilmour, asked,

'Had you also forgotten that, Mr Gilmour?'

'No, I had not.' His tongue unlocked by her look, he boldly took up the challenge in it. 'But I have a strong hand for plucking thistles, Mistress Isobel!'

'We were going to have a turn at the cards,' Wishart threw out the reminder, and in a general buzz of conversation they took their places at the table.

Gilmour glanced about him. It was a far cry, he thought, from the garish salons he had frequented in London to the sedate gentility of this room. His eye took in the candlelit polish of the furniture, the unpainted faces of the two ladies above the glowing silk of their dresses, and he felt a sudden sense of homecoming.

'You are deep in thought, Mr Gilmour.'

It was Mistress Wishart's voice recalling him to the present. He smiled, and said quietly, 'I was thinking how much your house reminds me of my own home in Perthshire, ma'am.'

'But Scotsmen will aye wander,' Wishart said with a sigh.

'They come back home,' Gilmour said, and looked at Isobel, 'when there is something to draw them back.'

Isobel blushed the colour of her dress, and in her confusion, failed to follow suit in her play. *'My trick, I see.'* Gilmour smiled at her, and drew the cards towards him.

The room was cool after the heat of the busy streets outside. It smelt of lavender and beeswax. In one corner, the gleaming keyboard of a harpsichord invited to music. A small, gilded clock on the mantelpiece ticked time slowly and thinly away. The light flip and swish of the cards on the table-top was a soothing sound. Isobel Wishart was a rose, a slender pink and gold flower in the candlelight. Watching her, across the hands moving through the game,

Gilmour was strangely content with the quiet passing of the evening.

When Mistress Wishart rose eventually to say it was time to sample the cold collation she had ready in the kitchen, he bowed both ladies to the door and sauntered back to the card-table thinking vaguely that he must make some inquiries of them about the social life of Edinburgh. It would be a very pleasant thing to squire Mistress Isobel to a ball – always providing, he amended the thought hastily – that his mission allowed of time for such trivialities.

Wishart turned towards him, a carafe of wine in one hand and a glass in the other. 'First you must sample this for me, Gilmour,' he said as he began pouring. ''Tis part of a shipment that arrived in –'

A crashing noise cut across his speech. It was the sound of a door being slammed violently back on its hinges, and this was followed immediately by a scream and a rattle of breaking crockery. Wishart's hand was arrested in its pouring. Gilmour whirled to the sound, which came from the hallway beyond the drawing-room, and moving swiftly towards it, he wrenched open the drawing-room door. Wishart followed, the carafe still clutched in his hand, and both men stopped short to stare at the scene in the hallway.

It was the outer door of the house which had been so roughly burst open. Inside it stood Sandy Maxwell, a ragged figure swaying drunkenly back and forward and barely recognizable under the dirt that streaked his face. The serving-girl who had screamed at the sight of him stood islanded in the midst of her broken crockery, and from the kitchen doorway on the far side of the hall peered the startled faces of Mistress Wishart and Isobel.

'*Sandy*!' His face thunderous with anger, Wishart stepped forward. 'What the devil d'ye mean by this!'

The apparition in the hall turned to the sound of his voice

and attempted to focus bleary eyes on him. A mouth opened in the dirt-streaked face but the sound that came from it was no more than a croak. The swaying figure sagged off balance, knees buckling under it, and Gilmour lunged forward to catch it as it fell towards the litter of broken crockery.

They had brought him into the drawing-room, Sandy realized, his opening eyes resting first on the ring of anxious faces around him and then travelling beyond them. He sipped at the glass of wine Mr Wishart was holding to his lips, then drank greedily. Full consciousness returned with its fiery bite in his throat, and he struggled to sit upright in the corner of the couch where they had placed him.

'Sir –!' Mastering a strange and unexpected thickness in his tongue, he managed to speak. 'I have something of the utmost importance to tell you, but –' his eyes flickered to Isobel and her mother '– it is secret.'

Wishart straightened to face his wife and daughter. 'Pray leave us, ladies,' he told them.

Mistress Wishart and Isobel exchanged glances. Plump face and pretty one settled into lines of determination. Mistress Wishart drew herself up and said briskly, 'James, for a man that is such a clever lawyer you can whiles be a terrible fool! That boy is near dead with exhaustion, and it is my duty to look after him.' She nodded to Isobel. 'Get water to bathe his face, miss! We must see if there are signs of fever under all that dirt.'

'Yes, *ma'am*!' Gathering up her skirts Isobel ran lightly from the room, and Mistress Wishart bent over Sandy. 'Talk away if you must, lad,' she told him. 'Mistress Isobel and I will not tattle your secrets over the teacups, but I could not face your mother with a clear conscience if she knew I had left you now.'

Sandy looked to Wishart himself for guidance and saw

him exchanging glances with Gilmour over Mistress Wishart's head. The Customs man shrugged resignedly in reply to the other's look, and Wishart turned back to meet the question in Sandy's face.

'I will go bail for the ladies' discretion, Sandy,' he said. 'Tell me your news – but take your time about it, for you certainly look to be in a very haggard state.'

He reached for Sandy's glass to fill it again. Isobel came back with a bowl of water and a cloth, and while Mistress Wishart counted Sandy's pulse Isobel gently bathed the dirt off his face. The result satisfied them that he had no signs of fever on him, but apparently feeling that he might topple over again at any moment, Mistress Wishart held her ground and Isobel stayed with her.

Sandy took the glass that Wishart was thrusting into his hand and smiled his thanks at the two women. He was not ill of course – there was no need for such a fuss – it was just that last hour trying to hold himself upright in Gambler's saddle that had done for him . . . Still, it was pleasant to be the centre of all this attention! He sipped his wine, trying to put his confused thoughts in order so that he could tell his story quickly and simply. Then looking up at Wishart, he began talking.

Half a dozen times as he spoke he saw that both Gilmour and Wishart were having to keep a tight rein on a desire to interrupt with questions, but no one spoke a word till he came to tell of the way he had used the sheepskin to help him escape.

'So that is why you smell so badly!' Isobel exclaimed then. Her remark broke the tension in the room and everybody, except Gilmour, laughed at it. Gilmour was regarding him, Sandy noticed, with rather a strange look. There was speculation in it and also a kind of grim approval that gave him a sudden feeling of elation. Diplomatically, he left out any mention of the panic that had struck him as he fled from the valley, and touched only lightly on the exhausted state he had reached before he started off on the course that led him to Archie's search-party.

'I got my brother's horse from him,' he finished, 'and rode straight to Edinburgh. I stabled the beast with Hoseah Eastgate, and then found that the city gates were shut for the night, but I managed to persuade the porter on duty at the Netherbow Port to let me through the wicket at the side of the main gate – and so here I am.'

His voice tailed away on the last words, and with the ending of his effort to concentrate on his story came sudden fresh awareness of the aches and pains which had made the long ride on Gambler such an ordeal. He felt limp. He was cold, in spite of the momentary warmth of the wine. The effect of it on an empty stomach was making his head spin and he was only vaguely aware of Wishart's surprised voice saying,

'And you rode straight here without even stopping to rest after such an experience!'

'I thought it urgent to reach you, sir,' he mumbled.

Mistress Wishart's voice came, suddenly loud, in his ear, 'It is more urgent now that you be fed, washed, and rested,' and he looked up to see her rising briskly to her feet.

'Isobel,' she commanded, 'fetch food for him while I get hot water and clean linen ready.'

'Are you very hungry, Sandy?' Isobel asked.

'As a hunter, Mistress Isobel,' he told her fervently, and laughing as she followed her mother from the room, she called back to him, 'I will heap the plate high!'

Wishart looked at Gilmour. 'This will take some unravelling before we get to the truth,' he commented, 'but St Clair is the key, and if we can –'

'Did I guess correctly about him?' Sandy sat upright to interrupt, his fatigue forgotten in a swift revival of curiosity about St Clair. 'Is he a Jacobite spy?' Eagerly he looked from Wishart to Gilmour, and it was the latter who spoke.

'Kevin St Clair,' he said slowly, 'has no politics. His services are for sale to the highest bidder, and in this case, it would appear to be the Jacobites who are making use of them.'

'But who is he?' Sandy pressed.

'An Irishman by birth,' Gilmour answered. 'One who has had many years' experience in various Continental armies.'

'And what services are these he has to offer?'

Gilmour and Wishart exchanged glances and then Gilmour said, 'He is a professional revolutionary.'

'A type,' Wishart added soberly, 'that crops up every so often in history – a man without attachment to any cause or religious faith, and therefore with no ideals to hamper him. A man to whom pity is only an expression of inefficiency, and mercy a tactical error. You were very lucky to escape from him, Sandy.'

Gilmour said suddenly, 'I think you should beware of taking all this too seriously, Mr Wishart. After all, Jacobite plots of one kind or another have been hatched every summer since the rebellion of 1715 was crushed. They are ten a penny, and none of them has ever come to anything.

'You apparently know St Clair's reputation as well as I do,' Wishart retorted. 'If the Jacobites have commissioned him to some enterprise, we *must* take it seriously!'

Turning away, he began his characteristic nervous pacing up and down. 'Let us look at such facts as we have,' he went on. 'St Clair is secretly buying horses which would make good cavalry mounts and disposing of them again through men who have all the appearance of cavalry officers. Now, what does that suggest? Think back to the circumstances of the '15 rebellion. Why did that fail?'

'Lack of organization – a weak command divided in itself,' Gilmour answered. 'We all know the reasons.'

'Ach!' Wishart shook his head impatiently. 'You have not given the campaign sufficient study. There was another reason for the failure of that rebellion – the Jacobites lacked cavalry. All the horse they had were several small troops of gentlemen volunteers who were never properly organized into an effective striking unit. And without an effective cavalry force they will never be able to mount the kind of campaign they need to win back the throne. Agreed?'

'Yes, sir, but –'

'And if St Clair is building up such a body,' Wishart bore on over Gilmour's objections, '– as seems very likely from what Sandy has observed – all our reasoning points to the fact that the Jacobites intend to rise again – in force! In force!' he repeated, glaring at Gilmour. 'And we must stop them, sir! We must track down St Clair, capture him, and make him disgorge the plans for this new rebellion – and we must do so speedily!'

'*We* must do so?' Haughtily Gilmour returned the fierce look the lawyer was bending on him. 'You may do as you wish, sir, but politics are not my concern – and in any case, I have no authority at all in that field. *My* duty is to continue with my assignment of capturing Robertson.'

Distress crumpled Wishart's long pale face. 'Gilmour, you disappoint me! Can you honestly mean that you intend to put the defence of the throne second to the small matter of an escaped smuggler – you, a trained investigator who are the very man to hunt St Clair down?'

'It is not a small matter,' Gilmour stated coldly. 'It is a part of a much larger scheme of things which – as I have already mentioned – is not for discussion outside the Service. But now, it seems, I am forced to speak of it to make my position clear to you – No, let him stay!'

Interrupting himself as he caught the changed direction of Wishart's glance, he nodded to Sandy and added, 'He is fairly deep in the matter already, and his actions have shown extraordinary resource so far. I may need to use him again.'

'I will be very willing to help, sir,' Sandy volunteered.

Gilmour surveyed him with a look that was not encouraging. 'You will be no help to me if you get into another such situation by exceeding your instructions. Remember that!'

'Yes, sir.' Prudently Sandy effaced himself again, and speaking to Wishart, Gilmour continued,

'In case you are not aware of the extent of the smuggling trade on the English coast, let me inform you that around sixty per cent of all taxable goods are now being brought into the country as contraband. In effect, sir, smuggling has become a major business enterprise – to the great detriment of the country's whole economy. The Customs Service is stretched to its limit in the attempt to crush this enterprise, and even with militia regiments to help us, we are just managing to hold our own in the struggle.'

'But Scotland –' Wishart began, and interrupting, Gilmour swept the words away from him, '– will go the same way unless we can stop the rot! It is only because the Scottish tax laws have so recently been brought into line with those of the rest of the kingdom that there has not yet been any attempt to build smuggling into the hugely profitable concern it is in England. But that will come – the signs are there! And until we can expand our forces sufficiently to meet that developing threat, we must strengthen those that already exist by rooting out such corrupt officials as the man I have just consigned to the Tolbooth. And even more importantly, we must quickly bring to book all such criminals as Robertson, and so repair the damage they have done to the prestige of the Service. Only thus can we deter others from following their example.'

In the pause that followed his words, Wishart studied him with surprise growing on his face. 'You talk,' he said, 'as if your assignment were part of a country-wide plan!'

'It is,' Gilmour told him quietly. 'I am only one agent

among many, and the case of Robertson is only the first on my schedule.'

There was another pause, a longer one, during which Wishart polished one side of his nose thoughtfully with a long forefinger, and Gilmour prowled restlessly up and down the room. Isobel Wishart came in with a tray of dishes and motioned Sandy to the table, and as he drew a chair in for himself the argument began again.

'You have produced a good theory for St Clair's activities,' Gilmour said, 'but there is one thing it does not explain, and that is Robertson's visit to the camp. Why did he go there? What action was he trying to persuade Lumsden and Rattray to take with him? What is this "trouble" he threatens to make for St Clair? Is he connected in some way with the Jacobite plotting? These are all questions to which I must find answers, for the answers might lead me to the man himself – and here, I suggest, we could find common meeting-ground for your duty and mine.'

'Aha!' Wishart pounced on his words. 'I think I follow you. You are suggesting that these two cases – Robertson's and St Clair's, might be investigated in parallel!'

'With Robertson himself as the connecting link between them.' Gilmour nodded. 'And, of course, with my continued pursuit of him as the focal point in the investigation. But remember, sir, that I have no authority in political matters. We must take steps to transfer what will be essentially a holding operation on my part to the proper authorities and to that end I suggest you start preparing a report of Sandy's discovery for forwarding to London.'

'I will draw up an affidavit,' Wishart announced. 'The boy will sign it and I will witness his signature in due legal order, and we will send it to – to –'

'That powerful patron of yours, the Duke of Argyll,' Gilmour supplied, smiling a little at the lawyer's enthusiasm. 'And a copy of it must also go to my Chief at Customs

House, with a covering letter from me asking him to press the Duke to send a political agent to take over that side of the case.'

'Good, good! We progress!' Wishart rubbed his hands with satisfaction and called jocularly down the table to Sandy, 'You approve, eh, Sandy?'

'Yes, sir, I do.' Sandy's glance slid from Wishart to Gilmour. 'But where do we start this new investigation – in Kidlaw Valley?'

'No, no!' Gilmour waved the suggestion aside. 'Your discovery of that camp will have put St Clair well and truly on the run from it! We start in the Tolbooth jail, where I have a prisoner – a renegade Customs officer who has been in league with Robertson. The possible link with St Clair will give me a new line of questioning for this man.'

'Can I be there when you question him?' Quickly Sandy slipped in his request before the conversation could turn away from him again. 'I will need to know what is said if I – if you still want me to help.'

'Very well,' Gilmour agreed.

'And my parents, sir.' Sandy turned to Wishart. 'How do I answer all the questions they are bound to ask when I appear at home again?'

'I will write them a letter that will explain enough without revealing too much,' Wishart assured him.

'Thank you, sir.' Suddenly remembering Wishart's other letter still lying where he had hidden it at home, Sandy fell discreetly silent again, and Wishart turned back to Gilmour.

'Just one more thing before I start work on that affidavit,' he said. 'That first time you saw St Clair – was there anyone with him, or did he speak to anyone?'

'No, he was alone – but my own theory, for what it is worth, is that he was attempting to make contact with someone. There was a clergyman – an elderly fellow, took the place St Clair had occupied at the book-stand, almost as if he had been waiting the opportunity to do so.'

'Did you know him?'

Gilmour shook his head and Isobel asked suddenly, 'That was on Thursday of last week, was it not – the afternoon of the day you arrived here?'

'Yes, Miss Isobel. Does that have some significance?' Gilmour's tone was very polite but it also conveyed quite clearly his opinion that this was not an affair in which a young lady should concern herself. Blushing, as she caught the note of faint disparagement in his voice, Isobel said lamely,

'Perhaps. I – that is, I will have to think about it.'

'Pray do.' Gilmour's courteous tone still showed his feeling that women should have no part in such discussions. Isobel's blush faded and a little frown of annoyance appeared between her brows as he turned from her to tell Wishart,

'It is late, sir. We should be getting to work on these documents.'

'Sandy,' Wishart asked, 'do you feel fit to dictate the broad lines of your story to my writing?'

'There was nothing wrong with me that food and a bit of rest would not cure,' Sandy answered, rising to his feet. And I have both now.'

'Then we will go into my office,' Wishart informed them. He led the way there, majestically, and sat Sandy down in a chair by his desk while he gathered writing-materials together.

Like a client! Sandy thought, leaning luxuriously back in the chair. The dangers of his captivity seemed very remote now. He glanced up to see Gilmour watching him, and smiled. The tanned face, so gravely handsome against the snowy white of the wig above it, smiled back at him. At Wishart's command he began to dictate, and as he did so, he meditated on this curious business, danger. It was an unpleasant, almost a nauseating thing at the time of its happening, he thought, and yet how exciting it was in retrospect!

'A penny for them!' Gilmour spoke to him during a pause in the dictation, and taken unawares he blurted out, 'I was thinking about danger, sir – what strange effects it has on one.'

'It is an acquired taste,' Gilmour said quietly, 'only suitable for those who have the physique to tolerate it, and the intelligence to know how far to indulge it.'

That, Sandy thought, described it exactly! And suddenly a problem resolved itself in his mind – the problem of his future. He knew now the kind of career he wanted to follow. He continued dictating, with his eyes fixed on the quill travelling rapidly across the paper in front of Wishart, but with his mind on the tall figure of the Customs man leaning casually against the lawyer's desk.

Tomorrow, he thought, tomorrow he would ask Gilmour how one became a Special Investigator in the Customs Service!

7. The Birds of Strange Plumage

MR WISHART had been indulging a rather snobbish fancy when he spoke about his wife's preparing a 'guest-chamber' for Deryck Gilmour, for his household was as cramped for room as every other in the crowded old city. It was only in Sandy's quarters in the clerks' room, therefore, that there had been space for Mistress Wishart to set up a bed for the guest, and as they made their toilet there the following morning, Sandy decided to take the best advantage he could of this circumstance. Carefully he began on the little speech he had prepared.

'Mr Gilmour, sir, I hope you do not mind my putting this

to you, but I am not content to follow the law as my father has devised for me. I would like to enter a profession that requires a hearty body as well as an active mind, and I was wondering – that is, I thought I might –'

Gilmour paused in the act of settling his wig on his close-cropped dark hair. 'You were wondering –' he prompted.

'– how one becomes a Special Investigations officer in the Customs Service,' Sandy finished in a swift, embarrassed rush.

Gilmour's eyes skimmed quickly over him and came to rest on his rough, country shoes, both made in identical shape so that the wear on them could be evened out by using them interchangeably on the right or left foot.

'Go to a shoemaker and have yourself a proper pair of shoes made,' he said quietly. He looked up again. 'Then pay a visit to a barber. Tell him to crop that untidy head of hair that makes you look like a wild Highland pony, and have him make you a good wig.'

Sandy looked at him without answering. His face had taken on a stubborn expression which outlined the adult features underlying its youthful roundness, and with approval Gilmour saw the strong, bony shape it would presently have. A boy like this, he thought, a young fellow just breaking into manhood, active, with an original intelligence and good powers of observation, was just the kind of recruit the Special Investigations branch needed – provided he was not too proud to accept the fact that other attributes were also necessary. He waited for Sandy to speak and presently heard him say sullenly,

'I was not brought up to be a drawing-room fop.'

'You are insolent.' Gilmour turned an immaculately groomed back on him and went off to breakfast, adding, 'Furthermore, you are stupid if you have not realized that such work as I do requires a presence acceptable in all ranks of society.'

They supped porridge together in a silence that was tranquil on Gilmour's part, hostile on Sandy's, until eventually Gilmour said,

'I take it you have some experience in handling small boats, Sandy?'

'Yes, sir.' Sandy glanced doubtfully at him. 'There is very little I do not know about that.'

'Good!' Gilmour nodded approval. 'You can build on that experience. But you will also have to acquire at least a first mate's ticket in navigation.'

'You mean ...' Sandy checked himself, and stared with the dawn of delighted understanding on his face.

'Yes,' Gilmour told him briskly. 'But there are other essential requirements for our kind of work. For instance –'

'What was that?' Mr Wishart's long face appearing around the door poked inquisitively at Gilmour.

'Nothing of importance.' Casually Gilmour dismissed the query and turned the conversation to ask, 'Have you breakfasted, sir, or will you join us now?'

'Lord save you, I was up and breakfasted an hour ago!' Wishart exclaimed, 'and I have sought you now to tell you that I have decided to go to the Tolbooth with you this morning. I have slept on the matter, and it seems only right that some responsible citizen in this town should warn Captain Porteous of the evil intentions Robertson has towards him.'

His words jerked Sandy abruptly from the rosy dream Gilmour had evoked for him. Staring at Wishart he asked, 'What evil intentions, sir?'

'Murder!' Wishart threw out the word with a grimace of distaste. 'It looks as if there will shortly be a reprieve for Porteous, and if that happens, Robertson has sworn to kill him himself in revenge for Drew Wilson's death.'

'A scheme which was probably the subject of the quarrel you overheard him having with Lumsden and Rattray,'

Gilmour added. 'You will recall his parting words after he had failed to persuade them to his purpose.'

'*May the ghost of Drew Wilson haunt both of you and the Colonel,*' Wishart quoted. 'I, too, have considered that theory, Gilmour.'

'Indeed? Your concern for Porteous does you credit!' Smiling slightly, Gilmour glanced quizzically at the lawyer. 'Yet I have heard that Porteous is a brute, much hated in the town, and certainly the deliberate killing of unarmed citizens would seem to merit death – whether by the hangman's rope or by the assassin's knife-thrust does not seem to make much odds!'

'Agreed, agreed,' Wishart admitted. 'Yet my conscience forces me to deliver the warning – as yours will no doubt force you to try to protect Porteous from his fate even while you set him out as bait to bring Robertson out of hiding.'

Gilmour chuckled and pushed his empty plate away. 'You read character well, my friend,' he remarked. 'Lead on! I am ready.'

'Sir!' Rising with him, Sandy caught Gilmour's attention. 'What makes you think Robertson will choose a knife to assassinate Porteous?'

Gilmour paused in the act of moving to the door. 'His face bears a scar that is evidently the result of a knife-cut,' he answered, 'and I have never yet known of a man so wounded who is not, himself, a knife-fighter.'

Did Gilmour *never* miss a point? Sandy pondered the question all the time they were threading a way to the Tolbooth through the morning chaos of the High Street, and thought he was beginning to see why his inquiry about joining the Service had been so coolly received. It was apparently not such a simple business as it had seemed last night at the moment of his inspiration, he thought ruefully, and wondered when he would have the opportunity to ask Gilmour what qualifications were needed apart from a knowledge of navigation and 'a presence acceptable in all ranks of society'.

Halting with the other two outside the main door of the prison, he noted curiously how Gilmour was taking in every detail of the narrow alley which was all the Tolbooth's peculiar position left of the High Street's width at this point, and while Wishart rapped to summon the porter from his lodge beside the prison entrance, he volunteered,

'They call this lane "the Krames", sir. The name comes from these wooden booths tucked against the wall of St Giles, there.'

He pointed to the trinket-laden stalls crammed between the buttresses of the church wall facing on to the prison. Gilmour nodded acknowledgement of the information and indicated the soldier in cocked hat and uniform of rusty-red colour parading slowly with fixed bayonet outside the prison door.

'That, I take it, is a member of the Town Guard?'

'Yes, sir,' Sandy confirmed. 'There is always one on duty here, and others inside the main hall of the prison.'

The gate-porter answered Wishart's knocking at that moment and they turned to the main door of the prison. It was a massive structure of heavy oak timbers, thickly bossed with iron, and it swung open under the porter's hands as slowly as a rock being levered from position. The foulness of the prison air struck them with its opening, and gasping under the impact, they stumbled up the flight of stairs inside.

At the top of these stairs was another door. Their porter hammered on it, shouting the while to some unseen colleague, 'Turn your hand! Turn your hand for Peter of the gatehouse!'

The turnkey inside obeyed the shout. The door swung open to admit them to the inner prison, and it did not need Wishart's word of explanation to let Gilmour know they had stepped straight into the prisoners' common recreation room.

They were in a hall measuring some twenty by thirty feet. Around three sides of this hall ran a waist-high wooden barrier which created a passage for patrolling Town Guard soldiers as well as visiting space for those crowding forward to speak to the prisoners milling around in the main body of the hall on the barrier's further side. On the hall's fourth side stood a high pulpit, and on this side also was the beginning of the spiral staircase leading to the prison's upper floors.

Tall, grimy-paned windows high up in the wall facing the entrance door threw pale light on the scene, and beneath these windows part of the wall had been partitioned off to make two small rooms – one a sort of guardroom holding keys, muskets, and handcuffs, and the other apparently serving as an office for a large, untidily dressed man hunched over a desk there.

Wishart waved a hand in the direction of the desk-bound man: 'There is Governor Andrew Monro, whom you will meet presently,' he told Gilmour, 'but meanwhile, let us have a look for Porteous among these rascals.'

Gilmour and Sandy moved with him to the barrier and searched the faces that turned towards them. They belonged to a strange assortment of humanity – some betraying their long imprisonment in ragged clothes and emaciated bodies, others well-fed and still sleek but yet with a sickening air of false bravado which showed the fear beneath the jaunty exterior. Others again – raffishly-dressed men these, in the main – had a careless ease of manner which showed a familiar contempt for their surroundings.

It flashed across Sandy's mind that Rattray would have looked like this last class of prisoner, and in that same instant he saw Porteous holding court among a small group of men whose air of seedy gentility was that of bankrupts serving a term for debt.

'There he is!' Exclaiming, he pointed Porteous out, and added for Gilmour's benefit, 'The one in the Town Guard uniform, sir.'

Gilmour gazed along the line of his pointing hand and saw Porteous as a thick-set man in his early fifties, with a sallow-skinned face deeply pitted by smallpox scars. The uniform Sandy had mentioned hung on him as if he had lost considerable weight since it was fitted and the white braiding on the cocked hat dangling from his fingers was soiled almost to the black of the hat itself. Nevertheless, he was talking volubly, one thick forefinger wagging his opinions at the men in front of him, and dryly Gilmour observed,

'Prison may have thinned your former Captain of the Town Guard, but it does not seem to have subdued him.'

'He was always an overbearing man,' Wishart returned, and raised his voice to call, 'Porteous! Captain Porteous, sir, a word with you!'

Porteous turned to the sound of his name being called, then strutted a way through the crowd towards their place at the barrier.

'Lawyer Wishart,' he observed. 'What brings you to see me? You are not my man of affairs.'

'I regret I have not that pleasure,' Wishart told him with no regret at all in his voice, 'but I considered it my duty to visit you since I have word of something that deeply concerns you.'

'My reprieve? You have heard it has arrived?' A sudden flush of excitement reddened the pock-marked skin, and slowly subsided again as Wishart said, 'No, not that, but –'

'It will come!' Vehemently Porteous interrupted. 'It will come soon!'

'How can you be so certain?' Wishart, his long face avid

99

with curiosity, stared at the other man. 'A man convicted of multiple murder as you have been surely cannot count on a reprieve.'

Almost snarling, Porteous told him, 'I have been a loyal servant of the Crown, and I was only doing my duty when I opened fire on that mob. Queen Caroline will recognize that! She will not refuse my petition.'

'Well, well,' Wishart pacified him, 'we must hope that will be so. But hear me, Captain Porteous. If and when you do go free, you will still be in mortal danger for Geordie Robertson has sworn to kill you in revenge for the death of his friend, Wilson. I have good warrant for thinking he means to carry out his threat, and I considered it my duty to warn you so that you can guard against it when you do leave prison.'

Quietly, before Porteous could reply, Gilmour added, 'I am an officer in Government service, sir, and I have an interest in capturing this man, Robertson. I am prepared to provide you with a suitable bodyguard whose duty it will be to arrest him when he shows himself in the attack he has planned on you.'

Porteous looked at them, his heavy face swinging to each man in turn. Then he laughed, a brief contemptuous sound. Speaking to Wishart he said,

'Lawyer Wishart, you may save your breath to cool your porridge! I know you for an old High Street gossip, and you will not panic me with your stories. And even if this one is true, I am a soldier and well able to take care of myself.'

He paused to survey Gilmour again, and with heavy irony in his voice added, 'Certainly I would not look to such a pretty young gentleman for protection!'

With a flourish of his shabby hat he turned away from the barrier and strutted back to the equally shabby group of his fellow-prisoners.

'Ass! Pompous ass!' Wishart fumed: 'I told you what sort of man he is, Gilmour, and now you have the proof of it. He is more overbearing than ever.'

'He is sick,' Gilmour said quietly. 'His mind is sick. I have known before of such cases – brutal men who suffered from delusions of grandeur which grew worse as time passed: And when the end came – when they found they could not defeat death itself, a curious paralysis overcame them. They died mute, immovable, death's prisoner, unable even to lift a finger to help themselves. I think somehow that Porteous is also marked out for that kind of death.'

A feeling like that of a cold hand running down his spine made Sandy shiver. He was aware of Wishart saying hastily, 'Yes, well – we will see Governor Monro now,' and shaking off his feeling of horror he moved after the two men.

'*I have known before of such cases . . .*' he recalled Gilmour's words as he moved. Did that mean he had studied medicine – and if so, was that another of the qualifications required of a Special Investigator in Customs? Making a mental note to ask Gilmour about this also, he turned to listen to the conversation going on between him and the Governor.

Monro had heaved himself to his feet, with difficulty easing his large belly out from behind his desk, and he was jingling a bunch of keys in his hand. 'Up on the third floor, Mr Gilmour,' he was saying. 'That is where I have penned the fox that was robbing *your* poultry-yard! I will lead you to him myself.'

He waddled off to the staircase beside the pulpit, the others following, and they began to climb. A rope, cleated to the wall at intervals, made an essential hand-hold in the steep, winding ascent, and as they climbed, the Governor's voice floated down to them from his leading position.

'Hold on to the rope, gentlemen, 'tis a good one! It was used once to hang a man!'

Sandy, bringing up the rear behind Gilmour, heard the hiss of his indrawn breath at these words and said quickly, ''Tis only his humour, sir. He makes that jest to everyone who climbs this stair for the first time.'

'Has he many more jests?' Gilmour asked dryly.

'Aye, indeed,' Sandy assured him. 'Enough to earn him the byename of "Merry Andrew".'

A grunt from Gilmour finished the conversation. They came out on to the third floor of the prison and the Governor turned to them, panting, but still grimly jovial.

'Here are caged all my birds of strange plumage,' he announced, 'the thieves, the murderers, the forgers, the coin-clippers – the felons all! Follow me closely now, gentlemen. This floor is a very rabbit-warren of passages, and I would not wish you to be like the man travelling from Jerusalem to Jericho!'

'Who "fell among thieves", eh?' Wishart chuckled. 'Well, Andrew, you may point the dangers of losing our way here with the parable of the Good Samaritan, but I think my nostrils catch a whiff of sulphur, all the same!'

'Ah, but you know what they say, James,' the Governor retorted slyly. 'The Devil can quote Scripture for his own ends!'

He laughed, and the jovial sound rebounded in strange, distorted echoes from the doors of plate-iron lining the passage into which he had led his party: *Like laughter in Hell!* Sandy thought, his imagination morbidly affected by the foul prison stench and the blank iron faces of the cell doors. The cold grue ran down his back again, and involuntarily he quickened his step till he was almost treading on Gilmour's heels down the gloomy passage.

They found their man behind one of the doors of plate-iron at last, after innumerable turns and twists through the passage-maze, and true to his reputation Merry Andrew quipped as he threw the cell door wide.

'Here is the hangman come to measure you for your gallows, Johnstone!'

The man in the cell stumbled to his feet, glancing uncertainly from one face to another. His own face was round, and lard-white now with fear, and he had pale eyes that came to rest eventually with desperate appeal on Gilmour.

'I am not for hanging, sir, am I?' he quavered. 'Say you will not make a hanging case against me! I was a good officer before I – before . . .'

Why did not Gilmour say something to put the poor wretch out of his misery, Sandy wondered, listening pitifully to the whining voice that choked itself out into sobs, and then silence. Gilmour was regarding the prisoner steadily, and his face might have been cast in bronze for all the expression on it. No one else spoke, and the tense silence endured till Sandy felt it like a living thing he could have reached out and touched with his hand. Gilmour's voice dropped into the silence, implacable, and icily cold.

'I might have considered your former good record,' it said, 'if you had told the whole truth about Robertson. But you did not, Johnstone. You shielded him, and shielded yourself in the process. So now you must take the full consequences of the crime you have not confessed.'

'But, sir – I told you everything!' Gaspingly the man replied, stretching out pleading hands. 'I told you the system – the smuggler's signal-code – how I get information to Robertson – how much he paid me. I told you everything!'

'Except the most important thing!' Gilmour rapped out. 'How long has Robertson been working for St Clair, eh, Johnstone? You did not tell me that, did you?'

With a long stride that took him across the cell he seized hold of the prisoner's coat and drew him close to himself. 'Did you?' His voice a soft snarl he repeated the question, staring down at the pale eyes in the lard-white face. They flickered away from his gaze. The slack mouth beneath them mumbled,

'Who is St Clair? I never heard of him.'

'Liar!' Contemptuously Gilmour flung the man from him, and turned to the Governor. 'There will be serious charges against this man,' he said curtly. 'See that he is chained while I go before the Procurator Fiscal to lodge a precognition of the evidence against him.'

'I will see it done immediately.' No longer merry, his fat belly now an added measure of dignity, the Governor drew himself upright on the promise.

'Mr Wishart, you will prepare the affidavit of my evidence, of course.' Ignoring Johnstone, Gilmour began to draw the lawyer from the cell with him 'And now that Robertson is in our hands at last, we will have to –'

'Wait! Wait, Mr Gilmour!' A cry like the yelp of someone trodden on came from behind them.

'What is it? What d'ye want now?' Impatiently Gilmour glanced back over his shoulder, and the prisoner came cringing up to him.

'Have you taken Robertson? Have you?' he stammered.

'What is that to you? You have told me all you know of him.' Indifferently Gilmour turned away again, but with a despairing clutch at his arm, the prisoner shrieked,

'Hear me, Mr Gilmour, hear me! I swear to God I had no hand in Robertson's ploys with St Clair, and if he is trying to blacken me with that charge he lies in his teeth and may he burn in hell for it! I never knew what was in the packets he carried – I swear it, Mr Gilmour, I swear it! All I ever did was to give him the position of the Customs sloops before he sailed for France. That was all, Mr Gilmour, that was all!'

With difficulty, Gilmour prised the clutching fingers off his arm. '*Johnstone!*' His voice cut sharply across the snivels of the man drooping in his grasp. 'Stand upright, man!

Stand straight, and make a report to me like an officer of the Service should, and when your case comes up I will see that your good record is taken into consideration.'

Slowly the man Johnstone lifted his drooping head. Slowly he straightened his shoulders. Gilmour watched him carefully.

'Be truthful,' he warned. 'You know the kind of charges that will be brought against Robertson. You know the penalty that attaches to them, and if you do not want to stand arraigned of high treason also, you will tell me the whole truth. Now!'

'Yes, sir.' Johnstone wiped his streaming eyes with his sleeve. His voice was still unsteady, but it grew firmer as he went on, 'St Clair came from France in Geordie's boat at the beginning of the year, sir. I warned him where the Customs sloops would be patrolling at the time of the trip, not knowing St Clair was on board, but thinking Geordie was carrying his usual goods for the Lothian run. Geordie was arrested for the robbery of the Collector not many weeks afterwards, but then he escaped from jail, and after that he began carrying packets for the Colonel between France and the Lothian ports.'

'What sort of packets?'

'Small ones, sir. Geordie said there were documents in them. He said he was working as a courier between the Colonel and the Jacobites in France, and I dug my heels in at that and said I would not tell him any more about the movements of the Customs sloops. But Geordie – Geordie had the advantage of me, sir. He said he could put me in jail any time with just one word to the Comptroller of Customs at Leith, and I knew that was true. I just had to go on helping him until –'

'Until when? Go on, man!' Gilmour prompted the faltering narrative.

'Until ten days ago, sir. Just a few days before you – before you found me out. Geordie came to see me then. He had one of the Colonel's packets on him, and he was very excited. He showed it to me – not what was in it, but the packet itself – and he said to me, *"You can stop shaking in your shoes about me blowing the gaff to the Comptroller, Johno boy, for I've got what I wanted off the Colonel and I'll not be needing you any more !"*'

'And that was the last you saw of him?'

'Yes, sir.'

'And what did he mean by saying he had got what he wanted off the Colonel?'

'As God is my judge, sir, I cannot tell you that – but I thought at the time he was crazy, for his eyes glittered so and that scar on his cheek was jumping like a live thing! I was glad to see him go that day, glad to get him off my back at last. I meant to mend my course then – repair some of the damage I had done the Service. And then you came along – turning up the records, asking questions, questions . . .'

Johnstone stopped speaking. He had been looking straight ahead at the blank wall of the cell all this time, but now his eyes came round to meet Gilmour's gaze.

'Now I *have* told you all I know, sir,' he said quietly. 'And I did mean to mend my course. That is the truth.'

'Very well. I passed my word to you and I will honour it when the time comes.' Gilmour nodded to Johnstone. To the others he said, 'Our business here is finished, gentlemen.' He strode from the cell, and in silence the others followed him. Governor Monro took the lead, and in this order they descended to the level of the hall again.

'You are a hard man to be up against, Mr Gilmour,' the Governor said as they took their leave of him at his office. He was still strangely subdued for Merry Andrew and, Sandy thought, it was no wonder after the ferocious intensity of the interview with that poor snivelling wretch on the third floor!

Outside the prison they paused to draw lungfuls of the purer air of the High Street. 'Well, Gilmour,' Wishart remarked, 'the link is fairly established now, is it not? Though mind you, we were slow not to have realized the nature of Robertson's connection with the Jacobites. A smuggler, with his knowledge of the Lothian run – he was an obvious choice for courier work!'

'Maybe.' Gilmour frowned, reviewing something in his mind. 'But there are still many questions that Johnstone's confession leaves unanswered. Why was Robertson so excited about that last packet he carried? Did he intend to steal it, instead of delivering it as he was supposed to? If so, is that packet the source of the "trouble" he threatens to make for St Clair? And what bearing, if any, has all this on his threat against Porteous?'

'You should have been a lawyer,' Wishart observed.

Gilmour laughed shortly. 'I almost was! But then it was whispered to me that the Service was looking for men with legal training combined with certain other abilities, and so I turned my experience to other purposes.'

'H'mm.' Wishart considered this, slyly noting the look that passed between Gilmour and Sandy as he did so. 'What next, then?' he asked. 'What will your next move be?'

'Routine according to Service procedure,' Gilmour told him. 'A very useful guide, sir! I have still to check the Customs houses on the Lothian side of the Forth, and I will do that now. There is no telling what I might turn up there!'

'And Sandy?' Wishart asked.

'Will go back to Prestonpans to do what he was told to do in the first place,' Gilmour answered.

'I thought you would say that!' Smiling, Wishart drew a sealed letter from his pocket and handed it to Sandy. 'There,' he remarked. 'That will stave off your father's curiosity for a bit. Was he angry with you when he read my first letter?'

Sandy drew a deep breath. 'I did not give it to him, sir,' he confessed. 'I have been thinking that I will not give up the law after all – not for a while longer, at least. I may need more knowledge of it for – for a plan I have in mind.'

'Which will also require some basic skill in medicine,' Gilmour added. 'Not to mention a good ear for languages, a knowledge of ciphers and shipping administration, together with the technique of knife-fighting and the ability to handle small boats, shoot straight and ride fast. It would also be advisable to acquire at least a first mate's ticket in navigation.'

Wishart and Sandy gaped at him, each for different reasons astounded by this speech. Wishart was the first to recover his breath.

'Correct me if I am wrong, Sandy,' he said carefully, 'but do I understand from this that you wish to follow Mr Gilmour's profession?'

Sandy shifted his feet uncomfortably. 'I would like to, sir – if he thought I was suited to it, but – I was not aware that all these skills would be needed.'

'There are ways of acquiring them that can be discussed later,' Gilmour told Wishart briskly. 'But the point you have to decide, sir, is – are you prepared to let him go?'

'Are you prepared to accept him if I do?' Wishart countered, and smiling, Gilmour answered,

'I will know that by the time this assignment is finished!'

'In that case,' Wishart said cautiously, 'I will think about my side of the matter.' He turned a warning glance on Sandy. 'But remember, it is not a decision to be reached lightly.'

'Yes, sir,' Sandy agreed, but his heart sang all the same for Wishart's glance had been more kindly than sharp, and it seemed to him that he could read consent, already, into it.

8. Live Bait

'SANDY,' Sandy's father said, 'you are a fool!'

'Mr Wishart told me that also, sir,' Sandy pointed out, 'but that was before Mr Gilmour arrived, and he is beginning to think differently now.'

'Nevertheless, he has not agreed to let you go!' Mr Maxwell said triumphantly. 'And Wishart is a man of good sense.'

'And so is Mr Gilmour,' Sandy argued. 'Besides, Mr Wishart has agreed to consider the matter.'

The argument was taking a hopeful turn, he thought, and waited expectantly for the reply to this reminder. His father was flicking Wishart's letter between thumb and forefinger, frowning, and glancing occasionally from him to his mother and brother as if he expected them to make some remark. Neither of them was foolish enough, however, to risk deflecting the master of the household's wrath in their direction, and eventually he said,

'You say this fellow Gilmour is to rendezvous here with you on his way back from Dunbar?'

'That was the arrangement we parted on,' Sandy confirmed.

'Then I will speak to him myself when he does come here,' Mr Maxwell said grimly.

He rose, and laying a hand on Sandy's shoulder added in a gentler tone, 'You think I am old and hard, laddie, and not in touch with your modern ways of thinking. I can see it in your face! But what *you* do not see is that I want only your happiness and success in life, and I have a responsibility to see whether this Mr Gilmour can help you to these things better than Mr Wishart can. So content yourself for the next few days, and we will see what happens then.'

He nodded to Archie. 'Come lad, we must get the rest of that barley field in.'

Archie followed him from the kitchen, turning at the door to flash an encouraging grin to Sandy and to make the gesture they both understood as a promise to talk secretly together when they were alone that night.

At Sandy's back, Mistress Maxwell said, 'You are being a sore trial to your parents, boy. I wonder your father was so reasonable with you in the end!'

'He is a reasonable man at heart, ma'am,' Sandy pointed out, 'or I would never have been able to risk being so frank with him!'

He moved to the door and Mistress Maxwell asked sharply, 'Where are you off to?'

'The harbour, ma'am,' he told her. 'I have business there for Mr Gilmour.'

'Aye. Aye, you did say that.' Her face troubled, she came forward to lay a hand on his arm. 'But you *will* be careful, Sandy? And you *will* be home for supper?'

Sandy smiled reassuringly at her. 'Be easy, ma'am. I am in no danger, and you can certainly count on hunger to drive me home again before dark!'

'You ate little enough dinner,' she told him mournfully, and he left her, thinking that was true enough! Between picking and choosing the right words for his first explanation to his father, and then holding his own in the fierce argument that had followed, he had had little chance to eat his dinner. Still, it was over now – for the time being, at any rate. And it had not been nearly as much of an ordeal as he had feared when he parted from Gilmour that morning!

Whistling cheerfully as he went, he reached the farm road-end. Before him now, the mile-long stretch of Birsley Brae dropped downwards, with the waters of the Firth of Forth beyond it and the village of Prestonpans straggling along the coastline at the brae-foot. His mind shifted to the task ahead, and frowningly as he strode down the brae, he considered how best to approach it.

The fisher-people of Prestonpans, he reminded himself, were a wary lot! And he – for all the summers he had spent working on their boats and the time he had passed at sea with them – was still one of the landward people they distrusted so much.

George Robertson, on the other hand, was one of their own kind. Moreover, they were all to a more or less extent involved in the smuggling trade, and they would be on their guard immediately anyone started probing for information about him. How could he disarm suspicion among them? How loosen their tongues so that, knowingly or not, they gave away the information he needed?

A week ago he had thought that all he had to do was to mention the subject of tea to set their tongues wagging, but now he was not so sure. It might just be, he thought, that talk of any smuggled goods would be the very thing that would make them clam up!

The problem, he found, was still very much with him by the time he reached the village, and sparing only vague reply to the numerous greetings called out to him as he strode along the High Street, he turned into one of the narrow vennels that led down between the houses, to the sea.

The harbour where the oyster-boats were berthed lay at the end of this vennel – though properly speaking, he supposed, it was not really a harbour at all. There was the sea-wall, forming a breakwater for the houses built on rocky foundations above it. At the wall's foot was a narrow strip of shingle, and beyond that a tiny, irregular bay with a tumble of huge rocks lining its foreshore. It was in the shelter of the inlets between these rocks that the oystermen found anchorage for their boats, and from the path that ran along the top of the sea-wall he looked down on their activities.

They were the ones normal to the start of a new season's fishing, which – he made a rapid calculation – would start in less than a fortnight's time now, on the first of September.

A row of boats, each twenty feet long and with a six-foot beam, lay upended on the beach, hauled up by the block and tackle fixed to a great iron ring let into the masonry of the seawall. A flat rock on the foreshore was piled high with oakum for caulking gaping seams, and buckets of steaming pitch with their round, long-handled brushes beside them were dotted over the shingle of the beach. Men with bare feet, brown bodies stripped to the waist, moved deftly through the confusion, crouching like monkeys to caulk the seams, swinging the long brushes with expert ease from bucket to boat.

They were singing as they worked – one of the chanties the oyster-men had made famous along the coast – and the rhythm of it was so catching that, on the impulse, Sandy joined in. Faces turned up to look towards the sound of the new voice, some curious, some smiling a cautious welcome as Sandy was recognized. There were shouts of greeting, some friendly, others with a mocking undertone:

'*Aye, Sandy! Home to help with the harvest, are you?*'

'*It's a fine, tuneful pipe ye have, laddie!*'

'*Seeking work for white hands, are you, then?*'

The answer to his problem flashed across Sandy's mind. Wary or not, the fishermen had never despised his help on the boats in the past, and if he did take a hand in the work now he would be in an ideal position to overhear any talk of Robertson or to plant remarks that might lead the conversation round to him.

'Look out below!' he yelled, and leaped for the shingle below the sea-wall. An elderly fisherman caught his arm, steadying his landing beside one of the boats. A face weathered to the colour of teak bent over him, and vividly blue eyes in wind-narrowed sockets regarded him with cautious amusement.

'Right, Rob!' Sandy straightened up, kicked off his shoes and rapidly began throwing off his coat and shirt. 'Where d'ye want me to start?'

Rob Grierson considered, rasping stumpy fingers along his fringe of stiff grey beard. He was behind with the work on his boat and it would not be the first time the Maxwell laddie had lent a hand at the harbour ... Half-questioning, half-teasing, he said,

'I heard tell they are making a fine lawyer of you in Embro', Sandy. Are you not over-proud nowadays to take a hand with the pitch!'

'Ach, lawyer's work is a dull thing compared to this ploy, Rob!' Sandy told him. 'Forbye, you can see I have not lost the skill you taught me in the school holidays!'

Seizing one of the long-handled brushes as he spoke, he twirled it through the hot, dark mess of pitch in a bucket and drew it accurately along the line of a seam in the boat. Rob watched him, grinning and nodding approval before he went off to fetch more oakum, and Sandy dipped his brush into the pitch again with his ears cocked to the buzz of conversation that had replaced the men's singing.

So far, he thought with cautious triumph, so good! The fishermen had accepted him into their midst – but the other side of that coin, of course, was that he had now laid himself out like so much live bait on a hook to tempt their secrets out of hiding, and there was no telling what form their hostility might take if they glimpsed the hook beneath the bait! A bucket of hot pitch 'accidentally' overturned on a bare foot, a 'mis-timed' axe-stroke that would find a mark on his hand – there were a dozen ways they could revenge themselves on a prying intruder, and they had the name of always being quick to do so!

He would have to be very, very careful not to show too keen an interest in their conversation, Sandy warned himself, and suddenly fearful that his long silence might already have drawn suspicion of this on himself, he began to sing again. A laugh came from behind him as his voice rang out, and someone jeered,

'Hoo, hoo! Listen to the lawyer's laddie singing away there like a lintie in a cage!'

Sandy looked round, and recognized the owner of the jeering voice. 'You are just jealous, Dave Geddes,' he retorted, 'because your own singing is as cracked as the sound of the town bell!'

There was general laughter at the expense of Geddes, who combined his oyster-fishing with the role of town crier, and Rob Grierson shouted, ''Tis pity they are trying to make a gentleman of you, Sandy! You will soon be too nice in your manners to put Dave down the way he deserves!'

Sandy grinned, straightening up to wipe a pitch-blackened hand across his brow. 'Man, but it's hot!' he exclaimed.

'Aye,' Rob agreed, 'near as hot as the women-folks get the kitchen on baking-day!'

His voice was friendly – friendly enough, Sandy decided, to justify an opening gambit. 'Ach,' he said casually, 'the women-folks can endure anything so long as they get their dish of tea.'

'D'ye tell me that!' Rob's answer came in a noncommittal tone, and with a laugh Sandy said, 'So my mother says, anyway – and maybe that is why she complains so much when she is out of the stuff, as she is now.'

Quickly then, for fear Rob had begun to suspect him of planting remarks to lead the conversation, he bent to his work again. Gently does it, he reminded himself. Let them become accustomed to his presence and gradually he would be able to follow up such remarks, and meanwhile, let others apart from Rob come to rely on his help in getting the boats ready. That would breed good will from them too, and good will could loosen even fishermen's tongues.

He looked for opportunities to help his policy forward, and found them in plenty.

The supply of oakum ran out and he willingly changed over to picking the frayed rope-ends for a further supply. The block and tackle man called for assistance and he bore his weight on the rope. With the delay over the oakum, the pitch grew too cool, and he took his turn of carrying the buckets back to the fire for reheating.

Conversation buzzed around him ... *a good start to the season if the fine weather held ... price of Pandores still going up ... Tab Morrison's new boat a fine craft ... rumours of English boats coming to pirate the oyster-beds ...* Ears pricked, he gathered it all in, and found it disappointingly dull listening compared to what he had hoped to hear.

A jug of the local beer was passed round as the afternoon lengthened into evening. He took his share of the heavy dark stuff, then passed it to Rob Grierson, but before he drank Rob paused to say approvingly, 'Ye've worked hard, Sandy. Will you be down the morn, by any chance?'

'Aye, I like this fine, Rob, and I have a day or two of leave in hand,' Sandy told him. He glanced towards the trail of gold the westering sun was laying across the Firth's waters. 'But I had better be winning home now, or there will be a rolling-pin ready for laying across my knuckles!'

'You do that, Sandy. You do that,' Rob agreed. He stood, hands in pockets, watching Sandy put his shoes on, and as he turned to hoist himself back up the sea-wall, said quietly, 'Oh, and Sandy, tell your mother not to fret herself about tea. There is some due to be dropped soon, and I will see she gets her share.'

He had been right – he had been right after all about his mother's tea being a perfect lead into a mention of smuggling! And he had been right, too, when he had so carefully avoided following up his first remark about it!

Exultantly as he trudged homewards, Sandy congratulated himself on the first success of his campaign. And lying that night beside Archie in the big feather bed they had shared for as long as he could remember, he kept Rob Grierson's remark as the trimphant tail-piece to the long, whispered story of his adventures since he had met Deryck Gilmour.

'You are a right reckless young devil, Sandy,' Archie told him. 'Do you not fear to get hurt – even killed, in all this?'

Sandy chuckled. 'Away, Archie! Y'are a pessimist, man! I am enjoying myself too much to be feared, and anyway, I do not believe my destiny is to be hit on the head by a smuggler on the Lothian run!'

'Rather you than me,' Archie commented. 'I like a quiet life, watching the land, seeing things grow.'

He was silent for a few minutes, then he said, 'Sandy, that beast Gambler is a hard-mouthed creature, and over-wild for a farming fellow like me. But he would suit fine for the kind of high jinks you are up to – if you want to have him.'

'To keep?' The bed creaked as Sandy raised himself to stare incredulously at the dim outline of Archie's face.

'Aye, to keep. You can call it an early present for your next birthday if you like.'

Did ever a fellow have a brother like Archie? Sandy asked himself. Somehow he managed to stammer his thanks, and long after Archie at last put paid to their whispering by hunching himself up for sleep, he was still indulging himself with dreaming fancies of the figure he would cut on Gambler. Even Deryck Gilmour, he thought, would approve his presence then, and closed his eyes on a blissful vision of his father's consent won and himself accepted into the Service at last.

With the next morning's daylight, however, cold caution came again. At breakfast, he listened with humble attention to his father's further lecture, and waited till he and Archie were well on their way to the fields again before he mentioned casually to his mother that Rob Grierson would likely be getting some tea for her soon.

Mistress Maxwell smiled delightedly at the news. 'You just tell Rob then, that I will not see *him* forgotten,' she said warmly. 'There will be a peck of oats from the new grinding for him, and a keg of butter, too. You just tell him that, Sandy.'

'I will, ma'am,' Sandy assured her. *And with pleasure!* he added to himself. Such a message would increase his stock with Rob!

In high spirits he made a leisurely way down to the harbour again. The work there was already under way, but shortly after he arrived there was a considerable snag developed over the running of the block and tackle, and it was not until the men broke off for their dinner of herring, bannocks and beer that he found a chance to speak privately to Rob Grierson. He began casually then, with the air of suddenly remembering his mother's message,

'Oh, by the way, Rob, my mother was right pleased to hear about the tea. She said to tell you she would be sending down a keg of butter and a peck of oats from the new grinding.'

'She is a generous woman, Mistress Maxwell,' Rob said cordially. He leaned back against the sea-wall, eyes closed, and added with just the slightest edge to his tone, 'But of course you made no mention of tea to your sire!'

'Devil a bit,' Sandy assured him. 'I know his views on the subject, and so does my mother.'

Rob laughed. The conversation drifted to other matters, and when Sandy judged the other's guard had sufficiently relaxed, he asked,

'What will be the arrangements for picking up the tea, Rob?'

'The carrier from Dunbar will drop it in to your mother in a wee chest labelled *Sugar*,' Rob told him.

Sandy glanced round at the reply and studied the other's face. 'Certes, Rob,' he remarked with a laugh, 'you must admit that Cove Harbour is God's gift to smugglers!'

'Maybe so.' Rob met his glance levelly. 'But I never said where the goods were to be dropped.'

'No, you never did,' Sandy agreed, and grinned with bold complicity at him. He knew, and Rob knew, that Dunbar was the distribution point for goods dropped eight miles away at Cove Harbour! Moreover, he reminded himself exultantly, the Cove had always been Robertson's favourite landing-point. The richest cargoes on the Lothian run were landed there . . .

He let his smile fade, as if some unpleasant thought had occurred to him, and asked hesitantly, 'But can you still bring stuff in safely there? I mean – well, times have changed for those that used to manage the drops at the Cove . . .'

He let the sentence trail away, and picking up a handful of pebbles began idly tossing them from hand to hand. Rob Grierson lay farther back, complacently turning his face up to the sun.

'The bold ones go where the money is,' he said, 'and the Cove is still a rich run.'

Sandy laughed. 'I can think of one bold one that would not let the money in such a ploy go past him,' he remarked. 'Not for all the Sheriff Officers in the county *or* all the Customs men on the Lothian run!'

He became aware of eyes watching him and turned to meet Rob's sharp gaze. 'You will keep such thoughts to yourself then,' Rob told him quietly, 'or the one you are thinking of might come at you with a knife some dark night.'

He sat up again, brushing sand from himself, and added with a sort of brutal humour which made Sandy's flesh creep, 'And then your mother would not relish the tea that is promised her!'

Sandy gave the laugh that was expected of him, but behind the stretched smile on his face his mind was ticking with feverish calculation. Robertson *would* be on that drop! He knew the fishermen's evasive turn of speech well enough to be certain of that now – but when would the drop take place? He had to risk finding that out. If it was to be 'soon' as Rob had mentioned yesterday, he had a pretty good idea of when it would be – but how to find out for sure?

He began throwing pebbles at an empty bucket far down the foreshore, gradually making his aim more and more vicious to underline the discontent in his voice as he spoke.

''Tis you fellows have the best of it – out there on the Lothian run, dodging the Customs sloops in the dark night between the moon's setting and its rising again. That is a game *I* would fine like to play!'

'You would maybe play it well. You seem to know all the rules!'

Grierson's voice came with a new hardness in it that made Sandy turn to look swiftly at him again. The bright blue eyes that met his own were slitted suspiciously, and in a spasm of guilty fear Sandy felt himself flush before that look. Quickly he covered up with an outburst of pretended anger that he hoped would account for his flushed face.

'Damn the law! It has me caged like a niminy-piminy miss in a parlour when I should be leading a proper man's life!'

'*Sandy Maxwell!*' Scandalized, Rob seized him by the arm, suspicion diverted as Sandy had hoped it would be by such an example of youth's base ingratitude. 'What a way to talk – you that has had so much good money spent on your education! Now, if I had had your chances when I was a laddie –'

The scheme had worked too well, Sandy thought ruefully, and seeking deliverance from the lecture that threatened, spied Dave Geddes approaching with a face that had news in it.

'Hold hard, Rob,' he interrupted, 'there is Dave Geddes with his town-crier's tongue all ready to bellow some tidings!'

Geddes saw them looking, waved and quickened his pace up the shingle towards them. 'Have you heard the news, Rob?' Panting, he dropped down to sit with them, face shining with sweat and importance. 'There was a stranger called at the Customs post here this morning – a smart young gentleman they say he was, in a blue coat and a haughty look to his face, and there is a rumour going that he is the same one that took Geordie's friend in the Customs off to jail!'

'Bedamned to him then, for a poking, prying Government spy!' Grierson exclaimed, and Sandy's heart missed a beat at the venom in his voice.

Gilmour! he thought. It could be no other from the description Geddes had given, and besides, the time fitted with the schedule of visits he had intended to make. As unobtrusively as possible he rose to saunter down to the boats, and back at work again he calculated how long it would take Gilmour to return to their rendezvous at his own home.

The Customs post at Dunbar was the only other one on the route he had taken and that, Sandy decided, meant that he would probably be back at Bankton Farm by the following evening. It also meant another day at the boats for him, for it would never do to rouse Grierson's suspicions afresh by deserting the work immediately he had got the information he wanted!

As if the thought had summoned the man he became

aware of Grierson facing him across the width of the boat, and said innocently, 'The caulking's near finished, Rob. What work is in hand for tomorrow?'

Grierson gave him a long, hard look, then slowly his features relaxed. 'Man, ye're keen!' he remarked. 'I have nets that badly need new hoops, if you care to give a hand with them.'

Sandy glanced towards the line of rigid-framed oyster nets leaning against the sea-wall. 'I will give you the best part of the day at them,' he promised, 'and then I must be off, for I am due back in Edinburgh tomorrow night and my mother will be sore vexed if I do not get the tar off me first!'

He held out blackened fingertips for inspection. 'Aye,' Rob agreed, ''twill take a good puckle butter to clear *that* off your hands!'

Exchanging grins they bent to their several tasks, and once again, Sandy permitted himself an inward chuckle of congratulation. Rob, he thought, had been finely caught on the hook, and the live bait was none the worse for it!

'I have found out everything I want to know,' he boasted to Archie that night. 'There will be a smuggling drop at Cove Harbour on the thirty-first of this month – that will be "the dark night between the moon's setting and its rising again." Geordie Robertson will be on that drop, and that is when we will catch him, for sure. Then you will see me win my reward, Archie!'

'You have to catch this other fellow, St Clair, as well – or so you said,' Archie reminded him.

Yawning, Sandy answered, 'We will soon find out enough to take him once Gilmour starts to question Robertson. You should have seen the way he drew information from that prisoner in the Tolbooth.'

'I am glad I did not,' Archie retorted. 'It sounded cruel to me.'

Archie had his own way of thinking, Sandy decided. He would never understand a man like Gilmour. Gilmour was not cruel. He was inflexible, because justice itself was inflexible and he was dedicated to the pursuit of justice.

A sense of exaltation possessed him with the thought of his own share in this dedicated pursuit, and the mood it bred persisted all throughout his work on the nets the next morning. Bending and shaping the willows that formed the hooped upper-structure of each net, he allowed the dream continued possession of his mind, but after the dinner-break was past his thoughts sharpened to focus on the hoped-for arrival of Gilmour that evening.

He would time his departure for four o'clock, he decided, listening to each hour striking on the clock of the parish church, and prompt on the stroke of four he reached for his shirt and coat.

'I am off now, lads!' With a general shout of farewell he scrambled to the path at the top of the sea-wall. 'Bankton's dame will be after my blood if I stay longer!'

They waved and shouted in reply, promising Mistress Maxwell a basket of Pandores from the first catch, but in his eagerness to be off Sandy hardly heard them. Through the town and up Birsley Brae he strode at his best lick, and arrived in the kitchen at Bankton, smiling, and all ready to tease his mother with the sight of his tarry hands.

His mother was not smiling. She sat at the kitchen table, hands clasped in front of her, neglected sewing in her lap and her face a picture of apprehension.

'He is in there,' she told Sandy, nodding towards the door of the parlour. 'Your Mr Gilmour is in there with your father, and God knows what is going on between them for they have talked for over an hour already!'

'I had better clean my hands.'

Sandy could think of nothing else to say at that moment.

He went out to the dairy to work butter into his tarry fingers, and when he had cleaned off the resultant oily mess, came back to the kitchen. His mother was still there, but now she had a tray set with glasses and a flagon of wine on the table before her. Nodding towards it she said hopefully:

'They will maybe compose their differences over a glass of wine, if they have quarrelled in there.'

Sandy groaned inwardly, thinking that neither his father nor Gilmour was the kind of man to yield a principle over a casual glass of wine! Tense with expectancy, he fixed his gaze on the parlour door and settled down to wait.

Five minutes passed, ten, twenty; then suddenly the murmur of voices behind the door grew in volume. The door swung open. Gilmour stepped through it into the kitchen, with Mr Maxwell following.

'– and there is no doubt at all,' Mr Maxwell was saying, 'that the planting of trees is an excellent method of conserving the soil. The Improvers Society has tested –'

He saw Sandy then, and broke off to laugh at the expression of surprised resentment on his face. 'We have not spent all this time in settling *your* affairs, Sandy,' he remarked teasingly. 'Mr Gilmour and I have been having a most interesting conversation about land improvement, and I must say I am obliged to you for the acquaintance of such an amiable and well-informed young gentleman.'

Smiling, Gilmour protested, 'You flatter me, sir. It is I who have learned from you!'

Mr Maxwell turned to his wife. 'Mr Gilmour will be taking supper with us, Mistress Maxwell,' he informed her, 'then he and Sandy will return to Edinburgh tomorrow morning.'

Mistress Maxwell came forward with her tray of glasses, her face beaming with relief. 'You will take a glass of wine,

Mr Gilmour?' she asked shyly. ''Tis elderflower champagne, made from this year's flowers – and though I do say
it myself, I have a name for my wines.'

Sandy could bear the suspense no longer. 'Sir,' he burst
out, 'you have said nothing yet of your decision about me. I
must know, sir. What do you intend?'

'I intend nothing,' his father told him calmly. 'I have
formed the opinion that Mr Gilmour's profession is an interesting and honourable one, although it is most unusual, and
I certainly could not wish you under a better influence than
his. The matter is therefore now up to him and to Mr Wishart to decide.'

'You agree!' With incredulous relief, Sandy stared at his
father.

'Unreservedly!' Mr Maxwell told him. And suddenly it
seemed to Sandy that the kitchen was full of people all
laughing and talking at once, each with a glass of elderflower champagne in his hand. Archie had appeared from
somewhere, and was nodding and smiling to him over the
rim of his glass. Gilmour was saying something to his father
about the East Lothian Customs posts all having been
cleared of suspicion. In a rush of excitement he remembered
his own news, and spilling champagne from his glass in
his haste he moved forward to tell it to Gilmour.

9. The Unpriestly Priest

RIDING back to Edinburgh the next morning, Gilmour
emerged from a long and thoughtful silence to ask Sandy
what troops the city held, and seemed delighted to hear
there was a company of Welsh Dragoons stationed in the
Canongate.

'And their Commander's name?' he inquired.

'Colonel Moyes, sir,' Sandy told him, and was surprised

then to hear Gilmour going off on an entirely different tack with his next question.

'Tell me, Sandy, have you ever met the Comptroller of Customs for the Lothian run?'

'No, sir,' he admitted, 'I never have,' at which Gilmour laughed as if enjoying some private joke.

'You will,' he promised cheerfully, 'and so will Colonel Moyes once I have completed my plans for dealing with the smuggling drop!'

'What have you in mind to do, sir?' Sandy could not resist asking then, but Gilmour was not to be drawn out on the subject. He retreated into his thoughtful silence, and they reached Edinburgh again with Sandy no wiser than before.

Mr Wishart met their arrival at his office with a face that hinted at news of his own to tell, but when Gilmour bade Sandy speak up with the story of his discovery at the harbour, he listened patiently and with every sign of close attention. By the end of the recital he was chuckling and rubbing his hands together in the manner habitual to him when matters were going well, and the look he turned on Sandy was one of benevolent and almost fatherly pride.

'Excellent work, boy!' He beamed. 'Excellent! Now you have justified the first assumptions I made to Mr Gilmour about you.'

'More than justified,' Gilmour added generously, 'for now we have our first positive information about Robertson with plenty of time in hand to gather forces to deal with it.'

'How long will it take you to make your arrangements?' Wishart asked.

'Several days possibly.' Gilmour began pacing up and down, throwing out words jerkily as he went. 'Colonel Moyes of the Welsh Dragoons – I will need him. The Comptroller of Customs – the captains of the Customs sloop patrol – seamen-signallers –'

'One moment!' Wishart held up a warning hand. 'Before you plan too far ahead, there is a further piece of information you must hear.'

To Sandy and Gilmour's surprise then, he opened the door of his office and called loudly for Isobel, then turning back into the room remarked blandly,

'I do not wish to forestall my daughter's telling of this news, but it will help understanding of what she has to say if you bear certain facts in mind. The first is, that the Episcopal Church in Scotland has always supported the Jacobites; the second, that many of its priests were dismissed from their livings for their part in the rebellion of 1715 –'

His lips tightening with annoyance, Gilmour interrupted, 'You waste time in reciting what is common knowledge, sir!'

'Not so commonly known,' Wishart retorted, 'is the third fact – which is that the braver spirits among these priests have continued to minister secretly to their former parishioners in defiance of the laws against them –'

'Ah, my dear!' He turned to Isobel, who had appeared at his elbow as he spoke. 'Be seated, my dear,' he told her, 'and give Mr Gilmour our news. And be brief, for he has much to do.'

'*My* news, sir!' With great aplomb as she swept towards a chair, Isobel corrected her father, then settling herself for the interview she looked demurely up at Gilmour.

'Briefly then, as I am bid,' she told him, 'my news concerns the clergyman whom you observed taking St Clair's place at the book-tray outside Allan Ramsay's shop. He is a Mr Henry Ogilvie, formerly the priest of a small Episcopal church in Aberlady – which is a coastal village about twenty miles east of Edinburgh. Mr Ogilvie was dismissed from this charge for taking part in the '15 rebellion, and is now living in retirement in this city.'

'Indeed?' With a touch of condescension in his tone, Gilmour asked, 'And how can you be so sure, Mistress Isobel, that this was the man I saw?'

'Because I happen to be a member of Mr Ramsay's circulating library,' she told him cheerfully, 'and so is Mr Ogilvie. His visits there are as regular as clockwork and therefore, Mr Gilmour, the day and time of your observation placed his identity exactly for me.'

She paused to allow comment on this, but when Gilmour offered none she continued, 'Mr Ogilvie was not one of those priests who continued his ministry secretly after being dismissed, but in this past year he seems to have suffered a change of conscience about this, for during that time he has frequently ridden forth upon what he has described to his housekeeper as "errands of mercy" –'

'To his former parish?' Gilmour interrupted.

'So Miss Crawford – the housekeeper – assures me,' Isobel told him. 'He leaves home on these errands late in the afternoon, as a rule, and does not return until the next morning.'

'You appear to have made considerable inquiry about the gentleman, Mistress Isobel,' Gilmour remarked. 'May I ask why you took it on yourself to do so?'

There was an odd mixture of curiosity and disapproval in the way he spoke, and this seemed to give Isobel considerable amusement. 'Certainly you may,' she told him. 'It seemed the sensible thing to do in view of the possible link between what you had observed and the common talk of his past activities with the Jacobites. Do you not agree, sir?'

Gilmour hesitated, and then said uncomfortably, 'I am not accustomed to young ladies exercising their minds over such matters.'

'You mean,' Isobel retorted with cheerful malice in her voice, 'you do not think they are capable of doing so. But there, sir, you are quite wrong for, as you will discover, the Edinburgh young ladies at least are quite as capable of exercising their minds over serious matters as gentlemen are!'

'I have already made that discovery,' Gilmour told her, 'of one Edinburgh young lady!'

He was beginning to smile, in spite of himself, at her neat choice of method to point the error of his views, and correctly reading the meaning of his smile, Isobel was generous in victory.

Smiling in reply she told him, 'Then I may go on to describe how the summons to such an "errand of mercy" reaches the Reverend Ogilvie.'

She leaned forwards, her face growing suddenly serious. 'It is brought late at night by a man wearing seafaring clothes – which is not remarkable in itself, of course, since Mr Ogilvie's former parish is on the coast – but Miss Crawford also mentioned that this seafaring man is small and scar-faced, and that she heard him addressed as "Geordie."'

It was Mr Wishart who broke the silence that followed this. In a voice of rueful triumph he exclaimed, 'Isobel, Isobel – such a lawyer I could have made of you! Why were you not born a laddie!'

'God forbid!' Gilmour exclaimed so fervently that Isobel blushed and Wishart looked abashed.

'Aye, well,' he conceded, ''tis sin, I suppose, to regret God's gift of a bonny daughter – but now, sir, what's to be done with this lead she has uncovered? You have time to follow it up before you make your plans for the night of the smuggling drop. And besides, it is one which could take you to St Clair as well as to Robertson!'

Gilmour nodded. 'That could well be the case,' he acknowledged, 'for it certainly seems to point to the fact that Robertson was acting as courier between St Clair and Ogilvie, as well as between St Clair and the Jacobites in France.'

He turned to Isobel. 'Mistress Isobel, I have not yet expressed the thanks I owe you. Pray allow me to do so now, and to say that you have fully convinced me of the error of my views on young ladies, before I ask you to direct me to the house of this priest, Ogilvie.'

Before Isobel could reply to this, Wishart asked curiously, 'What d'ye have in mind, Gilmour?'

'If our reasoning has been correct so far,' Gilmour answered slowly, 'Ogilvie must have lost his go-between when Robertson went into hiding. Also, the fact that Ogilvie was so uncommon regular in his visits to the bookshop indicates that this channel of communication was used only at stated times. But Sandy's discovery of the camp at Kidlaw has put St Clair himself on the run, and so even that contact is now denied them. In the case of emergency, however, Ogilvie would still find some way of getting in touch with St Clair – and I propose to create that emergency.'

'How?' Wishart and Sandy asked the question simultaneously.

'By frightening Ogilvie into believing it exists,' Gilmour answered. 'And now, Mistress Isobel, if you will direct me to his house . . .'

It was just over ten minutes walk away, Sandy realized, listening to Isobel's directions, and moved eagerly forward as Gilmour commanded, 'Come, Sandy! I will need you.'

'Oh, by the way,' Gilmour turned at the door to ask, 'is there any word yet of the reprieve for Porteous?'

'None,' Wishart answered, 'but I will know as soon as it does come, for I have arranged with Hoseah Eastgate that he will send me word of the first coach to arrive carrying a mailbag with the royal cipher on it.'

'And the next coach is expected – when?'

'On the twenty-fifth – three days from now. After that there is no mail-coach due till the first of September, and if the reprieve is not on that one it cannot have been granted after all, for there is no other mail-coach due before the

eighth of September – the day that Porteous is sentenced
to hang.'

Gilmour shrugged. ''Tis pity for him, I suppose, but it
makes no odds to us now that we are so sure of taking Robertson by other methods.'

'He thinks of everything!' Sandy remarked admiringly
of Wishart's part in this conversation as they crossed over to
the south side of the High Street a few minutes later. 'I take
my oath he will know the reprieve has arrived before the
Magistrates themselves get the letter!'

'Aye, because he thinks ahead,' Gilmour answered. 'As
we are about to do, Sandy!' They plunged into the maze of
closes and wynds providing passage through a huddle of
buildings that clung to the steep slope falling away from the
south side of the High Street. 'Can you find out where Ogilvie stables his horse?'

'Bowdy Jock – Eastgate's head ostler – will know,' Sandy
told him confidently.

Gilmour strode on in silence for a few minutes; then he
said, 'Listen carefully now. When we come out of this Ogilvie's house again, you will go quickly to Eastgate's stable
and arrange for our horses to be ready to ride out by a back
way at an instant's notice. Then you will use this as a bribe
to make sure there is as much delay as possible in Ogilvie's
obtaining a horse.'

'Yes, sir.' Sandy took the coin Gilmour was handing him,
and pointed ahead.

'There is the Cowgate, sir. We turn left when we reach it.'

They left the maze of buildings behind them, and turned
to walk eastwards along the Cowgate – the long street running parallel with the crest of the ridge crowned by the High
Street. Kennedy's Close, a narrow lane between the houses
on the far side of the Meal Market, was their objective now,
and they walked towards it without further speech.

They swung to the right off the Cowgate to enter it, and

at its far end found the small courtyard to which Isobel had directed them, and facing them across it the house with the white shutters just as she had described it. Gilmour walked unhesitatingly towards its front door. He knocked, then turned to scan the courtyard itself, and following his gaze, Sandy noted that it held no possible concealment from which Ogilvie's house could be observed. A shuffle of footsteps behind the door and the sound of its handle being turned recalled their attention, and they turned to see it being opened to them.

It was a plump, auburn-haired woman who had answered Gilmour's knock, but before she could utter more than a word or two of inquiry, a voice called from somewhere in the passageway behind her,

'Who is it, Miss Crawford?'

'On His Majesty's Service!' Gilmour answer loudly.

He shouldered his way past Miss Crawford as he spoke – an action so much at odds with his usual courtesy that Sandy was left agape on the doorstep – but quickly recovering he darted past Miss Crawford's outstretched arm and followed Gilmour into the hall, behind the front door.

The owner of the questioning voice stood in their path – an elderly man, very tall and thin with long locks of silvery-white hair falling down on either side of a pale face. He was undoubtedly the man they had seen at the bookshop, but now his face was blotched with angry colour. His voice came shrill and shaking with some strong emotion as he shouted at Gilmour.

'How dare you break in here! By what leave do you disturb my house!'

'I gave my authority, Mr Ogilvie – and I think you heard me.'

As he spoke, Gilmour bore Ogilvie firmly backwards through a door standing half-open behind him. Sandy followed, closing the door as firmly against Miss Crawford's prying eyes. Gilmour had something held ready in his hand – a sheet of thick, buff-coloured parchment with the red seal of King George the Second dangling from it. He held it out to Ogilvie.

'My warrant, sir.'

'A pox on your warrant!' With a violent sweep of his hand, Ogilvie struck the warrant to the floor. Gilmour bent to retrieve it, and in the same instant Ogilvie reached inside his coat.

'*Look out, sir!*'

Sandy's warning yell came a split second too late. Ogilvie already had a pistol in his hand, and Gilmour straightened up to find it trained on his heart. Ogilvie spoke breathlessly,

'Out of my house or I will kill you!'

Gilmour did not budge. 'Have you something to hide Mr Ogilvie?' he inquired calmly. 'I can think of no other reason for such unpriestly behaviour from one of your calling.'

'Even a priest is entitled to defend his house against a forced entry! Out, I say!' Ogilvie gave a threatening jerk to his pistol on the last words, and at that, Gilmour seemed to lose patience.

'Put down that pistol,' he ordered. 'I am an accredited agent of His Majesty's Government, with full entitlement for my actions. You, sir, are suspected of dealing in smuggled goods and are in no position to threaten me.'

'Smuggled goods?' As if wondering whether he had heard correctly Ogilvie repeated the words in an uncertain mutter, while a puzzled expression slowly replaced the anger in his face. The pistol began to tremble in his grasp. He let the hand holding it drop to his side and said stupidly, 'But your warrant ... D'ye mean to say it is a *Customs* search-warrant?'

'That, and something more,' Gilmour told him. 'It gives me authority to call all military and civil aid available to my assistance for the purpose of apprehending one, George Robertson, a smuggler. And I have information to the effect that this man has visited you at various times and at such an hour as to give rise to suspicion that you are involved in his illegal trade.'

'Who told you so?'

'I have to warn you,' Gilmour went on, ignoring the question, 'that if you have purchased contraband from this man you have been guilty of the crime of reset. I have further to warn you that he is a fugitive from the law and that anyone who shelters him will be charged with art and part in his crimes. If you have knowledge of his whereabouts, therefore, you conceal it from me at your peril of this charge.'

'Well – I – this is most distressing – I seem to have misunderstood your presence . . .' Slowly Ogilvie put his pistol away again, avoiding Gilmour's eyes, and continued lamely, 'I thought, perhaps – these disturbed times – wrongful arrest is not uncommon, you understand – But you are a Customs man!'

He paused, then seeming to collect himself went on more briskly, 'I certainly seem to have been in error, sir, but I think you are also. In all my life I have never smoked pipe tobacco or taken snuff. Nor do I approve of these habits for others, and being unmarried, I have no use for French dress-silks. What interest would I have, therefore, in smuggled goods? As for my – er – nocturnal visitors, I am sure you know that priests of my church sometimes receive requests from former parishioners which force them to choose between conscience and the penal laws.'

'I repeat,' Gilmour said, 'that one of your visitors, at least, answers to the description of Robertson.'

Ogilvie drew himself up to his full, thin height. 'Then you have been wrongly informed!'

'Would you swear to that,' Gilmour asked quietly, 'on oath?'

Without giving Ogilvie time to reply to this he went on, 'I warn you it may come to that soon, for we are hotly in pursuit of this man and will certainly take him before many days are past. Prepare yourself to be subpoenaed as a witness in his case, therefore, and look to your conscience before you take the Book in your hand, for his crimes are serious ones.'

He sketched a quick bow as if to take his leave, but Ogilvie said hurriedly, 'Wait – I – there were many seafaring folk in my former parish. Perhaps – if you were to tell me a little more of this man, I might be able to obtain some information for you.'

Sandy noted the look, almost of pleading, on his face as he spoke. Gilmour apparently did not notice this, however, or if he did, he gave no sign of it. He stood for a moment as if debating whether or not to continue the conversation, then with the air of merely seeking routine confirmation to previous replies, he demanded,

'Do you deny absolutely having purchased contraband from Robertson?'

'Absolutely!' Ogilvie's voice rang with sincerity and truth.

'You have never stored contraband for him, delivered it, or assisted in any way in its dispatch to purchasers?'

'Never!' Once again, the ringing truthful answer.

'You were not in any way concerned in the matter of the documents he has stolen?'

Silence, a small alarmed silence followed the last question, then with a determined attempt to be casual, Ogilvie said, 'But surely a theft of documents is not a smuggler's crime. You must have been misinformed, sir.'

'That is for me to judge,' Gilmour told him curtly, 'but as it happens, I have an eye-witness to the matter – a renegade Customs official who has been arrested for his dealings with Robertson.'

'Oh – so they are Customs documents!' Ogilvie was still fighting to give his remarks a casual air, Sandy noticed, but the look of strain on his pale face was now painfully obvious.

'No, they were not Customs documents,' Gilmour answered. 'I understand they belong to someone named St Clair – but their ownership, of course, is something we shall settle after Robertson is arrested. Meanwhile, in spite of the denials you have just given me, you are still under suspicion, and your offer to help in finding him must therefore be rejected as suspect also. So now, good day – and pray be careful whom you choose to threaten with fire-arms in the future!'

This time he did go, turning briskly on his heel and motioning Sandy out of the room with him. They swept past the figure of Miss Crawford hovering vaguely in the dimness of the hall, and heard her voice raised in agitated question to Ogilvie as the front door closed behind them. Gilmour said nothing as they continued their purposeful march down Kennedy's Close and Sandy did not dare to question him, but as the other halted on reaching the Cowgate again, he ventured,

'You fairly made him think you were on to his connection with St Clair, sir, when you called out "*On His Majesty's Service*".'

'D'ye tell me that!' Turning to face Sandy outside a coffee shop opposite Kennedy's Close, Gilmour favoured him with a sardonic grin, and then more kindly added, 'That was the purpose of the announcement – to prove beyond any doubt that there *is* a connection, and Ogilvie's reaction to it certainly established that fact.'

'But –' Sandy glanced uncertainly at him, '– if that was the case, why did you not challenge him with it?'

'And let him know we are on to that trail!' Gilmour exclaimed. 'No, no, my lad! The whole point of that exercise was to alarm Ogilvie into making contact with St Clair *without* revealing our own hand, and if I am any judge of men that is precisely what he will do now. So off you go to make the arrangements about the horses, and report back to me at this coffee shop.'

'And then, sir?' Sandy lingered a moment to ask.

'Then we wait for Ogilvie to come out and we follow him wherever he goes.'

'But suppose he sends someone with a message to St Clair? Suppose he –'

'Look you, Sandy,' Gilmour interrupted patiently, 'I have already considered all your suppositions. There is quite obviously no nearer point than this for mounting an observation post, therefore we can only watch Kennedy's Close and not Ogilvie's house itself. Nor have we any means of telling which of the people who are bound to come down Kennedy's Close in the course of a day will be a messenger from Ogilvie. But if he does send out a message, my guess is that it will only be for the purpose of arranging a rendezvous with St Clair.'

'But why –'

'For two reasons,' Gilmour bore on over Sandy's question. 'One – he will want to discuss my visit personally with St Clair. And two – he is an old man, and quite unfit to ride into the kind of wild country where St Clair is likely to be hiding out.'

'That is still only guesswork,' Sandy objected.

'Quite,' Gilmour answered flatly, 'and the more you know of this sort of investigation, the more you will learn how much of it relies, not on wild guesses, but on those based on a balance of probabilities. Now go, before I lose patience with you!'

And that, Sandy thought, was that! But speeding on down the Cowgate to regain the High Street again by way of Blackfriars Wynd, he had to admit that it was, after all, the only practical way of dealing with all the elements of chance in the situation, and the conclusion bred fresh confidence in the instructions Gilmour had given him.

He reached Hoseah Eastgate's yard with a clear picture in his mind of what he would say to Bowdy Jock, but for all his sense of urgency he was careful not to speak to the old man till he had drawn him out of earshot of the other ostlers. He took the precaution also, of letting him see the glint of the coin in his hand while he did so, and grinned at the light of greed leaping suddenly in Bowdy's rheumy eyes.

'Canny, now, canny!' he warned, holding the bribe back from the grasping fingers outstretched immediately agreement had been reached about his own and Gilmour's horse. 'There is one thing more to be done before you earn this fee, Bowdy. Are you by any chance acquainted with an old Episcopalian priest by the name of Ogilvie?'

'Ogilvie?' Bowdy looked at him curiously. 'The fellow that bides somewhere off the Cowgate – a tall figure of a man, thin, white-haired?'

Sandy nodded. 'Aye, you have him exactly. Can you tell me what stable he is in the habit of using?'

'This one, of course!' Bowdy exclaimed impatiently. 'How else would I be able to describe him so apt! He has no beast of his own, but he hires a cob here – a good, steady beast, whenever he needs one.'

'Then listen!' Sandy held the coin up in front of Bowdy's nose. 'He will hire a beast from you some time today and this is all yours, Bowdy, if you cause him as much delay as possible before he rides out of this yard on that good, steady cob of his!'

'That will be easy done!'

Bowdy's hand rose to clutch the coin, and stopped short in mid-grasp. He sighed. 'Eeh, Sandy, I am too old to rax my bones on a hard bed in the Tolbooth? Is it within the law – this thing you ask of me?'

'You will never have done a more legal thing in your life, Bowdy Jock,' Sandy assured him solemnly.

'Is that a fact!' The old man cocked a sardonic eye at him. He took the coin, tested it between stumps of teeth, pouched it, and turned away with a nod of satisfaction. Sandy watched his bandy-legged stride across the yard before he made off, smiling to himself at their conversation. He had managed that old rascal fine, he thought complacently. Now it would be up to Gilmour to make the best use of the arrangement.

He found the latter not, as he had expected, uneasily patrolling up and down the Cowgate, but comfortably established in the coffee-shop opposite the entrance to Kennedy's Close. Behind his seat near the doorway, the coffee-shop's dim interior was packed and noisy with groups of loungers exchanging opinions on the day's news-sheets. Waiters pushed back and forward, balancing trays one-handed above their heads, their shouted orders adding to the din of conversation echoing back from the low-beamed ceiling. Gilmour, lounging on the fringe of all this activity, looked the picture of bored ease, but the glance he lifted to Sandy had a sharp question in it.

He made room on the bench he occupied. Sandy slouched down beside him and said quietly, 'All arranged. He stables at Eastgate's place.'

Gilmour picked up a news-sheet lying beside him and pretended to scan it idly. 'The housekeeper came out,' he murmured.

'She could not take a message!'

'She could brief someone else to take it.'

'If Ogilvie has sent her to brief a messenger for him,' Sandy exclaimed contemptuously, 'he is a fool! Look at the way she clacked his secrets to Mistress Isobel!'

'You judge Miss Crawford too harshly,' Gilmour told him, 'and I think that is because you under-rate Mistress

Isobel. I suspect there was a good deal of shrewd cross-questioning went into her examination of the housekeeper.'

He snapped his fingers to summon a waiter, and when the man had come and gone again, turned to give a long look at Sandy. In a low voice he said,

'Sandy, you will attract attention with that uneasy look. Settle down. We are now two loungers with nothing better to do than to idle a day away in a coffee-shop.'

'The whole day?' Sandy looked at him in dismay.

Gilmour smiled and waved a hand to the milling crowd behind them. 'Why not? These others find it easy enough to do, and they have less to occupy their minds than we have.'

The waiter came with their coffee. Gilmour kept silent till he was out of earshot again and then said, 'If Ogilvie arranges a rendezvous with St Clair, it will be for the hours of darkness, but a man of his age will not be likely to make the journey itself after dark. My guess is that he will leave in daylight, and hide out somewhere near his rendezvous till it is dark enough to meet St Clair. And that will make it all the easier for us to follow him.'

'Following on horseback is different from following on foot,' Sandy objected. 'If we stay close enough to keep him in sight, he will realize he is being trailed.'

'Why does Ogilvie stable at Eastgate's place?' Gilmour inquired, and answered himself, 'Because that is a convenient one for anyone in the habit of riding out from the east end of the city. Now you, Sandy, are well acquainted with the countryside east of Edinburgh.'

Sandy nodded agreement. 'And,' Gilmour continued, 'you know there is a very limited choice of main routes available to the traveller. Furthermore, the countryside is mainly farm-land and very open to the view. D'ye begin to see what I have in mind?'

'I think so.' Sandy sat back, his eyes on Kennedy's Close

while he considered the question. 'The arrangement about the horses means that we can ride out of the city *ahead* of Ogilvie, instead of behind him. We find some vantage point to observe which route he takes, then we circle away and ride for another vantage point to observe the first crossroads on that route.'

'Precisely! And we continue doing so, always keeping ahead of him, each observation confirming the general trend of his route, until finally we have a fairly good idea of the particular place for which he is headed.'

Sandy glanced curiously at Gilmour. 'And what is your guess on that, sir?'

Gilmour made no direct answer to this. 'There are very few people, Sandy,' he said slowly, 'who have the imagination to compose a story that is entirely untruthful. Liars, in fact, tend simply to twist the existing facts in order to manufacture their lies – which is why I think there is a basis of truth in the story Ogilvie told me. I believe that his nocturnal visitor did come with messages from his former parish of Aberlady – but I also believe that visitor was George Robertson.'

'And Geordie would not sneak into the city with a message begging a priest to come to baptize a baby!' Sandy remarked.

'And so,' Gilmour went on, smiling at the form of the interruption, 'if Robertson was a courier between St Clair and Ogilvie, and if the messages he brought did come from Aberlady, the conclusion is that they contained St Clair's summons to meet him there. And that, Sandy, is where I believe they will meet again tonight.'

10. Canticle for Two Voices

THE bank by the roadside was high, and crowned by thick tree-scrub that grew tall enough to hide two horses and their riders.

'Up there!' Pointing towards the bank, Sandy urged Gambler forward, and with hoofs scattering the soft soil below the line of tree growth, the heavy beast charged up the incline. His face darkened with annoyance, Gilmour put his mount to follow and edged it into cover at the top of the bank.

In practice, he was thinking, his plan had proved absurdly simple to follow from the very moment, late that afternoon, when they had spied Ogilvie coming down Kennedy's Close. But – he glowered at Sandy perched beside him on Gambler – that boy *would* take chances! Time and again he had cut corners on their route, leaving only seconds to dodge back out of Ogilvie's sight. Now this was the second occasion he had led them to cover that was far too near the road, and instead of circling to gain it, had dashed into it headlong leaving a trail that clearly advertised their presence.

And yet . . . Gilmour tried hard to push his annoyance aside. He could never have tracked Ogilvie himself in this way. He needed Sandy's knowledge of the countryside.

If only the boy were not so impetuous! He sighed, wondering if it had been a mistake to take Sandy so far into his confidence. Rashness like this, after all, could so easily endanger the success of a mission – perhaps he should never have encouraged his desire to join the Service . . .

'I can see him!' Sandy spoke low in his ear. 'Look, coming through the village!'

Gilmour looked to where the village of Longniddry lay on

his left, and saw a mounted figure outlined black against the westering sun.

'Now he has a choice of two roads,' Sandy said. 'That level road to the right will take him inland to Haddington, and so on towards the Lammermuir Hills. The downward-sloping road to the left will take him towards the sea.'

Gilmour looked again at the prospect from the bank. The right-hand and left-hand roads formed two sides of a great walled-in triangle of park and woodland, with the Firth of Forth as the base of its downward tilt. Between the village on their far left and the left-hand fork of the road, lay rough moor-land, and as if reading his thoughts, Sandy said,

'We can circle round across that moor and reach the coast well ahead of him.'

'And from there?'

'The road bends sharp right and runs straight on to Aber-lady.'

'How far in all?'

'Five miles from here.' There was a note of suppressed excitement in Sandy's voice. 'Your guess was the right one, sir – he *must* be headed for Aberlady!'

'If he does not see that trail you left up the bank and guess at our spying on him!' Gilmour retorted.

Ogilvie was nearing the bank. Ignoring Sandy's muttered apology, Gilmour surveyed Ogilvie, thinking that his carriage was still remarkably alert for an elderly man who had already spent almost three hours in the saddle. The lower slope of the bank momentarily cut off their view of him, then they saw him reappearing again and heading down the left-hand road towards the sea.

Gilmour judged the time available before they could carry out their flanking movement unseen and fired a series of rapid questions at Sandy.

'How much cover on the road after it swings right towards Aberlady?'

'None. We have only the sea on our left and this walled land of Gosford estate on our right until we are almost in the village.'

'And then?'

'A farmhouse on our right, a small patch of open woodland and a deserted church on our left.'

'Ogilvie's church?'

'I suppose so. It has not been used for worship in all the time I have known Aberlady.'

'We will hide the horses in the wood,' Gilmour decided, 'and observe him from the cover of the churchyard. Hup!'

Kicking heels to his horse's flanks he galloped for the moorland, and heard Gambler thundering close behind him. There was no doubt about it, he acknowledged to himself – the boy knew how to give sharp, decisive answers to questions. And he could ride! He was sticking like a burr on that wild, hard-mouthed beast his brother had given him!

'Drop your pace after we have out-flanked Ogilvie,' he called. 'The horses will need to be cooled down if we are to leave them standing in that wood.'

'The breeze off the sea will hit us as we turn right. That will help to cool them,' Sandy replied, and after that there was neither time nor occasion for further exchanges.

The road to Aberlady stretched empty before them at the end of their gallop across the moor, sweeping in a wide curve round the sand-flats of Gosford Bay. The waters of the Firth were grey and cold-looking in the fading light. The sea breeze Sandy had predicted cut obliquely across their faces and went howling away to their right over tree-tops shaped by centuries of such cold, salt winds. Blinking against the sting of its passage, Gilmour peered ahead for the first signs of the village and thought how well Ogilvie had judged the time of his journey for a rendezvous in darkness.

The 'small patch of open woodland' when they reached

it, proved satisfactorily dense enough to hide the horses. Full marks again to the boy, Gilmour thought, and said aloud,

'Over the churchyard wall now, and keep well down beside me.'

Side by side they vaulted the wall separating the churchyard from the wood, and ran for cover again among the tombstones. Gilmour bore to his right, towards the section of wall between the churchyard and the road, and stopped beside a mausoleum that looked like a clumsy miniature of a temple in marble.

'He is not far behind us,' he whispered. 'Listen!'

Very, very faintly in the stillness of the churchyard, the sound of hoofs came to them. They crouched, hearing the irregular thud and clack of iron striking the stone-scattered earth of the road grow steadily in volume. The horse trotted past the churchyard wall, and came to a stamping halt. A gate creaked open and banged shut again. A horse and rider, moving slowly through the dusk enfolding the churchyard, came into their view and progressed in ghostly silence over the thick grass between the graves.

The long lines of tombstones swallowed them up, and disgorged them again as a dark shape against the frozen white flight of a marble angel near the church door. The rider dismounted. The angel's white gleamed unblemished again as he drew the horse after him into the deep shadow of the church's walls.

Gilmour's fingers digging into Sandy's arm checked an attempt at speech. They crouched in silence till he judged the time was ripe for his purpose, then drawing Sandy's attention with another touch, he whispered,

'I am going into the church. Listen carefully. You are to stay hidden inside this mausoleum till I come back to you. No matter what happens while I am away, you are not to move from here, or make a sound, or show yourself. If I do not return, you are to wait for daylight and then you will ride at your best speed for Edinburgh.'

'I cannot do that, sir.' Sandy's whisper in his ear was protestingly loud. 'If St Clair comes – if he attacks you – you might be killed. I could help you if I came –'

'Fool! Stupid fool!' Savagely Gilmour tightened his grip on the boy's arm. 'If I am killed, *you* must survive to report back to Wishart! Now, for once, *will you do as you are told*!'

A very subdued mutter of agreement reached him. 'Swear it!' he insisted. 'Swear on your honour there will be no heroics, no romantic gestures!'

The whispered answer came slowly – dragged, Gilmour thought, from God knows what reluctant depths, but that did not trouble him. The boy might be foolhardy, impetuous, and much too cock-a-hoop with his new importance, but he was still not the kind to take honour lightly. He released his grip on Sandy's arm. Half in commendation and half in farewell he tapped him lightly on the shoulder, and began crawling away through the tombstones.

A few feet from the marble angel he halted to reconnoitre his position. There was no sign of Ogilvie's horse but he could hear its shuffling movements from behind the church. Ahead of him the porch of the church's door yawned a mouth of darkness. He ran lightly towards it, feet soundless on the grass that grew right up to its steps.

Enveloped by the darkness inside the porch he paused to listen, and heard nothing. No line of light showed under the door, and involuntarily he shivered at the thought of the old priest sitting alone, in total darkness, in the silent church. Flattening himself against the wall of the porch, he edged round it, fingers searching the stone for the small door that must give entrance to the bell-tower. He felt wood, splintered in places, with the cold iron edge of a lock hanging loose from it, and his exploring fingers traced the outline of the door into the bell-tower above the porch.

The door was made to open outward, and fraction by fraction of an inch he eased it towards himself. A gap sufficient for his shoulders to slip through was all he needed. The door yielded unwillingly to his pressure, and he took his first silent step up the winding stone stairway behind it. Fervently he hoped he had assessed the interior structure of the church correctly.

Creeping slowly up the steps, he went back over his calculations. The church was a small one, but the tower was high enough to allow for the existence of a gallery below the level of the belfry itself. He had rested all his hopes on that!

His hands, reaching out on either side to steady himself against the walls of the spiral stair, suddenly plunged into space. Sliding a cautious foot forward, he found level floor instead of another step, and realized he had reached a landing at the top of the spiral's first flight. Above him now, if he had reckoned correctly, would be another flight of steps leading to the belfry, and across the landing should be the door leading into the gallery traversing the west wall of the church. He groped for this door, and felt it standing agape, half torn off its hinges. Gently he eased himself through it, and saw away below him at the east end of the church, two small yellow stars of light in the gloom.

Something silvery-white lay in the pool of pale light where their beams crossed, and staring at it Gilmour recognized the shape of a human head. Superstitious dread touched him. Then gradually, as his eyes adjusted to the light, he realized that he was looking down at the Reverend Henry Ogilvie kneeling with his head bowed in prayer before the candle-lit altar of his church, and was suddenly moved by something that felt strangely like pity.

An old priest, faithful to his charge, praying in near darkness in a derelict church . . . Was there any man of sensibility, he wondered, who would not be moved by such a sight? Uneasily it occurred to him that it did not fit with his picture of the wary political agent who had faced him, pistol in hand, that morning, but with stern self-censure he argued this uneasiness away again. Ogilvie's faith, he reminded himself, was so closely allied to his politics that the two pictures were but opposite faces of the same coin. And in any case, it was not his business to debate these things. He was not a philosopher, but a Government agent with a duty to perform.

He tried to visualize his own position in the gallery. Could he be seen standing there? The darkness around him was impenetrable to his own eyes, and must inevitably, therefore, conceal him from the sight of anyone in the church below. But the white patch of his wig might betray him! Quickly he whipped it off and stuffed it in his pocket. Sliding his hand inside his coat, he drew his pistol and settled himself to wait.

The smell of the church's interior rose to him – a sickish smell compounded of wood-damp and stale incense. The church was cold. After a while he had to tense himself to keep from shivering, and he wondered how Ogilvie could endure to stay for so long kneeling on the cold stone of the sanctuary steps. Mirthlessly he told himself it would be a fine jest at his expense if it was for that and nothing else the old priest had revisited his church.

Ogilvie stirred at last. Rising slowly, he lifted the candlesticks off the altar, and with one in either hand walked slowly down the chancel towards the nave of the church.

The chancel's floor was on a slightly higher level than that of the nave. Separating the two was a wooden roodscreen carved in a series of arches, and at the foot of the screen's central arch were two stone steps which bridged the difference in the floor-levels. Ogilvie set his candles down on the nave's floor, one at either side of the bottom step, then lowering himself to sit on the upper step he leaned his head back against a pillar of the central arch.

The light from one of the candles shone directly on to his face, leaving every other part of him in deep shadow. His eyes were closed. His face, bone-white with exhaustion, hung like a death-mask on dark velvet against the surrounding darkness.

A martyr's face? Gilmour asked himself the question, and once again his senses bespoke pity for Ogilvie. A fanatic's face! His reason gave the warning, and once again his sense of duty rebuked him.

In the stillness that had descended once more on the church, the faint creaking of the door from the porch being opened reached him with sudden and startling clarity. He saw Ogilvie lift his head and look towards the sound, and with delicate precision, cocked both hammers of his pistol. The door beneath his gallery creaked gently shut again.

Footsteps marched down the nave, quick and very purposeful steps advancing to the two small pools of light cast by the candles. A man's shape loomed up suddenly in front of Ogilvie's seated form. A harsh voice said,

'Well, reverend sir? Is your news as urgent as your message?'

In the empty church, the words rang with a loud and hollow sound. Without waiting for a reply to them the newcomer seated himself on the other end of Ogilvie's step, and by the light of the second candle Gilmour saw the thin, dark features of St Clair.

Instantly he decided his course of action. A silent sortie down the steps of the tower and into the church by way of the main door from the porch; a challenge, backed up by a single shot to warn St Clair he had the advantage of shooting into the light, then a swift move forward to arrest him and march him at pistol-point out of the church – that was his best plan! But meanwhile, he was in an unrivalled position to overhear their secrets. He would give them at least a few minutes to talk before he moved.

'I deemed it urgent to see you, and you have not previously questioned my judgement.'

Ogilvie had been slow in replying to St Clair's question, but now his voice sounded on a note of injured self-esteem, and magnified as St Clair's had been by the church's emptiness.

"'Tis safe enough to meet here, in any case,' he went on, 'in spite of all the useless locks and broken doors! The local people say the church is haunted since that time someone glimpsed my light through its windows!'

'I do not trust a ghost to guard me,' St Clair told him curtly. 'I have thirty men disposed round the church for that purpose.' He peered uneasily into the darkness all round him and added, 'Nevertheless, we will not meet here again. There is the smell of a trap about this place!'

With his free hand clenching in a fist of impotent rage as he listened to this, Gilmour reproached himself fiercely. What stupidity to think St Clair would have come unguarded to such a rendezvous! How could he have been fool enough to expect to take him so easily – but thank heaven, at least, that he had put the boy outside on his honour to stay hidden! That was something saved from the wreck of his high hopes. He strained forward, suddenly aware that his preoccupation had made him miss part of the conversation below.

'. . . and when he first came to the house,' Ogilvie was saying, 'I thought he must surely be a Hanoverian agent who had discovered our organization. Then it became clear that he was an official of Customs – from his bearing and speech, I guessed, someone highly placed in that Service – who had been assigned to bring George Robertson to justice. And worse than that, St Clair, he knows about Robertson's theft of your last dispatch to France.'

'The devil he does!' St Clair exclaimed. 'Does he know it holds the plans for the rising?'

'I do not know how much he knows!' Ogilvie cried. 'That is the whole problem. He made only a brief reference to Robertson's theft of the dispatch, and I dared not press him on the subject.'

'But if he is a Customs man and not a Hanoverian agent,' St Clair persisted, 'how did he know Robertson had stolen it?'

'He said something about a renegade Customs officer who had been arrested for dealing with smugglers. I suppose Robertson must have talked to this man.'

St Clair sat in silence for a few moments, apparently considering Ogilvie's reply, and eventually he said,

'As I see it, whatever your Customs man may know about us, he can prove nothing without that dispatch. But if he does succeed in taking Robertson before I do, then the fat will be properly in the fire for us!'

His voice trembling, Ogilvie said, 'He spoke as if all Robertson's movements were known to him. And he was positive that he would soon be able to take him. He even warned me I would be subpoenaed as a witness at his trial!'

'Then he was wasting his breath!' St Clair retorted. 'George Robertson will never stand trial, either for his smuggling crimes or for killing that Porteous fellow – as he has sworn to do. If he is captured for either reason, he means to sell the plans he stole from us, and the price he will ask is a free pardon for himself. A kingdom for a smuggler's life – can you doubt the Government will accept the bargain he offers!'

Dark face and pale stared at one another, each held momentarily frozen in its little pool of candlelight, then Ogilvie's lips moved in a harsh cry,

'Who told you this?'

'Robertson came to the camp I had in Kidlaw Valley,' St Clair answered. 'He tried to persuade Rattray and Lumsden to join his scheme to murder Porteous, but they were afraid the pardon would not extend to them. Lumsden gave me warning of his intention.'

'Oh, God!' Ogilvie buried his face in his hands. His voice came muffled through them. 'The names that will be discovered! The men who will be hunted if that happens!'

He looked up at St Clair again, his white face gleaming now as if a sweat had broken suddenly out on it. 'We could claim the whole document a forgery,' he suggested desperately.

St Clair shook his head. 'There is a snag to that,' he objected, 'an eye-witness to events – a boy who found his way into the Kidlaw camp and observed it for the three days he was held prisoner there before he managed to escape from Rattray and Lumsden.'

'*Sandy, Sandy!*' Gilmour prayed silently. '*For the love of God, boy, stay hidden. Stay hidden!*'

The silence that had fallen between St Clair and Ogilvie endured for another few seconds, and then Ogilvie said, 'St Clair, it has been bad enough knowing that Robertson was running loose with that document in his possession, but this twist to events makes it ten times worse. You must redouble your efforts to take him, St Clair. You *must take Robertson* before that Customs officer does so.'

'I am doing everything to that end that mortal man can do!' St Clair snapped. 'D'ye doubt my ability to handle this affair, Mr Ogilvie?'

'Yes, I do,' Ogilvie told him bitterly. 'You should never have chosen such a creature as your courier in the first place – and as for allowing an eye-witness to penetrate your camp –'

'That matter has been taken in hand,' St Clair interrupted angrily. 'The boy has been tracked to his place of work and I have sent Rattray there with orders to kill him at the first opportunity that offers.'

'*Kill* him?' Ogilvie echoed in horror. 'Kill a boy! St Clair, what sort of man are you!'

'A professional at affairs of this kind,' St Clair told him calmly. 'Whereas you, Ogilvie, like the rest of your Jacobite friends, are a bungling amateur.'

'But – but – there is no honour in such methods,' Ogilvie stammered.

St Clair rose to his feet. From the shadows into which his face had disappeared with the move, his reply came contemptuously, 'What has honour to do with winning a war – or a throne?'

'Who chose you, St Clair?' His voice now soaring hysterically, Ogilvie also rose, unfolding his tall, thin height to face St Clair. Peering towards him through the shadows he cried again, 'Who chose such a monster to carry out God's pure purpose of restoring King James to the throne?'

St Clair laughed. 'Spare me the sermon, reverend sir,' he mocked. 'I offered my services to your king's advisers. I guaranteed to raise and train an efficient cavalry force if they offered me a free hand and paid me well enough. They accepted my terms.'

'They did not know you for what you are!' Ogilvie's voice was a shrill cry of agony now. 'You cheated good men, St Clair. You hid your true self from them!'

'If I give your good men success they will not question how I achieved it,' St Clair told him sardonically. 'Men are passing strange creatures, Mr Ogilvie, and I have often observed how wonderfully easy they find it to forgive a wrong that brings benefit to themselves.'

'God will not forgive,' Ogilvie warned him. 'If you kill that boy, St Clair, God will not forgive you, or me, or anyone concerned in this affair.'

'They told me you were an intelligent man, Ogilvie – a reliable agent. I think you are a fool!'

St Clair began to walk away on the words, calling them back over his shoulder as he went. Ogilvie started up the aisle after him. 'You have to take Robertson,' he shouted. 'You hear me, St Clair – you must take him before that Customs man does! But you must not kill that boy – you must not!'

'Keep your voice down!' St Clair flung back at him. 'That boy could send you to the gallows – and me, too!'

He had reached the space underneath the west gallery and the sound of his voice came muffled by it. Ogilvie replied with a fierce whisper in which Gilmour could distinguish no separate words. The long creak of the door being opened and shut again reached him, then he heard footsteps returning up the aisle.

It was Ogilvie coming slowly back to snuff out the candles before he left in St Clair's wake. His head was bowed. He looked, Gilmour thought, a beaten man. In the darkness and silence that followed his departure, Gilmour relaxed on a long sigh, then groped his way back to sit at the head of the spiral staircase till it would be safe for him, too, to leave the church.

Crouched there on the cold stone of the topmost step, he tried to put his thoughts in order but found he could not budge his mind, at first, past the revelation of Robertson's plan for revenge on Captain Porteous. It was the audacity of the thing, he thought, the sheer wild simplicity of the whole idea that took the breath away. To plot a theft that meant he could barter the safety of a kingdom against a pardon for murder – who would have thought an ignorant fisherman-cum-smuggler could conceive of so cunning a strategy!

Robertson, his thoughts ran on, must bear a more than

mortal hatred against Porteous. Or perhaps he was crazy – hatred could turn a man's brain! That snivelling renegade in the Tolbooth had said he looked crazy at their last meeting.

Leaning back against the wall of the staircase, Gilmour decided gloomily that there was more than a touch of madness also in the complex pattern of pursuit that had developed from his original assignment. He visualized it in his mind like a frieze of running figures. Robertson hunting Porteous – himself hunting Robertson and St Clair – St Clair also hunting Robertson, and both of them racing against time now in the effort to capture him first – the horse-thief, Rattray, hunting young Sandy Maxwell –

With an effort as this final thought struck him, Gilmour checked his mind's aimless wandering. He had been responsible for bringing the boy into the affair in the first place, he reminded himself. It was his duty now, therefore, to look after his safety – and to do so in such a way, moreover, that he would not be aware of the danger hanging over him. A boy of his age, after all, could hardly be expected to face up calmly to the threat of being murdered!

He turned various schemes over in his mind, and decided on one that should have settled the matter for him, but as he rose to begin his silent retreat from the church he was visited again by the fear that Sandy might already have come to grief at the hands of St Clair's men. And creeping downstairs he admitted the reason to himself.

It was more than a sense of duty that moved him to concern for Sandy's safety – dammit, he *liked* the boy! There was good stuff in him – fine brave stuff that would make him a valued colleague some day when that brash confidence of his had been trimmed by experience!

He gained the churchyard, and saw the white marble angel gleaming at him in the light of a waning moon. Before him, the tombstones stretched like a pale, stone forest empty of any signs of life, and crouching he ran for the shelter of their ranks. Crawling rapidly then, he came into sight of the mausoleum and paused a few yards from it. In a hissing whisper he called,

'*Sandy!*'

A few seconds passed, and then the boy appeared, a dark shape against the moonlit pillars of the mausoleum. His answering whisper came,

'Mr Gilmour? All clear now, sir. They have gone.'

The boy had obeyed orders – he was safe! Sudden blessed relief flooded Gilmour's mind. He rose to his feet and advanced to the dark, stocky figure waiting confidently for him by the mausoleum, but already his thoughts had raced beyond the moment of greeting and his first words to Sandy were,

'Back to Edinburgh, boy. The plan for dealing with the smuggling drop must be put in hand without delay now.'

11. Two Kinds of Strategy

THE Comptroller of Customs for the Lothian run was a man in late middle-age, wirily built, with eyes like chips of steel and a face which looked as if it had been assembled from old saddle-leather and whipcord.

It was at his office in Leith, the port of Edinburgh, that Gilmour held a council of war, four days after he and Sandy returned from Aberlady. By courtesy, therefore, the Comptroller himself presided, and watching him there Sandy realized that there had been grim undertones to Gilmour's amusement at the prospect of their meeting. This steely-eyed man, he thought, had a presence in which even the bravest would walk warily!

On the Comptroller's right sat the Welsh Dragoons' Commander, Colonel Moyes, flanked by Major Shadwell, his second-in-command. Shadwell, Sandy noticed, wore a pee-vish expression on his large, rather florid features, and he was much older than Moyes – a dark, restless-eyed man who seemed very young to be a Colonel.

Facing the soldiers across the table headed by the Comptroller, sat three burly sea captains, arms folded, cocked hats laid neatly in line before them. It had been the difficulty of recalling all three ashore at once that Gilmour had allowed for when he forecast it would take him 'several days' to make his arrangements, for the Customs sloops, *Princess Anne, Princess Carolina* and *Prince William* had a wide area of patrol. But this delay had served useful purposes too, Sandy thought. It had given Gilmour opportunity to make secret reconnaissance of Cove Harbour, and himself plenty of time to carry out his instructions to make a detailed map of it for the benefit of the military.

From the decent obscurity to which he had retired after unfolding the map, he watched Gilmour pointing out the features of it, and hoped virtuously that the soldiers would appreciate such an aid to action. To his chagrin, however, Colonel Moyes spoke up eventually in very different vein.

Leaning forward he stabbed an accusing finger at Gilmour and challenged, 'Tell me, Mr Gilmour, why cannot I examine the terrain of this exercise for myself? 'Tis folly to campaign on a map-reading only when there is still time for me to make a personal reconnaissance.'

'Secrecy, sir, is our first essential of success,' Gilmour told him. 'Military persons surveying this area would quickly be recognized as such by the local people and word of their presence reported back to our quarry.'

'Added to which, Colonel Moyes,' the Comptroller said, 'there can only be one man in over-all command of the action. And since this is a Customs matter, all those taking part in it are under Mr Gilmour's orders.'

Steely eyes challenged the restless dark ones and Colonel

Moyes' gaze was the one which yielded. As he looked away, Gilmour said tactfully, 'But of course Mr Comptroller is aware that the action would be crippled at the outset without the assistance of your Company, and I personally, Colonel, look forward to the pleasure of co-operating with you.'

Colonel Moyes nodded grudging acknowledgement of this. His peevish expression growing more pronounced, Major Shadwell whispered some comment to him but he did not reply to it, and Gilmour went on,

'To recapitulate briefly on the question of terrain, then, gentlemen; as you see from the map, Cove Harbour lies eight miles east of the port of Dunbar. It is the exact shape of a horseshoe, with a stone jetty running across its outlet to the sea and leaving passage for nothing bigger than a fishing-boat between the prongs of the horseshoe.

'Backing the east half of the harbour is a very steep rise of grassy ground, about a hundred feet high. Sheer rock cliffs of similar height enclose its western aspect, and bored right through these cliffs there is a capacious tunnel which gives the only access from the harbour to the landward side of the cliffs. Now, to show you how we will net that harbour!'

He turned to the sea captains. 'Gentlemen, what is the complement of your craft?'

One of the captains, a man with the soft lilt of the West Highlands in his voice, answered promptly, 'One Commander, one Mate, eleven men, and a boy.'

'Can you each spare me one agile seaman who is also a skilled hand with a signal lantern?' Gilmour inquired.

The West Highlander looked doubtful. 'Good seamen iss ferry hard to come by, Mr Gilmour,' he objected. 'What wass you wanting the men for?'

'The smugglers will have a signaller planted somewhere on the cliff-top,' Gilmour explained. 'We will have to capture that man and put our own man in his place. Our second signaller will be in hiding behind the jetty with a party of men under the Comptroller's command, and our third one will be on the seaward side of this headland – here!'

On the map he indicated the headland that enclosed the east side of the harbour. 'Your sloops will be hiding behind that headland, gentlemen,' he told the captains, 'and the chain of action will be as follows. Number 1 Signaller on the cliff-top will flash a false "All Clear" to the smugglers, and once their boats have been thus lured into the harbour, the Comptroller's party will draw a boom across its opening. Number 2 Signaller will flash Number 1 when this part of the operation is complete. Number 1 will pass the signal on to Number 3 Signaller, who will then flash the orders for you to sweep out and further blockade the harbour mouth.'

'It is possible some boats might break out of the trap,' the Comptroller added, 'and it will be your task to capture any who do succeed in this.'

The three captains whispered together, then the West Highlander who seemed to be their spokesman said, 'A ferry good plan, Mr Gilmour. We will lend you the men.'

'Gentlemen, I am obliged.' Gilmour bowed his thanks, then turned to Colonel Moyes.

'Your men, sir,' he told him, 'will be stationed in the concealment of this dip of ground, some fifty yards back from the harbour's landward side. When Number 1 Signaller receives the flash from the Number 2 man with the Comptroller's party, he will pass it on to you as well as to the Number 3 man, and you will then advance your men in rapid order to ring the cliffs overlooking the harbour.'

'Who guards the tunnel-mouth?' the Colonel asked. 'You said that was the only access from the harbour to the land.'

'A picked party of your men,' Gilmour answered. 'Two

picked parties, in fact – one to blockade the seaward end of the tunnel, and one its landward end. Take as many of the smugglers alive as you can, but make sure that not one of them escapes from the trap.

'Not a single one,' he emphasized, looking searchingly at each man in turn. 'That is the whole importance of this operation. And now, gentlemen, your questions please!'

There was a considerable number of questions. Sandy listened conscientiously at first as Gilmour and the Comptroller dealt with them, but they were all on points which he and Gilmour had already discussed over the map-making and gradually his attention wandered to the activities of the docks outside the windows of the Comptroller's office. His eye traced the flight of gulls across the harbour, the rigging of ships berthed at the quayside, and the old restless urge to be up and about seized hold of him.

After all, he told himself defensively with a guilty look around to see if his inattention had been noticed, it was high time he had *some* freedom! Mr Wishart had kept his nose relentlessly to the grindstone these past four days – to make up, he said, for all the office work he had been allowed to put aside since that day of Gilmour's arrival in Edinburgh. Making the map had occupied his evenings, and between the two things he had hardly smelled fresh air since the night they had tracked Ogilvie to Aberlady.

He caught Shadwell's eye on him and smiled vaguely, wondering if he had missed some remark addressed to him, but the Major's florid features wore a distinctly unfriendly look. Ignoring the smile he studied Sandy briefly, then turned away again. A moment later there was a lull in the conversation, and to Sandy's dismay, Major Shadwell pointed suddenly to him and said in his peevish voice,

'And may I ask what this young fellow is doing here? You have not explained *his* presence on this so-secret exercise, Mr Gilmour.'

Sandy felt himself turning hot under all the eyes unexpectedly focused on him. He opened his mouth to speak, caught the warning look Gilmour flashed him, and remained silent.

'This young fellow,' Gilmour replied for him, coldly emphasizing the words, 'is the source of the information which has made the exercise possible. The Customs Service, Major Shadwell, is very pleased to have his help.'

For the life of him, Sandy could not have told what reply the Major made to this. His mind was soaring, his thoughts flying on swifter wings than the seagulls swooping over the harbour. It had all been worthwhile, he told himself exultantly – the terror of his captivity, the tense days at the oyster-boats! Even the grind of work in the office again had been worth having Gilmour speak like that of him!

A general rise to leave brought him back to earth again. He listened to Gilmour and the Comptroller arranging to rendezvous with Moyes on the night of the drop at the village of Innerwick, a mile or so inland of Cove Harbour, and smiled as the Comptroller suggested,

'We could meet at the house of John Drummond, the schoolmaster at Innerwick. He is my very good friend and will gladly accommodate us.'

They would make a good pair – the Comptroller and the Dominie – he thought, remembering the forbidding aspect of the latter.

Colonel Moyes said, 'Is he loyal and discreet, Mr Comptroller? That is of more importance, surely, than friendship?'

'All my friends,' the Comptroller retorted, 'are loyal and discreet,' and for a moment it seemed to Sandy that his steely eyes gleamed with savage amusement at the Colonel's discomfiture.

Striding out on the two mile walk back to Edinburgh, he ventured to say as much to Gilmour, adding with a chuckle,

'The Comptroller does not seem to be over-fond of the military, sir!'

'He is very thankful to have action at last against the smugglers of the Lothian run,' Gilmour said drily, 'but like the rest of the Service, he does not take kindly to the necessity for outside help.'

He was striding along at a pace that made conversation awkward, and wondering why he was in such a hurry, Sandy remembered eventually that this was the night he was taking Mistress Isobel to the ball at the Assembly Rooms. Mistress Wishart would be going with them as Isobel's chaperone, of course, and he knew that Mr Wishart planned to attend a meeting of the Law Society that evening – which meant he would have to think up some amusement for himself if he was not to spend the time dully alone in the house!

What should it be? A visit to the playhouse in the Cowgate to see Mr Phipps and his company presenting *The Beggar's Opera*? A cock fight? Or should he wander down to Candlemaker Row and join the University students who debated the fate of the world every evening in Loupity Joe's ale-house?

The pleasure of choosing how to spend his evening's freedom occupied him for the rest of the way back to Wishart's house, and once there he had time to consider half a dozen other prospects before Mistress Wishart announced that supper was ready. By the time that happened, however, he was decided. A visit to the playhouse it would be, for the tunes from *The Beggar's Opera* were all the rage in the city and so the one and sixpence for a place in the pit was sure to be money well spent.

Gaily whistling a snatch of *Beggar* music, he went in to supper and found the rest of the company looking very festive in their evening finery. Even Mr Wishart, he saw, had been persuaded out of his rusty black and into a coat of dark brown silk with gold braiding on it, while Mistress Wishart in her full-hooped gown of green silk with a show-petticoat of gold, was in the very peak of fashion! Deryck Gilmour, also, was even more than usually elegant in scarlet and black, but it was Isobel, of course, who outshone them all in a dress of billowing white satin over a silver show-petticoat, her fair hair, dressed high and powdered, holding a silver coronet with pearls.

Gilmour, Sandy noticed, could hardly take his eyes off her, and she seemed to have softened considerably towards him for she was accepting his compliments with a very pretty grace now. Mr Wishart had joined in with his own kind of bantering gallantry, and as for Mistress Wishart, she was fairly beaming good humour at the sight of her daughter being so gracious to the handsome guest!

None of them paid the least attention to him slipping into his chair, and he settled down to enjoy the conversation, comfortably aware that their lack of interest meant he would be able to slip away eventually without even asking permission to spend the evening abroad. Which was just as well, he decided, remembering how unreasonably strict Mr Wishart had been these past few days!

Patiently he waited for the right moment to take his leave unnoticed, and found it in the ladies' usual last-minute flurry of searching for cloaks and fans. As unobtrusively as possible then he edged towards the door, but to his dismay, Mr Wishart saw his move and called sharply,

'Sandy! where d'ye think you are going?'

'I thought, perhaps, a visit to the playhouse, sir,' Sandy said lamely, 'I would like –'

'I thought so! I thought so!' Wishart interrupted, his smiling face stern now, his eyes cold. 'Well, you can just put such ideas out of your mind, my lad. Your father does not approve of playhouses, and neither do I. *Or* of cock-fighting, *or* of arguments in rowdy taverns, *or* of strolling the streets after dark in defiance of danger to life and limb from these ruffians of the Hell Fire Club. D'ye hear? You will stay at home tonight and improve your mind with some study – as you should have been doing all these months past instead of idling about letting strange ideas breed in your empty head!'

'But, sir –!' Sandy attempted to protest. Gilmour had escorted Isobel out of the room without a backward glance at this sudden tirade. Mistress Wishart had followed them and he was alone with none to whom he could appeal except this terrible, tyranical old man. 'But, sir, you said you –'

'– would consider this fantastical idea of allowing you to break your articles with me – is that what you wanted to say, eh?' Wishart glowered at him. 'Well, I will, boy. I will – provided you, on your side, begin to show me some signs of steadiness of character for a change. That is the conclusion my thinking has come to. Now, d'ye understand? So long as you are under my rule I will not have you stravaiging the streets of Edinburgh. Therefore I forbid you to leave this house tonight. D'ye understand, I said!'

'Yes, sir.' In spite of the sense of outrage swelling in him, Sandy's gaze faltered before the stern authority of the look the old lawyer bent on him.

'See that you obey me then, or you cannot expect any concessions from me,' Wishart said, and with a final black glance of warning, he left the room.

The outer door of the house slammed behind him. Sandy stood motionless for a moment longer, then slowly he picked up a taper to light a candle for himself in the clerks' room. With dragging steps he carried the little light through, tipped a candle into flame and held it up to make his choice from among the fat black volumes on the shelves of law books there. Disconsolately then he sat down at his desk with the book laid open in front of him, and staring down at the solid mass of print it presented, felt a fresh wave of anger sweep over him.

It was monstrous, he told himself passionately – a monstrous injustice to keep him always thus chained to his desk. Yet what could he do but submit to it? Mr Wishart had the whip-hand so long as he was bound by the articles of his apprenticeship, and there was no way of winning freedom from these except by pleasing him.

For a long time he continued to stare unseeingly at the lines of print wavering in the candle's uncertain gleam, then with elbows on the desk and forehead propped in his hands he began unwillingly, at last, to read.

. . . a monstrous injustice! With a start that set his heart lurching Sandy heard the words echoing again in his mind, and became aware of something hard pressing against his cheek. The book – it was the hard outline of the book he could feel! He had fallen asleep over his reading. Groaning he sat upright and glanced at the grandfather clock in the corner of the office. Midnight! Good lord, he had slept for hours! Were the others back yet?

He listened, inclining his head for the sound of voices from other parts of the house, and heard nothing. The air in the room was stale – and how his head ached from lying in that awkward position! Stiffly he made for the casement window, jerked it open, and leaned out over the dark street.

Facing him across its width a jumble of steep-pitched roofs and gables cut a crazy pattern against the light of a dying moon, and along its length he could see a lantern still burning dimly in its bracket against the occasional house-front, but no life moved on the cobbles far below him. It was a street asleep, a dim canyon of dreams under the moon-haunted sky.

Drawing deep breaths of the cool night air Sandy visualized the pleasure of walking through its silence, and thought that even Wishart could surely not deny him the right to clear away his headache with a few minutes' stroll in the fresh air. It was ridiculous even to suppose otherwise, he told himself, and turning decisively away from the window, made for the outer door of the house.

Once outside, he walked slowly, relishing the pleasant feeling of expectance that being abroad at night always seemed to give, but alert all the same to any sudden noise of shouts or running feet, for – in justice to Mr Wishart – the High Street *could* sometimes be a dangerous place. At this late hour especially, any one of the dark alleys opening off it might spawn a horde of the wealthy young hooligans who called themselves the Hell Fire Club, and then he would be set on, beaten, kicked, pinched, trampled, and very likely left for dead before they swept on to their next victim!

He had turned to the right when he left Wishart's house, walking westwards up the High Street, and on his left now he could see the steep slope of the street called the West Bow running down from the south side of the High Street to the open space of the Grassmarket. From there, he thought, he could strike off east along the Cowgate in order to circle back to the High Street again, and with this in mind he turned down the West Bow.

Its narrow passage, with houses towering high and leaning at crazy angles on either side of it, closed in on him like a tunnel swallowing him up, and instinctively he quickened his pace to reach a patch of light that showed ahead of him and on the opposite side of the street to the one he had chosen.

Its position placed it for him as coming from the tall building which housed the Assembly Rooms, but beyond it was blackness again where the street continued its winding course down to the Grassmarket. It had not been a good choice of route after all, he thought and decided he would walk only as far as the light before turning back to the High Street again.

There was music as well as light spilling from the Assembly Rooms. Now that he was closer he could hear it drifting through the open doorway at the top of the outer stair which gave access to the building. There were people standing just inside the doorway taking leave of one another, and as he strolled on looking across the street towards them, he saw one of the ladies being handed down the steps by her escort. At the foot of the steps they both turned to wave gaily to the rest of the group before they started off up the West Bow. A voice which had a familiar ring to it called out in farewell to them, and a tall man in a scarlet coat stepped out to hand a lady in a white dress down the steps.

Sandy halted in swift embarrassment as he recognized Gilmour and Isobel Wishart. If they saw him there, he realized, they might think he was prying into their private affairs. On the other hand, he was now well within the perimeter of the light from the doorway. If he turned to hurry away they would see him just the same, and so there was obviously nothing for it but to walk steadily on hoping that they would be too engrossed in conversation to glance over to his side of the street.

He walked on again, quickening his pace towards the darkness beyond the outer rim of light from the doorway, and heard the air split with a crack that reverberated in roaring echo from the house-fronts lining the narrow street. In the same instant, something struck his shoulder a blow that pitched him headlong to the cobbles underfoot.

There was a blank space of time in his mind as he fell, and during this, a woman screamed loudly. Then his face hit the stones and his mind jerked into action again with the realization that someone had shot at him. And hit him?

There was no pain. Rolling over to grope for the place where he had felt the blow, he heard voices shouting and the thunder of feet on the cobbles.

His fingers encountered torn cloth and padding hanging loose from the shoulder of his coat, but there was no blood. His left arm was numb and it was difficult to rise again using only one arm. Pushing hard against the cobbles with his right hand, his hearing was assaulted again by the crack and roaring echo of another shot, and panic heaved him to his feet.

Crouching, he achieved a stumbling run to the safety of the Assembly Rooms' door, only vaguely aware of the babbling voices coming from the group of people milling round inside it. Hands reached out to draw him in. The group took him into its midst and he saw Isobel Wishart in front of him, her face as white now as her dress, her eyes dilated with fear. Shakily he said,

'I am not hurt, Mistress Isobel. The shots missed me.'

She stared wordlessly at him. Her pale lips moved and she whispered, 'Deryck was carrying a pistol. He – he ran after the man who shot at you.'

A man standing behind her said, 'That second shot, too, must have been fired by the assassin. It was not nearly a sharp enough report for the toy that Gilmour carried.'

Isobel swayed as if about to fall, and the man steadied her in sudden alarm at the effect of his tactless remark. Sandy turned as its meaning struck him, and made a plunge for the doorway. Voices called to him as he blundered down the steps but no one tried to stop him from leaving. He reached the street and glanced wildly right and left for a sight of Gilmour.

Left, he decided. The first shot had come from behind him. He ran up the street's winding slope, feeling the blood waken painfully to life in his numbed arm as he ran, and heard a third shot ring out. He followed the direction of its sound and in the High Street, twenty yards from its junction with the West Bow, came to the end of the chase.

Gilmour was there, stooped over the body of a man sprawling on the cobbles. He rose as Sandy came pounding towards him, and the light of a house-lantern glinted on the pistol in his right hand. Sharply he asked,

'Are you wounded?'

Sandy shook his head, staring past him to the face of the sprawling figure upturned to the lantern light. Its misshapen head lolled, the thin curve of its mouth drooped slackly, the eyes were dark slits in an empty mask. A jagged hole in the forehead showed black against the wax-paleness of the features.

'*Rattray!*' His voice came in a shocked whisper.

Gilmour slid his pistol back inside his coat. 'Listen to me,' he said carefully. 'When the Town Guard patrol comes – as it will in a moment – I will identify this body as that of Sandy Maxwell, a colleague of mine who was shot at and killed by an unknown assailant. I will claim it immediately for burial and insert a notice of the death in tomorrow's news-sheets. D'ye understand?'

'You want it given out that I am dead!' Incredulous, Sandy stared at him.

Gilmour nodded. 'So that word to that effect will be reported back to St Clair,' he explained. ''Tis the only way to keep you safe till the smuggling drop is over.'

'Of course!' Light dawning suddenly, Sandy glanced back to the body. 'You and Mr Wishart have been keeping me shut up like a prisoner – and tonight Rattray tried to murder me ...'

Gilmour was glancing down the street. 'Here they come,' he said abruptly. 'Get back to the Assembly Rooms and back up my story by explaining that you were accidentally caught up in the cross-fire between the dead man and his assailant.'

'But my parents . . .' Sandy objected. 'What if they see this false announcement in the news-sheets?'

'I will see they are kept informed of the truth. They will have no cause for worry,' Gilmour answered, and with his words, the plan suddenly took on reality for Sandy.

With quick excitement he peered towards the sound of marching feet and the dim gleam of bayonets far down the street. 'Go!' Gilmour commanded – and he ran, with an inclination to macabre laughter rising in him, to announce the death of Sandy Maxwell.

12. Land and Sea Force

IN the long thick grass of the headland overlooking Cove Harbour, Sandy lay with his hand curled round the butt of a pistol and waited for Lieutenant Daventry's signal to move off ahead of the tunnel-party.

'Daventry will need to be guided by someone familiar with the path down to the tunnel if his party is to surprise any sentries posted there,' Colonel Moyes had pointed out at the rendezvous in Dominie Drummond's house. Gilmour had immediately cast Sandy in this role, and the Comptroller had provided him with the pistol as well as a cutlass from the extensive armoury carried by his own party.

'If you are old enough to risk death by a stray shot from a smuggler's pistol,' he had remarked, 'you are old enough also to bear arms in your own defence.' In the safety of the schoolhouse the words had sounded with a dramatic ring. But now, in this dark world of whispering grass and silently crowding soldiers, Sandy recalled them as the flat tones of common sense and was glad of the pistol-butt lying heavy in his palm and the hard line of the cutlass against his hip.

A rustling noise behind him warned him of the approach of the runner keeping contact between Gilmour and the tunnel party. Beside him, Daventry stirred and turned his head. The scout crawling up to them eased himself forward till he was in position to whisper,

'Mr Gilmour's compliments, sir, and a message to say you can proceed now. The smugglers' cliff-top lookout has been captured and our own man put in his place.'

Daventry's hand reached out to touch Sandy's shoulder. In the darkness his teeth gleamed white as he whispered, 'Lead on, Maxwell,' and Sandy guessed at the grin on his face. Daventry was only a couple of years older than himself and, he thought, was enjoying this as much as he was! Carefully he rose, and began a crouching, soundless descent of the headland.

Far below on his left were the shifting white lines of waves breaking against the cliffs bounding the east side of the harbour, but the path leading down to the tunnel was a bare twenty feet below him and it was his task to pick the spot from which Daventry could launch a silent, surprise attack. He moved slowly, aware that the party had to keep close enough order for each man to follow exactly in the steps of the man in front, and listened as he went for any sound that might break the careful silence of the men creeping behind him.

When he saw the two smugglers standing guard over the tunnel entrance, he froze in position long enough to let Daventry guess what had happened, then he turned, grasped the other's arm, and drew him forward. He pointed down. The men were standing side by side at the edge of the cliff path, their backs to the headland as they gazed out to sea. Daventry pressed his arm in acknowledgement, and he crawled aside to allow Daventry room to bring his sergeant alongside.

Long moments of waiting passed after the sergeant had surveyed the smugglers' position and then dropped back to rejoin his troop. The faintest of rustlings reached Sandy, and he held his breath, guessing at an attack party crawling down towards the cliff path. The men there had apparently heard nothing. Silent, they continued gazing out to sea, motionless until a sudden small clink of rock on rock made one of them turn to face inland.

As he moved, the sergeant's party launched themselves across the cliff path, clubbed pistols swinging high and descending again with almost soundless force. The sagging figures of the two smugglers were caught before they fell. Sandy followed Daventry's scramble down to the cliff path, and heard his whispered order for an escort to take them back as prisoners to the base camp at Innerwick.

He waited while the guard for the landward end of the tunnel was posted under the sergeant's command, and then turned to lead off again with the whispered warning,

'*Remember to hold on.*'

He felt Daventry grasp the skirt of his coat. The next man laid a similar hold on Daventry, and so on right down the line. The tunnel ahead of them, Sandy knew, would engulf them in seventy yards of pitch darkness. Daventry had agreed to this way of having the party advance as a unit through it, and so linked like this, Sandy led them forwards.

The tunnel's floor was wickedly uneven. Feeling his way along the moisture-dripping curve of the wall he thought of the dozens of times he had raced backwards and forwards along it on swimming or fishing expeditions to the harbour, and tried hard to remember exactly where the roughest parts of it lay, but still could not avoid an occasional stumble. Behind him, when this happened, the whole line wavered in temporary disarray, but the Dragoons were well-disciplined and each man retained his grip of the one in front until the tunnel lightened to grey with the approach of its wide, seaward end.

Daventry released his grip on Sandy then, to bring his men forward in close order. At the tunnel mouth he checked them, and stood with Sandy looking out over the horseshoe of deserted beach sloping gently up from the water of the harbour. The tide was making. In an hour's time, Sandy calculated, it would be full and the smugglers' boats would be riding it into the harbour.

'There!' he whispered. 'And there!'

His pointing hand indicated the huge alcove that high tides had hollowed out at the base of the cliff on the seaward side of the tunnel's entrance, and the great sandstone boulders flanking its landward side. There was room for at least half of Daventry's troop in the alcove with ample cover among the rocks for the rest, and once caught in their crossfire, the smugglers would have little hope of forcing the tunnel mouth.

Daventry's hand descended on his shoulder. Daventry's voice whispered delightedly in his ear, 'Perfect, Maxwell! A thousand thanks!' and in a glow of achievement, Sandy turned to work his way back up the tunnel again.

'*Land and Sea Force.*'

In a low voice he gave the password in reply to the murmured challenge that greeted his approach to its farther end.

'All in order with Mr Daventry, sir?' the sergeant whispered.

'Aye, all in order.' Hurriedly he answered before he swung himself up from the cliff path and began to climb towards the point where Gilmour lay hidden with Colonel Moyes and the rest of the Dragoons.

The outposts had been warned to expect him, but still did not let him pass before he had given the proper reply to their whispered challenge. The last sentry was posted only a few yards from where Moyes and Gilmour crouched together in the long grass of the ditch that sheltered the Dragoon troop, and both men looked round as he answered the sentry's challenge and came crawling forward.

'Tunnel parties posted, sir,' he reported to Moyes first, as

Gilmour had instructed him. 'Sergeant Morgan at the land-ward end, and Lieutenant Daventry in ambush at the sea-ward end.'

To Gilmour he said, 'Mr Daventry captured two men who were guarding the landward end of the tunnel, sir, and sent them back under escort to Dominie Drummond's house. The tide should be full in less than an hour from now.'

Gilmour murmured to Moyes, 'I leave the action in your hands now. I am going forward to Number 1 Signaller's post.' He nudged Sandy, 'Come on, lad.'

Together they crawled forward to where the signaller crouched a few yards back from the edge of the cliffs over-looking the harbour.

'Commence landing signal, sailor,' Gilmour told him. 'One long, two short, two long, at two minute intervals.'

'Aye, aye, sir. Commence landing signal it is.' Rising to his feet the man began operating the shutter of his dark lantern. Gilmour crawled forward to join Sandy at the very edge of the cliffs and they lay in silence taking stock of the position.

Their view seawards was a surprisingly clear one for a moonless night, for in spite of a light breeze blowing off-shore, there was little or no cloud to dim the brilliance of the stars. The harbour water gleamed coldly with their light. The jetty that concealed the Comptroller's party was a bar of solid black against it, and beyond the jetty the dark waters of the Firth were tipped occasionally with sudden sparkles of silver.

'The weather is working against them,' Gilmour mut-tered, and Sandy nodded silent agreement. The soldiers would be dark against the darkness of the land, he realized, but the smugglers' shapes would be clearly lined against this sea-gleam of starlight. His heartbeat quickened with the thought that in less than an hour they would have

Robertson in their hands, and he could not resist whispering this comment to Gilmour.

There was no answer for a few moments, and then Gilmour said softly, as if to himself, 'And I will see him at last!'

He turned to peer at Sandy. 'D'ye realize how strange a thing it is to hunt a man you do not know – have never even seen? There is a feeling of unreality to it – almost as if one were running through a nightmare in pursuit of a faceless man . . .'

Sandy shivered, wishing Gilmour had not spoken his final words. Robertson was real, he told himself stubbornly. He was cunning and violent, but he was still flesh and blood – not the weird fantasy-figure Gilmour had conjured up. He drew his coat collar up round his ears, telling himself it was the cold touch of the offshore breeze that had made him shiver.

The signaller behind them was still patiently flashing away at two minute intervals, and suddenly they heard him say,

'Here they come, sir!'

'Flash every minute now, sailor,' Gilmour ordered.

'Flash every minute it is, sir.'

They strained to catch the next flash of the answering signal their own man had noted, and saw it presently gleaming west of the harbour.

'Get back and warn Colonel Moyes to stand by,' Gilmour said, 'and keep well down in case your movement is seen.'

As rapidly as he could, Sandy crawled back to report, and immediately Moyes demanded, 'How long do we have before the signal that they are safely in?'

'Fifteen to twenty minutes, sir, I make it,' he answered. 'They are coming in on the tide.'

'Good!' The word came out on a sigh of relief from Moyes. 'The men have been getting tense with this waiting!'

With a dismissing wave of his hand he turned away, and Sandy hurried back to Gilmour.

'You can see them clearly now.' Gilmour pointed out for him the cluster of dark shapes bearing down on the harbour. 'No sails and no sound – they are coming in on muffled oars.'

The man behind them had closed the shutter of his lantern. Soundlessly advancing, the first of the boats swept into the harbour.

'Seven craft,' Gilmour muttered, 'each with probably a six-man crew. A good haul, Sandy!'

The noise of a boat scraping on the shingle reached them, and a laugh that was cut off suddenly in mid-sound.

Three in, four to come, Sandy counted silently, and wondered how their timing would go. Would the last boat be in to the harbour before the men from the first boat made for the tunnel?

'It will take time to unload each boat and rope the goods for carrying,' Gilmour's whisper sounded in answer to his unspoken question.

The signaller came to crouch down beside them. In a voice of quiet desperation he said, 'Sir, the shutter of my lantern has stuck!'

Gilmour cursed under his breath and snatched the lantern out of the man's hand. 'A knife, quickly!' he commanded, and waving away the large blade the signaller offered him, took the small penknife Sandy held out. With rapid precision he ran its point along the shutter-groove, and then shielding the flame with his body, tried the effect. The shutter slid smoothly open and shut again.

Fiercely he whispered to the signaller, 'Captain's report for you tomorrow, sailor, for allowing grit to collect in that groove!'

'Sir!' Sandy touched his arm. 'They are all in!'

Their little group froze into watchfulness, all eyes on the

jetty. There was movement there now – a boat being pushed out from the concealment of the rocks behind the jetty, a flurry of white water across the harbour-mouth, and then suddenly, men's shapes appearing on the jetty itself and hauling away at unseen ropes.

A reddish-yellow flash split the darkness, and a shot cracked across the harbour. One of the men on the jetty threw up his arms and toppled towards the water. More shots followed from the beach, and answering fire came now from the jetty. Shouting mingled with the noise of the shots, and a boat slid out across the harbour towards the jetty.

A single voice screamed, 'Swing her hard round by the head! Hard round! *Hard* round!'

'The Comptroller,' Gilmour identified the voice. There was a sharp edge to his own voice. He had his pistol in his right hand, and his left hand was tightly clenched.

'There she goes! I read you, Jack, I read you!'

Number 2 Signaller was flashing his message from the jetty, and exclaiming aloud as it leapt across the darkness, their Number 1 man swung to face inland with the shutter of his own lantern working furiously.

A swift rattle of shots from the beach told of Daventry's party opening fire, and hard on the sound came a hoarse yelling as the Dragoons in the ditch broke from cover and surged towards the edge of the cliffs.

Gilmour bounded up roaring, *'Stand clear to signal the sloops,'* and their signaller broke through the rush of soldiers to flash his signal to the Number 3 man waiting on the seaward side of the headland.

The noise from the beach had reached pandemonium level. Crouching shoulder to shoulder with the Dragoons on either side of him, Sandy peered downward at the flashes and the turmoil of dark figures scurrying over the sand. The whine of bullets ricochetting off rock warned him that some of the smugglers had taken cover to shoot it out with Daventry's party, and he thought grimly that there would be a great deal of mopping-up to the operation. Not all the smugglers would walk tamely into the net!

The voice of Colonel Moyes blared out along the line of Dragoons. 'Dragoons – *ready*! Warning volley – fire!'

The volley fired into the air rang out with appalling loudness that momentarily blanketed every other sound. In the hush that followed it, Gilmour cupped his hands to his mouth and roared,

'You are surrounded! You are surrounded! Throw down your arms! I repeat, throw down your arms and advance to surrender!'

A scatter of shots from the beach answered him. Colonel Moyes blared again, 'Dragoons – ready! Take aim! Fire at every man not raising his hands in surrender!'

The ragged shooting from below continued as the Comptroller's men battled with the boat-crew which had tried to break out through the boom, but there were no more shots from the beach.

'Come up!' Moyes roared. 'Come up with both hands raised!'

The surrender began slowly, with one man clawing his way up to the headland and shouting, 'Hold your fire! Hold your fire!' to the Dragoons watchfully poised above him. Halting a few yards from them he held empty hands above his head, and was curtly ordered to advance. Two Dragoons seized him, and held him at pistol point while Gilmour briefly shone the signaller's lantern on him. The face of a youngish man, fair-skinned and unscarred, glowered back at him.

'Take him away,' Gilmour ordered, and the Dragoons pushed him towards the escort party Major Shadwell was mustering to take the prisoners back to Innerwick.

In twos and threes after that, they struggled towards captivity, helping one another up the steep slope and pausing

as the first man had done, to show empty hands to the soldiers waiting to seize them. Gilmour continued to stand
beside Major Shadwell, the lantern held high to inspect each
man pushed towards the escort party, and anxiously waiting
with them, Sandy watched face after face loom into the light
and vanish again.

Sullen, angry, or fearful, according to the way they had
accepted defeat, they hovered momentarily in his vision –
nineteen men in all, and none of them Robertson. But there
was still every chance he would be among the dead men or
the prisoners down on the beach, Sandy argued to himself.
After all, it was much more likely he would be among those
who had put up the fiercest resistance than the ones who had
accepted capture!

Gilmour seemed to share his views. 'Down to the harbour,'
he ordered after the last man to surrender had been checked.
'We will see if Daventry or the Comptroller has taken him.'

Glancing seawards as he led the way to the cliff-path,
Sandy saw that the battle by the harbour-mouth was over.
The jetty was crowded with dark figures making their way
beachwards, and the occasional shot that sounded as they
hurried down to the tunnel mouth seemed to come from
directly below them, on the beach itself. Daventry rooting
out the last hard core of resistance, he thought, and recklessly increased his pace down the stony path in a sudden
fierce desire to seize the last chance of playing an active part
in the fight.

At the tunnel mouth, Sergeant Morgan stepped forward
on the sound of his reply to the sentry's challenge. Gilmour
identified himself and the sergeant said jovially,

'Just as well Mr Daventry posted us here, sir. We got two
that managed to break through from the other end!'

'Let me see them,' Gilmour ordered.

'There they are, sir,' Morgan stood aside and gestured to
two men lying face down on the path with their hands

clasped behind their heads. Gilmour took a swift step towards them and motioned back the Dragoon standing over them with a pistol at the ready.

'Turn your heads!' he snapped.

Two sullen faces turned slowly into the light of his lantern, one fleshy and bearded, the other sharp-featured and sallow.

'Sandy?' Gilmour gestured to the sharp-featured man.

'No, sir.' Sandy shook his head. 'That is not Robertson.'

Gilmour turned away, telling Morgan, 'We are going down to join Mr Daventry,' but the sergeant checked his move and said apologetically,

'Beg pardon, sir, but I must warn you that the tunnel may be dangerous. I have had a scout keeping contact with Mr Daventry's party and they told him it was not two men, but three, who broke past them.'

'But your scout has passed backwards and forwards since then,' Gilmour said, 'and the man has not shot at him.'

'Correct, sir,' Morgan agreed, 'and so we reckon he must be in hiding somewhere, hoping to escape unseen after everything is over.'

'In that case,' Gilmour told him drily, 'he will not reveal his presence by shooting at me either!' He turned to Sandy. 'You know this tunnel, Sandy. Where could he hide himself?'

'There is a cave opening off the right-hand side, near the seaward end of the tunnel,' Sandy told him. 'That is certainly where he will be.'

'And it could be Robertson,' Gilmour said thoughtfully. ''Tis the kind of move we could have expected of him!'

'Then all you can do is starve him out,' Sandy answered. 'The cave mouth is very narrow, sir, and one man could hold it indefinitely against an army.'

Gilmour stood thinking for a moment, then decisively he said, 'Sergeant Morgan! Kindly detail a Corporal and five men to accompany Mr Maxwell and myself down the tunnel.'

'Yes, sir!' Morgan turned to select the men, and Gilmour said quietly to Sandy, 'I am going to leave you at the cave mouth with these men, Sandy. I want you to talk to the man inside the cave, and try to get him to answer you. Can you tell Robertson by the sound of his voice?'

'I should be able to, sir,' Sandy told him. 'I have heard it often enough.'

'Very well. If you find it is not Robertson, you may proceed to join me with Mr Daventry's party on the beach. Leave the Dragoons on guard, with orders to shoot if the man tries to break out of the cave.'

'Detail ready, sir,' Morgan reported.

'And if it is Robertson?' Sandy asked.

'Send the corporal at the double to fetch either myself or Daventry, or the Comptroller – whichever he can find first. Now take this, and lead on.'

Sandy took the lantern from him, and holding it wide to light the way for the rest of the party, led the way down the tunnel to the cave mouth. When he stopped beside it, Gilmour took the lantern and held it up to examine the opening. It was narrow, as Sandy had said, and high enough to allow a man of average height to enter without stooping. With signs, he indicated that it continued into a passage opening out to a fairly large cave, and Gilmour nodded understanding.

Placing the lantern where it would light the cave's entrance, he stationed the corporal and his men so that they could block any attempted escape from it, then with a brief clap on Sandy's shoulder, continued on his way to the seaward end of the tunnel. Stolidly, as his footsteps faded, the Dragoons regarded Sandy.

They were waiting quite incuriously for his next move, but he still felt slightly foolish at the thought of it. Squaring his shoulders, he put the feeling aside and shouted into the cave,

'Hey! You, in there! Come out, your friends are all taken!'

'... *taken* ... *taken* ...' the echo of his voice rebounded from the walls of the tunnel and died into silence.

He tried again. 'We can starve you out if you will not come freely. There is no escape!'

'... *cape* ... *escape* ...' the echo mocked, but still no voice came in the silence that followed it.

'I could fire into the entrance, sir,' the corporal suggested softly.

'The passage twists. The bullet would ricochet,' Sandy told him. He bit his lips. This parley was a stupid business. If he could think of a better idea . . .

It came to him suddenly with a memory of the time he had been 'it' in a long-ago game of hide-and-seek at the Cove with Archie and a gang of boys from Innerwick. There had been a large hole at the foot of the cliffs behind the great boulders flanking the seaward end of the tunnel – a hole not more than eighteen inches high that was almost blocked by soft, dry sand. He had crawled through the hole, and found a sloping shelf of rock above his head. The shelf had been the roof of a small, irregular-shaped recess opening off the main body of the cave, and lying there he had heard whispering – Archie and Neil Drummond, the Dominie's son, plotting to dash out to a new hiding place if they heard him coming up the tunnel to the cave entrance.

And he had taken them by surprise!

'Corporal!' Whispering with his lips close to the man's ear, he said, 'I am going into the cave by another way. Stand fast to guard this entrance.'

The corporal saluted in silent acknowledgement of the order. Sandy bent to slip off his shoes and then ran sound-lessly in stockinged feet for the tunnel mouth. The password took him by the sentry on guard there, and for a moment he stood, temporarily distracted from his purpose by the scene on the beach.

The foreshore was darkly littered with beached boats and the packages that had been spilled from them. In the alcove where the Dragoons had waited in ambush, a row of bodies was laid out neatly. A group of prisoners squatted on the sand, hands on their heads, a starlit ring of steel pointed at them from the Dragoon guard's sabres, and everywhere there were men scurrying through the darkness – men running along the jetty, men heaving packages ashore, men leaping about among the rocks.

Gilmour's voice shouting, 'Search that place again, Mr Daventry! Search it again!' reached him above the babble of other voices, and broke the spell on him with the realization that they had not yet found Robertson. Dropping down, he crawled to the place where he remembered finding the hole.

He discovered it again, still almost blocked by sand, and with slow, silent movements pushing this aside he wriggled through into the little chamber with its sloping rock-roof. Lying there, he listened for movement or breathing from the cave, but could hear nothing. Gently and slowly he eased himself out of the recess, and with infinite caution, rose to his feet.

The cave was pitch black. Its floor, he knew, was as uneven as that of the tunnel, but it was covered thickly with damp sand which meant he would be able to move silently across it. He inched forward, keeping the wall nearest to the tunnel as a guide, testing every step before putting his weight on it, and pausing after each step to listen.

Still no sound! Either the fugitive knew he was there and was holding his breath, or else he was in the L-shaped passage leading from the cave to the tunnel. He counted his steps and advanced an exploring hand when he calculated he had reached the passage. His fingers encountered the sharp angle it made with the main line of the cave, and he turned to follow their careful groping along the passage wall.

Now he *could* hear breathing! Heavy and slow – the sound a man under tension would make! He reached the end of the L's long leg, and turned again, slowly, slowly ... The man *must* be in front of him now ...

He leapt, left hand outstretched to the darkness, right hand thrusting his pistol forward, and crashed against something that yielded to his weight. His left hand clutched it, his right hand jabbed the pistol against it. In a breathless shout he threatened,

'Drop your pistol, or I fire!'

The man in his grip stiffened in his half-bent position. 'Drop it!' Sandy repeated hoarsely. A second pause, and then a dull thud as something heavy fell to the sand.

'Corporal!' Sandy yelled. 'I am bringing out a prisoner. Shoot if he tries to run.'

'Now walk!' he ordered through the corporal's answering shout, and the man walked slowly to the cave's entrance. In the light there, they saw one another's faces.

'*You!*'

Sweat gleaming on his weathered skin, narrowed blue eyes glaring, Rob Grierson snarled the word out at Sandy, and in equal astonishment he stared back at his captive.

'You dirty wee spy you!' Shouting, Grierson lunged, and was dragged back by two burly Dragoons.

'Bring him out, Corporal.'

Sandy gave the order as he bent to retrieve his shoes, and then walked out of the tunnel ahead of the prisoner and escort. He was trembling, both from the shock of the encounter and from the release of tension, and with a feeling of intense relief he saw Gilmour standing with Daventry and the Comptroller a few yards from the tunnel mouth.

They turned towards him at the sound of the sentry's challenge and he called to Gilmour, 'Sir, I have taken the man in the cave!'

'Who is he?' Gilmour moved towards him, throwing the question out sharply.

'Rob Grierson of Prestonpans,' Sandy answered, and asked, 'Have you got Robertson, sir?'

'No, we have not got him,' Gilmour said sourly, and whipped round in quick amazement – as they all did – at a loud cackle of laughter from Rob Grierson.

'And you never will!' Grierson shouted through his laughter. 'You never will this trip!'

'Be quiet, d'ye hear!' Gilmour caught Grierson's chin in his hand and jerked his face up. 'Stop that cackling and say what you mean, man. Why will we not take Robertson this trip?'

'Because he fooled you – that is why,' Grierson told him spitefully. 'Geordie changed his mind at the last minute and never came with us on this drop after all. He fooled you *and* your spy, Mister Clever-dick Customs man!'

Gilmour snatched his hand away as if he had been stung. He muttered something, and Daventry asked, 'What did you say, sir?'

Gilmour stared at him, then slowly and distinctly he answered, 'I said, Mr Daventry, that I am still pursuing a faceless man. Now form up your men to march the prisoners back to Innerwick.'

13. Red Herring, Black Dawn

WITH sombre gaze, Dominie John Drummond of Innerwick surveyed the transformation that had overtaken his house, his schoolroom, and his garden. A tall man, with a wild lock of greying hair falling over a pedant's broad brow, he had subdued generations of schoolboys with the hawk-like intensity of that same brooding stare. But far from wishing to impose his will on anyone at that moment, the Dominie was quietly satisfied with what he saw.

His orchard had been spoiled beyond redemption by the trampling of a troop of Dragoon horse. His schoolroom had been commandeered for a full-scale interrogation of some thirty prisoners, and the rest of the house converted to a makeshift infirmary for dead and wounded men, but the Dominie was a firm believer in law and order and these things did not trouble him. With long, rangy strides stalking through his domain he laid them sternly at the altar of his principles and put out of his mind the reckoning there might be, the next day, with Mistress Drummond.

That lady was in the kitchen, her long black hair streaming over the shoulders of her bed-gown as she busily ripped sheets into bandages for the medical orderly standing obediently by her side. With some relief the Dominie saw that the night's turmoil had not stopped her conversing graciously with Colonel Moyes as she worked, and turned to watch his daughter, Harriet, dishing up soup to a group of Dragoon officers and that boy – What was his name – Maxwell? Yes, that was it, Sandy Maxwell.

The Dominie's brooding gaze became even more forbidding. There was a brother in that family, he remembered, and the two of them had robbed his orchard one day when they had gone swimming with Neil at Cove Harbour. But he had caught them, and tanned their backsides for them – and very likely it had done them some good, for according to the Comptroller, the boy had behaved well in the battle against the smugglers. A pity Neil was not at home just now, he thought, walking through to the schoolroom. He would have enjoyed meeting the Maxwell boy again.

The press in the schoolroom had eased somewhat he found when he opened the door and looked out over the rows of prisoners slouched on the scholars' benches. The Comptroller had apparently removed his men to deal with the great pile of contraband that had been brought up from the harbour, and there were now no more Dragoons than were necessary to stand guard over the prisoners. The Comptroller's colleague, Gilmour, was still seated at his desk, engaged in questioning one of the prisoners standing in front of him, and with a touch of dismay at the haggard look on his face the Dominie went forward to ask,

'How goes it, Mr Gilmour?'

Gilmour drew a hand wearily over his face. 'I have still not found out any more than the fellow, Grierson, told us at the harbour,' he admitted, 'but I must press on – all night if need be. One of the prisoners is bound to know something of Robertson's whereabouts, and I must get it out of him.'

The Dominie drew a stool towards himself and sat down beside Gilmour. Grimly he said, 'I taught some of these fellows as boys, Mr Gilmour, and the old fear of the Dominie's power is not an easy thing for them to forget. Furthermore, I am in the habit of keeping late hours at my books, and an all-night session of questioning will not trouble me – if you care to accept my assistance.'

'I would be glad of it!' Gilmour's voice showed how genuinely he welcomed the offer of help, and the Dominie smiled slightly before he turned the full force of his hawk-like gaze on the man in front of the desk. In a voice that had menace rumbling under its even tones he began,

'I know you, William Dodds, and I know when you are lying and when you are speaking the truth. Now tell me, my lad . . .'

'Put out the candles, Sandy,' Mistress Drummond said quietly. She handed him an extinguisher, and he moved round the schoolroom nipping out the flames of the candles that had been allowed to burn on beyond the dawn. Sleepily, as he moved, he glanced through the window to the Dominie's garden. The sun was well up now, sparkling on the dew in the orchard, and the men on duty in the horse lines were yawning and shivering in the morning air.

Going back to the little group that had come gradually to gather at the Dominie's desk, he noticed how haggard they all looked. The Comptroller, Moyes, Daventry, Shadwell, Gilmour, the Dominie – even Mistress Drummond herself had not closed an eye that night, and now they all looked the worse for wear. The prisoners, he thought, had fared better than their captors, for while one was being questioned the others had simply lolled asleep on the benches!

'Well, Mr Gilmour?' Irritably the Comptroller broke the gloomy quiet that hung over the group. 'You see how useless it is to try to break this law of silence they have – so what d'ye propose now?'

Gilmour focused tired eyes on him. 'I have one shot left in my locker, Mr Comptroller,' he said in a low voice. '''Tis a trick – an interrogator's trick, but I will not give up till I have tried it.'

The Comptroller reached out to stop him as he moved back to the desk, but the Dominie brushed his hand aside and said,

'Let him go, my friend. He is the kind that can break, but will never give up.'

Gilmour faced the prisoners lying half-asleep on the benches. He had picked up a heavy leather strap from the desk – the 'tawse' the Dominie used to punish erring scholars, and suddenly he brought it down on the desk with a crack as loud as a pistol-shot. The lolling forms in front of him jerked drunkenly awake, and harshly he shouted at them.

'Listen to me, you scum, or you are dead men, every one of you!'

The prisoners' eyes rested vacantly on him. Glaring back at them he went on, 'You think to hide George Robertson behind this law of silence you have among yourselves, but one thing you have not counted on is that Robertson is not only a smuggler, he is also a traitor, engaged in seditious work that will make him stand guilty of treason! And you – by the fact that you are admitted associates of his, stand accused now of the same crime.'

He turned to the group of colleagues silently watching him. In the same harsh voice he said, 'Dominie, Mr Comptroller, I call you to witness that I hereby charge these men with being art and part in the crime of high treason. And, Colonel Moyes, I request that you immediately deliver them to the Sheriff of this county for the appropriate trial and sentence.'

Rob Grierson leapt to his feet. 'You will not make that charge stick, Mister Customs-man,' he bawled. 'No one will believe we were in on this game Geordie was playing!'

'Will they not?' Gilmour asked mockingly. 'You fool, Grierson – look at my witnesses! A Colonel of Dragoons, a Dominie, the Customs Comptroller – respectable men of position and authority! Who will believe the word of a gang of smugglers against their? No, no, my good fool – you can stow that kind of sea-lawyer talk! You are for the rope, the drawing-iron, and the quartering-axe – all of you, if you have not the sense to tell me where George Robertson is!'

Prisoner turned quickly to prisoner and a wild buzz of talk ran through their ranks. With the mocking smile still on his face Gilmour watched their confusion, and noted particularly the face of a young, fair-haired man – the William Dodds whose silence the Dominie had tried to break so many hours before.

Cracking the tawse on the desk to draw attention to himself again, he shouted, 'You have had plenty of time to consider whether you want to be hanged, drawn and quartered for George Robertson's sake. Now I give you five seconds to decide which charge you want to face – smuggling or treason!'

He began to count, slowly, looking at a different face with each number he called. On the word 'four' his eyes rested on William Dodds. The man half-rose, and before Gilmour had finished saying 'five' he called desperately, '*Sir!*'

'Sit down!' Grierson yelled, and other prisoners joined the shout, 'You dirty traitor, sit down!'

Dodds rounded on them, yelling in reply, 'I have a wife and bairns, mates, and so have you all. Why should we sacrifice them for Geordie Robertson!'

'We will burn your boat if you speak,' a voice threatened him.

'I can build another boat,' Dodds retorted, 'but who will feed my bairns if I am killed for a traitor?'

'Mr Comptroller,' Gilmour called, 'kindly take note that William Dodds has turned King's Evidence in the case of His Majesty versus George Robertson, and arrange for him to be protected against any violence offered as a result.'

'That will not stop us,' Grierson shouted. 'We know how to deal with those who betray us!'

'Do you indeed?' Gilmour asked quietly. His gaze swept over the rows of hostile faces glaring at him and Dodds, then shooting out a hand to point at Grierson he yelled, 'Then deal with this man, my merry lads! There sits the one who blabbed to the Customs about this smuggling drop!'

A howl of denial burst from Grierson and was drowned in an angry roar from the rest of the smugglers. Men rose to hurl themselves on him, and cracking at heads with the flat of their sabres, the Dragoons moved in to restore order. Gilmour and Moyes leapt to drag Dodds clear of the mêlée. 'Speak up!' Gilmour commanded him, and glancing in terror at the uproar behind him he gabbled,

'Geordie landed at Dunbar last night, instead of at the Cove with the rest of us. He had horses waiting there for him and the rest of the fellows in his boat, and I think he had guessed that someone had blabbed about the drop and was only letting it go on to make a red herring that would draw you away from his real intentions.'

'Why? Why should you think that?' Gilmour demanded.

'Because – because of the horses, sir, and – and because he said his business was at Soutra Hill,' Dodds stammered. 'It is a long way from Dunbar to the road running over Soutra, and he must have planned well ahead to have had horses ready for the journey.'

'Soutra Hill?' Gilmour shot a general question at the rest of the group around him and Dodds. 'Where is that – and what would take Robertson there?'

The Dragoon officers shook their heads, but Sandy and the Comptroller exchanged swift looks as each read the answer in the other's face.

'It lies some thirty miles inland from Dunbar,' the Comptroller told him, 'and the road running over it is the coach-road from Edinburgh to London.'

'The coach-horses always have to slow to a walk by the time they reach Soutra's crest,' Sandy joined in breathlessly. 'It is a notorious place for ambush – and there is an Edinburgh-bound coach due to pass there this morning.'

'The Porteous reprieve!' Staring at him, Gilmour blurted out the words. 'Wishart said it was almost certain to arrive today. D'ye mean to say –'

'Lieutenant Daventry!' Moyes said sharply. 'Have "Assembly" sounded. Major Shadwell, take charge of the post in my absence.'

'Thank you, Colonel!' Quickly Gilmour turned to follow Daventry running from the schoolroom, but checked as the Comptroller said gloomily,

''Tis no use, gentlemen. The Lammermuir Hills lie between Innerwick and the crest of Soutra, and if we go roundabout as Robertson did, it will be too late to stop him robbing the mailcoach.'

'Not so, my friend,' the Dominie contradicted. 'There is a way that would enable you both to cut across the long route and avoid the high one – a bridle track that runs directly southwest to Soutra over the low reaches of the Lammermuirs. But you would need a guide.'

'Speak plainer,' Gilmour demanded. 'Are you offering your services?'

A gleam of battle leapt in the Dominie's eye. 'Can you give me a good horse?' he answered, and as if his words had been a spring that released them all, they rushed in a body for the schoolroom door. The brazen notes of 'Assembly' sounded as they ran, and they reached the orchard to find Daventry hastily bringing order out of the trampling chaos of men and horses there.

'To horse – all troopers not on guard duty!' Colonel Moyes roared. 'Daventry, give Mr Drummond the Major's horse!'

Sandy ran for Gambler. Swinging into the saddle he wheeled in time to see the Dominie urging Shadwell's mount forward, with Colonel Moyes and Gilmour riding neck and neck behind him. The Comptroller was following hard on their heels, and kicking Gambler into a spurt ahead of the Dragoon troop, Sandy gained fourth place in the riders streaming out of the orchard.

Westward through the village they raced, the Dominie's wild lock of hair flying like a pennant in the lead, and the sound of the massed troop of Dragoon horses behind Sandy rolling thunderously between the walls of the sleeping houses. A noisy marriage of rooks wheeling on ragged wings above them cawed alarm to the startled morning, and in the fields sliding by on either hand sheep and cattle ran in panic from their passing.

The fields gave way to moorland, and abruptly the Dominie wheeled his mount southwest on to a narrow ribbon of brown track rippling over the moor. Gilmour had to drop into single file behind Moyes. The Dragoon troop also deployed into single file, and with its pace settling down to a steady gallop the column surged forwards over the moor.

The path ahead of them ran twistingly, in the manner of its kind seeking the easiest route over the rising ground of the ridged and hummocked moorland. With an occasional glance aside from it, Sandy became aware that the landmarks he could glimpse around him were familiar things seen from unfamiliar angles, but the Dominie was cutting a straight line southwest that ignored the natural twists of the path, and he was too intent of keeping his place in the column to do more than hurriedly identify them.

Gambler was not an easy beast to handle. Hard-mouthed and powerful, it took main strength to pull him round when the Dominie shot off at an angle to the track. But that, Sandy thought, only made the business of mastering him all the more satisfying! Exhilarated by the rush through the clear, sunny air of the morning and by his control of the great, powerful beast gripped between his knees, he turned in the saddle to wave to Daventry riding at the head of the Dragoon troop, and received a wave and a screeching war-whoop in reply.

Grinning, he faced about again. He and Gambler, he decided confidently, could keep up this pace for long enough, and so apparently could Daventry and the Dragoons. But the Dominie was an old man – fifty if he was a day. How long could he continue to put out such effort?

The long ridge of Lothian Edge slid by on their left, to be

replaced by Deuchrie Edge with the green, blunt-topped mound of Deuchrie Dod rising up to the right, and still the hard pace continued. Deuchrie Dod fell behind them, and the blue waters of Danskine Loch came into sight. The wild lock of the Dominie's hair still waved like a flag in the lead, and still he was charging on in a straight southwesterly course, taking ridge and stream in his stride, without so much as a backward glance to see if the column continued in tow.

Passing Danskine Loch the sun had risen high enough to be hot on their right side. Sandy eased his cravat from his neck, feeling sweat start out on him, and saw the steam beginning to rise from Gambler's hide. The Comptroller was still riding steadily in front of him, ramrod-stiff in the saddle. The Dominie was still triumphantly guiding them straight over the rises and troughs of moorland, and with a glance ahead at them, Sandy withdrew the last of his reservations about old men. In these two at least, he acknowledged, the years had seemingly bred a toughness that rivalled any strength young limbs could put forth!

Beyond Danskine they struck a road again. Sandy took his bearings from the peaks of Priest Law and Lammer Law rising away to his left, and realized they were on the road leading through a string of farms and hamlets to the last stretch of moor before the ambush point. And that stretch, he thought grimly, would be the real testing-point for both men and horses, for there the gentle rise of the moorland would lead them to Blegbie Hill and a sudden steep rise of at least another eight hundred feet before they could plunge down on to the road running over the crest of Soutra Hill.

The pattern of hoofbeats behind him changed as the Dragoons took advantage of the road to double up their ranks again. Colonel Moyes drew level with the Dominie and began a shouted conversation with him. The Dominie gestured ahead to their left, and Sandy guessed he was warning Moyes of the climb that would face them eventually.

One mile after another of grey road sped by under them – but not so swiftly as the moorland had done. The horses were begining to feel the strain, Sandy realized. He could sense the labouring that had crept into Gambler's stride. Thinking that the rise of Blegbie Hill might well cause them to founder altogether, he glanced behind and found his fears heightened by a straggling in the tail of the Dragoon column.

Longyester fell behind them. They pounded on through Newton Hall, Longnewton and Kidlaw, and with the pace still dropping, reached Stobshiels, the last of the farms on their route. Beyond Stobshiels, the moor spread a wide swath of brownish-green in front of them again, and there again was the brown ribbon of bridle-track leading over it.

The Dominie pulled to a halt beside the track, Colonel Moyes bellowed an order for the Dragoons to close ranks, and they came jostling past Gambler to crowd around him. Pointing to Blegbie Hill rising out of the moor on their left, Moyes shouted,

'Our objective is an ambush party lying in wait for the stage-coach which will shortly pass along the road on the other side of that hill. Your orders – to advance in single file as before, to the foot of that hill. There you will deploy into depth. You will climb the hill in that order, and charge from the summit to capture as many as possible of the ambush party alive. Now, forward again!'

'Charge, he says – and our horses blowing like bellows already!' A muttered complaint from a Dragoon reached Sandy in the rapid reshuffle to form up in advance order again.

Gilmour drew alongside him as the Dominie led off. In a voice harsh with fatigue he said, ''Tis wearing on to nine o'clock. D'ye reckon we will reach the ambush point before the coach is due to pass it?'

'I think so,' Sandy told him cautiously, and went on to speak of the time the coach was due in at Edinburgh, but Gilmour did not stay to listen. Swinging out from the path he regained his position behind Colonel Moyes, and rapidly Sandy considered his own prospects of being allowed to take part in the Dragoons' final action. They were not high, he decided, and rode on across the moor considering how he could avoid being sent to the rear when the charge did take place.

The idea of outflanking the Dragoon lines and rejoining them at the top of the hill occurred to him; and when the Dominie yielded his lead to Moyes at last and dropped back to join the Comptroller at the rear of the Dragoons deploying into order of charge, he was ready with his plan.

Wheeling Gambler sharply round, he sent him scrambling for a deep cleft splitting a level platform that jutted from the body of the hill at the right of the Dragoon ranks. Beyond that, he had realized, he would have an easier passage up the hill than the soldiers themselves, and there would be nothing to stop him rejoining the flank of the troop at its crest – always providing that Gambler did not baulk at the jump!

But he would not. With as much confidence as he could muster, Sandy reminded himself it was for that very reason Archie had named the creature. Gambler would take a chance on any jump.

With shortened rein, knees gripping hard and elbows squared for balance, he rode Gambler at the cleft, and with nicely timed judgement changed his stride to the quick, prancing step for the take-off of the jump. Gambler shot forward, neck arched, hindquarters stretched out, forelegs bent under – perfect leap, and landed in a spurt of stones and earth on the farther side of the crevice.

Looking up in triumph to where the Dragoons had forged ahead of him, Sandy saw his easier path running parallel to theirs, and urged Gambler into a rapid upward scramble. Moyes was shouting something across the gap that separated him from Gilmour, gesturing to the crest of the hill as he shouted, but Sandy could not make out the words. A few moments later, however, he understood without the need of any explanation. It was the rattle of firearms that Moyes had indicated, and it was continuing in a manner unmistakable even to his untrained ear. There was a battle going on at the road beyond the hill!

It would be cruel to push Gambler harder, Sandy thought in dismay, but it had to be done. It had to be done! And closing his heart to remorse, he used heel and hand and voice to force every last ounce of effort out of him. The Dragoons were doing the same with their mounts, and somehow the poor beasts were finding the strength to respond – somehow they were narrowing the last spurt for the summit to a distance measurable in yards ... a hundred ... seventy ... fifty ... twenty – And then, so suddenly that he could hardly believe it was so, Sandy realized there was no rising green ahead, but a long smooth drop to a band of grey road and he was part of a yelling horde thundering down towards it.

From the corner of his eye he saw Moyes with a pistol in his right hand, and arm extended to point it at their target – puffs of white smoke coming from the ridge of the hill on the opposite side of the road. The downward sweep of his vision registered a stagecoach lying tilted against the bank fringing the nearer side of the road, with two bodies sprawled beside it and its team fighting vainly to break free of the shafts holding it jammed against the bank.

He had drawn his pistol – he could not remember when – and with a shout he raised it as the facing hillside suddenly leapt alive with the running figures of men and horses. In the same moment another horse collided with Gambler.

The reins in his left hand were roughly snatched away and Gilmour screamed in his ear,

'The coach, Sandy! Stop at the coach!'

His grip had Gambler locked closer to his own horse than twin traces could have brought them, and in futile rage at his sudden helplessness, Sandy yelled,

'But they will get away!'

'They will anyway! Their horses have rested all night – ours are foundered!'

With brutal skill keeping the heads of the two horses under control, Gilmour forced them down towards the coach, and as he brought them to a slithering halt behind it, the Dragoon charge swept on past them. Gilmour was swinging out of the saddle even before the horses had stopped, but Sandy stayed perched aloft a moment longer, biting his lip at the sight of the horsemen on the farther hillside fleeing ahead of the Dragoons.

The noise of breaking wood brought his glance downward, and he slid from Gambler's back to see Gilmour reaching through the wrecked and tilted door of the coach to the pile of satchels lying on the seat inside.

Two of the men who had apparently been defending the coach crouched watching him, one silently nursing a hand from which blood dripped, the other holding a pistol still smoking from the last shot he had fired and looking round from the sprawling figure of a third man to say excitedly,

'– and after they shot the guard and the driver, they would have taken the coach entire if Mr Symonds had not driven them back with his own pistol shots. Then he bade us hide down behind the coach and crawl out into the road to get the guard's weapons, and –'

'Quiet those horses!' Gilmour snapped out the interruption as he withdrew from the interior of the coach, and after one glance of startled respect for the authority in his voice, the man scrambled to his feet and ran to obey.

'Look, Sandy!' Gilmour flung all but one of the satchels to the ground, and their eyes met over the Royal cipher blazoned on the one he had retained. Gilmour wrenched at the straps that held it closed. The flap burst open, and tipping the satchel up he caught the sealed and stiffly folded letter that fell out. Briefly he scanned the inscription on it, then looked up to say exultantly,

'This *is* the Porteous reprieve! We have beaten him there at least, Sandy!'

'And there is still time to catch him!' Snatching at Gamblem's reins in the sudden realization that the halt had left them only a minute behind the Dragoons after all, Sandy made to swing into the saddle but Gilmour checked him roughly.

'Use your intelligence, boy!' he snapped. 'It was plain, even before we charged, that we could not hope to do more than frighten them off! Let Moyes carry on with the useless gesture of pursuing them on foundered horses. We will do more good by attending the wounded here.'

'Look to Symonds, then.' The man with the bleeding hand had been waiting an opportunity to speak, and now he did so quickly. Gilmour glanced from him to the bodies lying in the roadway, and then to the third man still stretched motionless where they had first seen him.

'The guard and the driver are dead,' the man said, following his look, 'but you may still be in time to help Symonds.'

'You are hurt also.' Gilmour thrust the letter of reprieve into his pocket and made to lift the bleeding hand, but with surprising vigour the man waved him away and said sharply,

'I have a lot of blood yet to lose before I am in danger!'

Gilmour shrugged, and moved to kneel by the third man. Sandy followed, and kneeling down opposite Gilmour, echoed his gasp of dismay as he saw the blood-specked froth bubbling on the man's lips.

'Sit him up before he drowns in his own blood!' Gilmour commanded urgently.

Gently between them, they eased the man to a sitting position. The man with the bleeding hand called, 'Can you do anything for him?'

'No, he is shot through the lung,' Gilmour answered quietly. He glanced up to the other passenger, still busy at calming the horses, and then back to the second man. 'Your friend spoke as if this Mr Symonds had organized the defence of the coach,' he said. 'Was that so?'

'Aye,' the man nodded. 'He did that for us, God rest him!'

'He is coming to, sir.' Sandy nodded downwards at a flicker of eyelids. Gilmour watched their movement, then putting his lips close to the man's ear said distinctly,

'Mr Symonds, you will need a surgeon's help. We will try to get you to Edinburgh.'

'No use – no use ...' The bloodied lips moving feebly managed to get the words out at last. Another one followed them, but a rustle of footsteps approaching over the grass partly covered its sound. Sandy looked up to see the Dominie and the Comptroller approaching, then his attention was drawn back to the wounded man by Gilmour saying urgently,

'Hold him steady for me, Sandy.'

Sandy extended his support for the man's weight. Gilmour slipped a hand inside the blood-stained front of his coat, and drew it out again holding a red-sealed sheet of parchment similar to his own warrant of authority. Once again he put his lips close to Symonds' ear and spoke clearly,

'I have your warrant, Mr Symonds. What do you wish me to do with it?'

Once again there was the awful struggle to speak. In the midst of it the Comptroller and the Dominie arrived beside them and the Comptroller said bitterly,

'So he got away again, Mr Gilmour!'

'Hush!' Gilmour held up his head, and nodded to the wounded man. His drooping eyelids were lifting slowly. His lips were working, and the sound that came from them eventually was the whispered word,

'*Gilmour?*'

'That is my name,' Gilmour told him gently, 'Deryck Gilmour.'

'Of His Majesty's Customs.' The Comptroller, unable to resist making an official announcement of it, added the description, then stared in amazement as the others did, at the sudden light of life flaring in the dying man's eyes. He spoke, the lit eyes moving slowly from face to face around him, the words spaced out through the terrible difficulty of his breathing,

'*Witnesses . . . all present . . . hereby . . . invest . . . Deryck Gilmour . . . in full authority . . . my warrant . . .*'

With a swift movement the Comptroller bent to take the red-sealed warrant dangling from the hand that Gilmour held supporting the man's back. Flicking it open he glanced rapidly down it and then looked back at Gilmour to exclaim,

'This warrant –! He is – this man is the political agent you sent for to take over the case of St Clair!'

Gilmour did not reply to him. His eyes were still fixed on those of the dying man, and gently he said,

'We have all witnessed your words, Mr Symonds. Rest easy now, and I give you my solemn oath that I will carry out all the terms of your warrant as you would yourself.'

'*. . . rest . . .*' The last word Symonds was to speak came like a sigh from his lips, and with it, the light went out of his eyes as suddenly as it had come.

Gilmour remained kneeling by him a moment longer, then quietly he said, 'Lay him down, Sandy.'

Slowly Sandy let his burden sink back to the ground,

wondering vaguely as he did so why the Dominie's normally stern eyes were now resting on him with such kindly concern, and then realized that he was shaking almost as if he had an ague.

'Break a promise to a dying man and it will haunt you,' he heard the Comptroller say acidly. 'So tell me, pray, how you propose to fulfil this one!'

'With this!' Rising to his feet, Gilmour pulled the Porteous reprieve from his pocket and showed it to the Comptroller.

'If Robertson had succeeded in stealing this,' he continued, 'the hangman would have taken revenge on Porteous for him. But now the release of Porteous means he must come out of hiding to do the murder himself, and St Clair knows that as well as I do. He will be waiting to pounce on Robertson – and that is when I will get them both!'

'Are you so certain?' The acid gone from his voice now, the Comptroller searched Gilmour's face for reassurance, and with a last look at the dead man he answered,

'As certain as I am that here lies a very brave man, Mr Comptroller. As certain as that!'

14. Riot

THE party of Customs men was strongly armed and well placed to observe the Tolbooth from the many points of concealment offered by the buttressed wall of St Giles facing on to it. In the deepening September dusk they stood watching for Porteous to walk a free man through its great, iron-bossed door, and peering from his own particular place of concealment, Sandy wondered impatiently how much longer they would have to wait.

It was hours since the Magistrates had announced the

reprieve! The scaffold that had been standing ready for Porteous in the Grassmarket had been dismantled and stored away again, and the crowd listening sullenly to the reading of the reprieve had long since dispersed. But they had left threats of riot and an unofficial hanging for Porteous lingering in the air behind them, and now he was afraid to leave the safety of the prison walls. Now there was nothing Gilmour's men could do but wait for the moment when he had plucked up sufficient courage to face the city that hated him so much.

Uneasily glancing to right and left through the gloom, Sandy marked where the rest of his party were stationed and tried to guess which of the many other dark hiding-places round the prison might be holding Robertson, and which St Clair. They were bound to be waiting, too, for that moment, he thought – but what if the crowd attempted to storm the Tolbooth and seize Porteous before he made up his mind to leave? What would happen to all their plans then?

Restlessly he changed his stance so that he could watch both the Tolbooth door and the west porch of St Giles where Gilmour and the Comptroller had chosen to wait, and then suddenly unable to bear the inaction any longer, he walked quietly towards them. Mounting the steps of the porch he saw the pale blur of their faces turned towards him, and as casually as he could he said,

'I was thinking it might be useful to have a scout round, Mr Gilmour. I could maybe pick up a crumb or two of news about what the mob intends tonight.'

'I want everyone here,' Gilmour told him sharply. 'This is where the action will happen – where Porteous is!'

'Ach, let him go,' the Comptroller persuaded. 'To tell you the truth, Mr Gilmour, there is something in the atmosphere that makes me considerably uneasy. I would be glad of a first-hand account of the state of the streets.'

'You think there will be a riot tonight,' Gilmour said.

'But why? The crowd dispersed peaceably enough, for all their threats, after the reprieve was announced.'

'That only means they are nursing their wrath,' the Comptroller argued, 'and there is always more to fear from a smouldering fire than from an instant flame! Indeed, I promise you it will take only one determined man to blow that smouldering fire into a most astonishing conflagration, for the Edinburgh mob is a fearsome beast – and never more so than when it has had time to brood on its wrongs.'

Gilmour shrugged. 'You know the city better than I do, of course,' he allowed.

'Aye, I do,' the Comptroller agreed dryly. 'You have not noticed there is no member of the Town Guard patrolling in front of the Tolbooth tonight, but I have, and it is the first time I have ever known that to be the case.'

Gilmour did not reply to this, and turning to Sandy, the Comptroller went on, 'Take a run down to the West Port, boy. The porters on duty there will likely know if there is trouble brewing in that part of the city.'

'In Portsburgh? Is that what you mean?' Gilmour asked, and the Comptroller answered, 'Aye, 'tis a wild place, Portsburgh, and the people there have more cause than most to remember how brutal Porteous was in the days of his power.'

'Very well, you may go – but make good use of the time.' Gilmour dismissed Sandy, and like a hound unleashed at last, he was off down the porch steps.

It was almost dark now. Turning westwards up the High Street he made briskly towards the West Bow, but had been walking only a few moments when a man stepped from a doorway and seized hold of an arm to prevent his passing.

'You are not wise to be abroad tonight, sir.' A dimly seen face leaned towards him. The smell of the streets on ragged clothes reached him as the voice threatened softly, 'Pray be warned and take cover before harm befall you.'

'I can take care of myself, fellow!' Swiftly jerking his arm free Sandy gave the man a push that sent him staggering away, and hurried on, with a quick, backward glance to see if he was being followed. The man had recovered himself but he was making no attempt at pursuit and suddenly the reason for this occurred to Sandy.

That voice, he thought, that softly threatening voice! This had been no ordinary encounter between a cut-purse and his prey. The man had been ragged and filthy, yes, but his voice had been that of a gentleman!

He glanced across the street. Two chairmen carrying a sedan-chair had halted there, and there were another two of the ragged fellows talking to the lady in the sedan-chair. As Sandy watched, one of them handed her out and escorted her to a doorway, where he took leave of her with a flourish of his bonnet and a bow that would have done credit to a courtier.

Looking round then, Sandy noticed how unusually deserted the street was. The tavern lights burned, but there were no groups of revellers passing in and out. No gossiping citizens leaned over window-sills or lounged in doorways, and the few people passing up and down the street were hurrying along almost as if some pursuer were on their heels.

Quickly he walked on again. *Something* was being planned for that night. That much was clear, and it was clear also that the planners were taking the trouble to clear the streets beforehand. But who would have done so – and why? Who were the ragged creatures with the accents and manners of gentlemen?

With the questions racing through his mind Sandy hurried down the West Bow and across the great, empty space of the Grassmarket to the West Port. The big main gate was shut for the night, he saw long before he reached it, but the two porters on duty were standing by the wicket gate at its side. By the light from their lodge he saw that they were gazing out to the ramshackle houses of Portsburgh clustered on the far side of the West Port, and panting to a halt beside them, he caught the sound of a distant chorus of voices coming from that direction.

Faintly through the voices came the sharp, military beat of a drum. There was menace in the sound, and pointing towards it one of the porters turned a frightened face to the other. His voice shaking he said, 'You hear that? They are coming – and I am not staying to be over-run by them!'

'Nor I!' Turning on his heel the second porter fled to the safety of the lodge. The first man followed without sparing a glance for Sandy, and the door of their lodge slammed closed behind them.

Whoever 'they' were, Sandy decided, he did not want to meet them either – but if they were the mob the Comptroller had feared, it was up to him to find out as much as possible about them, and darting into the dark shadow cast by the lodge, he pressed himself flat against its wall.

The noise beyond the gate grew steadily nearer, but as it grew in volume, he noticed, the character of it changed. The ragged shouting died away, and the scattered sounds of people running steadied to the heavy tramp of feet marching in orderly procession. The roll and paradiddle of the drum had set the time of the march and now it was no longer a mob he could hear but an army, treading fast and rhythmically towards him.

In a crescendo of sound it reached the gate and stamped to a halt. The drum marked time softly and over it a voice bawled,

'Waste no time on the main gate! Break down the wicket!'

A burst of yelling followed the voice, then came the sharp crack of axes against the wooden slats of the wicket gate. A dark figure came running, sword in hand, past the angle of the wall that hid Sandy, closely followed by a man with a drum bumping at his hip. Another and another came on behind the drum, then a knot of figures and finally a stream of both men and women all rushing to join the first man.

He had halted in the Grassmarket, holding his sword high in front of him as he turned to face the rest of the mob. The drummer stood at his side, steadily beating, and with amazement Sandy saw the discipline the sword and the drum were imposing on the mob's rough ranks.

Swiftly he reconsidered his own position. Whatever plan was inspiring the mob to obey their leader, he reckoned, there was only one way to find out about it, and breaking from cover he ran to join the stream of people pouring through the wicket-gate into the Grassmarket.

A glance backwards as he ran showed him a body of men, swords and muskets in hand, lining up to mount guard over the main gate of the West Port. Other men were tugging over a heavy country cart to form a barricade before it, and still more men were running swiftly towards the houses climbing up the slope that separated the Grassmarket from the west end of the High Street.

There was no time to note more. The man with the sword was commanding his rabble army forward, and it had swung into motion again, advancing at a rapid trot towards the east end of the Grassmarket. Treading blindly on the heels of the man in front of him, pushed by those behind, Sandy had to trot with it.

He was near the head of the column, not near enough to see the leader himself, but only his sword as it flashed high in the air again. 'Swing right! Swing right!' voices yelled at him as the sword's flashing signal turned the head of the column towards the narrow opening of Candlemaker Row at the Grassmarket's east end.

The leader held his position, his sword now pointing their

route of Candlemaker Row, and realizing that only the
leading section of the mob was to be diverted up it, Sandy
guessed at his purpose. Candlemaker Row led to Bristo Port,
the city's south gate, and the purpose of the diversion could
only be to capture it as the West Port had been captured!

It was impossible to turn back against the tide of this
movement – but it was possible to slide out of it; and taking
refuge in the first doorway that offered, Sandy let it go past
him. Peering from the doorway then, he saw that the main
force in the Grassmarket was once more on the move, making farther eastward down the Cowgate. He caught a
glimpse of the leader's sword at its head, heard the continuing rattle of the drum, and ran to join them again.

And now, he saw as he ran, there were others doing the
same – many others. The Comptroller had been right when
he said it would take only one determined man to blow the
mob's smouldering wrath into flames!

From all directions they were coming – both men and
women running from alleys, vennels, and wynds; some
with torches held high, some with weapons waving. And
all of them, astonishingly, taking their cue from the orderly
marching of the main body as they joined its ranks.

Running hard, Sandy outpaced those on his own side of
the marching column, and succeeded in gaining a position
close behind the leading ranks before someone roughly
checked his progress and shouted,

'March orderly, boy, like it was planned, or you will not
even get the chance of breaking Porteous out of jail!'

The man who had seized him was a flesher, a burly fellow still wearing his blood-stained butcher's apron and
hefting a meat-cleaver in one large fist.

'Aye, I will that, Master Flesher,' Sandy agreed, a wary
eye on the meat-cleaver, and fell prudently into step with
its owner.

Drum beating, torches flaring, feet pounding an ever-growing volume of sound from the cobbles, the marchers swept down the long dark canyon of the Cowgate, and almost at the foot of it, the man with the sword turned to halt them again. Sword pointing to his right he yelled,

'Front ranks up Blackfriars' Wynd to take the Netherbow Port! Rear ranks follow me to take the Cowgate Port!'

The head of the column swung to its left, up Blackfriars' Wynd to the High Street. Sandy was carried with it and in the light of a flaring torch as he passed by the leader he saw the face of St Clair. Then, with his head turning back over his shoulder to stare, he realized he had been recognized in his turn. The man with the drum on his hip was his onetime captor, Jock Lumsden, and Lumsden was pointing after him and shouting excitedly to St Clair,

'The Maxwell boy, sir! There he is – alive!'

St Clair's voice roaring, 'After him! Get after him, men!' reached him as he ran wildly on the heels of those already surging up the long, narrow passage of Blackfriars' Wynd, and instantly he tried to fox the pursuit by taking up the cry himself. Bellowing *After him! After him!* he shouldered desperately forward, and other voices took up the cry as those before and behind him leapt mistakenly to the conclusion that he was urging on their vengeance against Porteous.

A man landed a thump of approval on his shoulder. A woman looked back to shriek delighted laughter at him, and on a wave of howling excitement he was thrust forth among the rioters bursting from Blackfriars' Wynd into the High Street.

The impetus of the rush carried him briefly eastwards with them towards the Netherbow Port, but the High Street was wide enough for the forerunners of the mob to spread out and dark enough for him to slip through their thinning ranks to the cover of an alley on the side opposite to Blackfriars' Wynd. A voice yelling, *Spread out! Search the doorways for him!'* sent him running silently on his toes down the alley and at the end of it he found himself in a courtyard overlooked by the towering height of the High Street's houses and with a choice of a further two exits opening off it.

He chose the westward one, and ran silently through it to another, smaller court. Beyond this, a passage ran northwards between walled gardens, but it was joined by another that led him back to his westerly direction. A leftwards twist off this passage brought him to the back doorway of a house that he realized must front on to the High Street. There was a gleam of light behind the door. Unhesitatingly he knocked, and almost immediately it was opened a cautious inch.

It could only be the man of the house who had dared open to a stranger on such a night, Sandy guessed, and rapidly he said, 'Sir, I am pursued by the rioters. For pity's sake, open to me!'

His voice apparently convinced the owner of the house that he was harmless, for almost immediately again, there was a response. The door swung open, a hand grasped his arm and pulled him, blinking, into the light of candles held high by a woman and two young girls clustered in the passage behind the door.

'He's only a lad!' the woman exclaimed in astonishment, and the man who had pulled him in added, 'And a foolish one, to be out tonight!'

The passage ran right from the back to the front of the house, Sandy realized, seeing the strong outer door at its farther end, and rapidly he improvised for his helpers' benefit.

'I must get home, good people, and my pursuers will not guess I have come this way. Pray let me out through the farther door.'

He was moving towards it as he spoke, and anxiously

the whole family crowded with him, exclaiming and shaking their heads at his foolhardiness, and with his hand on the latch, he spoke directly to the woman of the house.

'My parents, ma'am,' he pleaded, mentally begging forgiveness for the lie. 'I am a younger son and they will be deathly worried if I am not home soon.'

He had struck the right chord. 'Thomas!' the woman commanded, and turned pitying eyes on him as her husband drew a massive door-key from his pocket. The door creaked open under it, and with its opening the distant sound of the rioters came into the house.

Sandy peered out, feeling the man crowd behind him to look over his shoulder. Nothing moved in the street for as far as he could see – but his pursuers could be waiting in hiding for him! It was a chance that would have to be taken, Sandy decided. 'Good night, sir and ma'am,' he whispered. 'And thank you.' Then stepping lightly from the doorway he fled westwards again up the High Street.

No voice was raised to check his flight, no footsteps sounded in furious pursuit of him. The only sound was the distant yelling of the mobs attacking the Cowgate and Netherbow Ports, and exulting in the thought that he had managed to shake off the men St Clair had set on his track, Sandy pounded rapidly on. Yet, for all the deserted aspect of the street, he had the feeling of being watched by many eyes, and remembering how ready his rescuers had been and how aware of the night's events, he guessed at eyes spying from every darkened window of the houses soaring tall on either side of him.

With only a couple of minutes still to go before he reached the Tolbooth at last, he passed the barracks of the Town Guard, and saw its door swinging idly open to the deserted street. No sentry patrolled before it, and beyond it was darkness – no soldiers lounging off duty, no patrol arming for a foray into the streets. St Clair's plan, he thought, must have included a warning threat to the Town Guard, and they had fled before the prospect of the same brutal anger the mob had turned against them on the day of Andrew Wilson's hanging!

Still running he reached the west porch of St Giles and almost fell into the arms of Gilmour and the Comptroller hurrying out to meet him. 'We heard a drum beating and shouts,' Gilmour began. 'What –'

'St Clair!' Sandy gasped. 'He has roused the mob and organized them like an army to capture all the gates to the city. They mean to attack the Tolbooth and seize Porteous!'

Exclaiming, the two men turned to one another, and Sandy raced on, 'The West Port is taken, and Bristo Port, the Cowgate and Netherbow ports too, and they are barricading each one and mounting guard over it. The city is cut off completely from outside help now, and the Town Guard has deserted. I saw their barracks empty as I ran up the High Street.'

'We could call out troops from the Castle –' the Comptroller began, but Sandy interrupted, 'No, sir, that will not be possible either. St Clair sent men up to the west end of the High Street as soon as the West Port had been captured, and that means they will have barricaded the approaches to the Castle by this time.'

'Is Robertson with the mob?' Gilmour demanded.

'I cannot tell you that, sir,' Sandy answered. 'I only saw St Clair.'

'What's to be done then, Mr Gilmour?' The Comptroller asked urgently. 'Do we take St Clair when he leads his mob against the prison?'

'And turn the anger of his whole rabble army against ourselves? That would be madness! No,' Gilmour decided, 'St Clair has evidently decided to force the issue in this way so that he can stake Porteous out like bait for Robertson. We must wait till the mob has its hands on the wretched fellow, and then we will be able to seize both Robertson and St Clair without interference from them.'

'But they will kill Porteous!' Sandy exclaimed. 'Surely we could warn Governor Monro to get him out of the Tolbooth before they arrive!'

Gilmour had started down the steps while he spoke. From halfway he flung over his shoulder, 'Tell him, while I brief the men,' and the Comptroller said curtly, 'The prison doorkeeper has bolted from his lodge. There is no way of communicating with anyone inside the Tolbooth.'

'We could hammer on the door,' Sandy suggested. '*Someone* might hear.'

'Nonsense!' the Comptroller snapped. 'The stairway behind the door and the inner door at the head of it would muffle any noise less than that of a battering-ram!'

'But –'

'Listen, boy!' Rounding on Sandy, the Comptroller told him fiercely, 'Murderer though he is, Porteous has been reprieved and is legally entitled to live. Moreover, he stood for the rule of law in his time, and so do I now. Do you suppose for one moment I would permit the mob to have its way with him if I could see any way of preventing it?'

He moved away without waiting for an answer, and after a moment's hesitation, Sandy followed him. From the foot of the steps then, he saw Gilmour's men taking up position on either side of the Tolbooth door, and hastened to stand beside Gilmour himself. Cutlasses were to be the order of arms, he noted, and drew his own weapon. As the steel hissed from the scabbard Gilmour said in a low, bitter voice,

'I pray to God no innocent citizens will get caught up in the mob's advance.'

'I do not think that likely, sir,' Sandy reassured him, and went on to recount his experience with the ragged man who had warned him off the streets.

Gilmour listened in silence to him and then asked, 'Was

there anything else of note happened while you were with the mob?'

'Aye, sir,' Sandy answered wryly, 'I am no longer officially "dead". The man with the drum is Jock Lumsden, and he recognized me. But I managed to trick the pursuit that was set up when he shouted out to St Clair about me.'

With a ripple of laughter in his voice Gilmour commented, 'Well done! And they will be too busy seizing Porteous when they get here to bother about you yet awhile – but stay close to me, all the same.'

'I will, sir; I am all for safety in numbers now,' Sandy assured him. Then he went on, 'And one thing more, sir. I think I must have been wrong in guessing that Lumsden was a cattle-drover, or something of that nature. There was a very military style to his beating of that drum, and my guess now is that he was formerly a soldier.'

'That would account for his connection with St Clair,' Gilmour agreed. Then half to himself he added, 'That man's military reputation is well deserved – there is a touch of genius, after all, in anyone who can successfully plan to turn a mob-rising into a strategic exercise for capturing a city!'

After that they stood listening in silence, and presently the first raucous sounds of the advancing mob reached them. From somewhere on the farther side of the doorway, the Comptroller's voice came then,

'That is near enough to be coming from the Town Guard's barracks, lads – which means they will be raiding the armoury there, so watch out for Lochaber axes!'

'And muskets,' another voice chimed in, but it was the thought of the Lochaber axes that stayed in Sandy's mind. Huge things they were, he knew, with a wide, curved blade that had a wicked-looking hook projecting from the back of it. Wiping sweat from the palms of his hands he took a fresh grip of his cutlass, and heard the thunder of running feet suddenly added to the sound of the mob's yelling.

15. The Face of the Enemy

'STAND fast, men!'

Gilmour's sharp warning rang out a second before the howling, hooting vanguard of the mob came surging down the narrow lane between the Tolbooth and St Giles, and the Customs men braced themselves against the impact of the first wave of bodies.

In shrieking confusion the rioters milled and eddied about the prison door, those behind crying 'Forward!' and those in front now crying 'Back!' as men swinging Lochaber axes aloft strove for a way through. Torchlight glinting redly on their great curved blades, they cleared a passage at last. The mob formed a solid semi-circle to watch and cheer them on and the attack on the door began.

The axes bit home against the wood, stroke after stroke landing with hard and vicious impact against it, but the Tolbooth was a fortress built to withstand such attacks and the heavy timbers of the door were weathered to the hardness of the iron bosses that studded it. For all the force that was put behind the axe blows they made only shallow scars on the door, and in rage, one of the attackers turned to the mob yelling,

''Tis like striking iron! We will never break in this way!'
He leaned on his axe, glaring at the poor sum of his labours thus far and in the mob behind him a voice bellowed,

'Fire! Burn it down, you fools! Burn it down!'

The crowd heaved and parted, shooting the form of St Clair out of its ranks. 'Break up these booths!' Fiercely he gestured to the wooden booths tucked between the buttresses of the church wall, and with a wave and a yell of 'Come on, men!' led the axe-men charging towards them.

The noise of splintering wood was added to the pandemonium of yelling from the crowd. Broken planks, shutters, and window-frames were tossed from the wreckage of the booths, and seized on by men and women alike, were heaped up against the prison door. A torch-bearer in the mob – a creature made witchlike by the black shawl that hooded her face – rushed to thrust her torch into the heart of the pile. Another followed her, and another, and the whole great mound of dry fuel roared into fierce life.

Legs astride, his face ruddily lit by the flames, St Clair waited for it to eat the door away. Behind him a knot of men stood with their axes raised, ready for the word to break through once the fire had done its work, and capering all round, the mob howled its triumph to the night.

St Clair's head was turning restlessly this way and that as he waited, and it passed through Sandy's mind that he must have noted the contrast between the mob's wild excitement and Gilmour's men, standing so still and silent on either side of the doorway. But he gave no sign of having done so and it was evident that, like them, he was deferring every other action in favour of the need to be ready for the vital moment when George Robertson should suddenly appear.

The roaring flames that had seized the door began to die away until they were only licking at the charred shell that remained of it, and St Clair's restless attention concentrated on the dying fire. His hand shot up in a signal. *'Now!'* he roared, and rushing forward the axe men smashed a great jagged hole in the charred and smoking panels of the door.

To renewed whoops of triumph from the mob St Clair disappeared through this hole, followed by the axe men and a laughing, scrambling band of rioters armed with muskets, swords, meat-cleavers, hammers, and every conceivable variety of weapon. Even the women were armed, Sandy noticed, watching the woman who had fired the pile of wood dancing around with a long, thin knife in her hand,

and then suddenly found himself jostled aside by a man who had clutched Gilmour by the arm and was shouting in his ear.

A surge of bodies behind them knocked off the man's hat, and catching a glimpse of long pale features with white hair flying dishevelled about them, Sandy recognized the Reverend Henry Ogilvie. From the shouted conversations with Gilmour he heard fragments: *impossible to rescue him now ... comfort to his soul if you can* ... Then a muffled shouting from inside the prison and a clattering of feet on stone steps brought his attention back to the hole in the prison door.

They were bringing Porteous out, and in the horror of that moment Sandy forgot everything else, for the man was as Gilmour had darkly prophesied he would be when death finally overtook him – too paralysed with fear to move so much as a finger. Two men carried him, their hands linked to form a chair. His arms were placed loosely round their necks. His head lolled forward on his chest and his feet dangled helplessly, ridiculously, like the feet of a puppet on slack strings.

The roar that rose from the mob at the sight of him was deafening. As it subsided a single voice screamed, '*To the Grassmarket with him! Hang him on the scene of his crimes!*' And immediately the cry was taken up by hundreds of voices yelling, '*To the Grassmarket! To the Grassmarket!*'

Ogilvie broke forward, urgently shouting to St Clair poised a step above Porteous, 'Stop them! For God's sake, *stop them!*'

St Clair ignored him, his head turning this way and that as he searched once more among the bobbing faces of the mob for the one this vital moment should have brought forth. But the cries to hang Porteous in the Grassmarket were continuing to swell in volume, and it was evident he realized he would lose control of the mob if he delayed in yielding to their demands.

'Forward to the Grassmarket, then!' he roared, and moved swiftly to head the little group in the doorway. Instantly Gilmour's men bore forward and closed in shoulder to shoulder behind the men carrying Porteous. The drummer struck up somewhere on the outskirts of the mob, and the procession moved off towards the High Street.

Westwards it surged, spreading out behind and before the slack figure of Porteous bobbing like a cork on a wave in its midst. Ogilvie strode alongside him with one of his nerveless hands clasped between his own, and in the weaving torchlight Sandy saw tears gleaming on his pale cheeks. As the procession neared the head of the West Bow, St Clair began forging ahead shouting something about 'a rope', and breaking into a run also, the men nearest him took up his cry.

People were looking openly down from their windows now, some silent and horrified, others cheering the rioters on. Matching his step to the steady beat of the drum ahead, Sandy felt some of the mob's fever enter his own blood, but a glance at Gilmour marching beside him showed none of that fever reflected there. Gilmour's face was hard and watchful, and as St Clair's had done, his eyes were roaming everywhere in search of one particular face in the mob jostling round their tight escort group.

Leftward down the West Bow the procession swung, and was forced to move more slowly by the narrower, twisting way. Yells, and the crash of axes on wood echoed back to them from farther ahead, and thinking of St Clair's call for a rope, Sandy shouted to Gilmour,

'They must be breaking into the rope-chandler's shop down there!'

Twenty yards from the street's junction with the Grassmarket they came on the rope-chandler's door swinging

wide, and saw St Clair framed in it triumphantly display-
ing a coil of rope to the vanguard of the mob swirling round
him. On one side of him stood the redheaded Lumsden with
his drum and on his other side was the shopkeeper, broadly
grinning as he held one hand aloft to show the glint of a
golden guinea held between thumb and forefinger.

'I would have given it free if you had told me it was for
Porteous,' he was shouting, 'but here is handsome payment
indeed for a murderer's rope!'

With cheers and howls of laughter the mob greeted his
words, and it seemed to Sandy that their present merriment
must be even more terrifying to the wretched Porteous than
all their previous anger. They were so sure of their revenge
now that they were taking time to relish the prospect of it,
he thought, and sickened by this realization, he moved off
unwillingly again when St Clair waved the procession on.

Like a river bursting suddenly from a deep, containing
bed to flood across a plain, its tightly packed ranks broke
out of the West Bow's narrow channel and spread across
the width of the Grassmarket. Those in front ran for its
north-side. The men carrying Porteous followed them, and
the ranks of those behind cast round in a circle to race for
vantage points at the scene of the execution. Keeping the
close formation in which they had marched, Gilmour's men
advanced stolidly behind the victim, and linking arms when
his bearers halted, they formed a line that stood firm against
the pressure of the mob behind them.

St Clair shouted for more light and a dozen men struggled towards him with torches. The light flaring up from
these showed him standing by the doorway of a barber's
shop, with the long striped pole which was the barber's
trade-sign projecting above his head. Lumsden was there
also, his drum on the ground by his side, the rope in his
hand. Porteous was still lolling on the linked hands of his
bearers and Ogilvie was trying to close one of his hands

round a crucifix, but the nerveless fingers could not grasp it.

Lumsden stepped forward and placed the noosed end of the rope round Porteous' neck. Taking up the slack he tossed it over the barber's pole, and grasping the loose end that fell towards him he pulled it taut. Like a sack of sawdust being toppled, Porteous was jerked to the ground beneath the barber's pole, and a long *'A-aah!'* of satisfaction went up from the crowd.

'Hands to pull on the rope!' St Clair yelled.

The words were hardly out of his mouth before a woman broke out of the crowd – the same witchlike creature, Sandy noticed, who had fired the pile of wood outside the Tolbooth door. With an eager agility that surprised as much as it shocked him, she sprang for the rope and grasped it with both hands, but St Clair seized her from behind before she could put her weight into a pull. 'This is man's work!' he shouted, and she kicked out fighting viciously to free herself of his grasp.

A roar of mingled impatience and excitement went up from the crowd at this check to their desire and from all parts of it came a rush of volunteer hangmen. One of Gilmour's men sagged, stunned by the flat of an axe as a man behind him tried to force a way forward, and with the breaking of their tight cordon the mob surged over them. Striking wildly out to keep his footing Sandy caught one glimpse of the woman pulling free from St Clair, leaving her shawl behind her as she fled. Then he went down, clutching at Gilmour as he fell and screaming,

'Robertson! I saw Robertson!'

The Comptroller and Gilmour between them saved him from being trampled to death, their backs crouched to take the impact of the wave thrusting forward to tread a way over him. He hauled himself up, clutched Gilmour again, and pointing beyond the mob that now surged closely round Porteous he yelled,

'He ran up that alley there, with St Clair in pursuit!'

'Then I know where he is headed,' the Comptroller shouted. 'Hold on, and follow me!'

Turning, he began forcing a way out of the mob. Heads down, each with one hand holding on to the Comptroller and the other arm clutched round one another's shoulders, Sandy and Gilmour trod on his heels, and their wedge-shaped formation bored compactly forward. Blows rained on them, hands tore at their hair, feet lashed out to trip them, and the screams and curses directed at them deafened their hearing to the overall sound of the mob's roaring. But still they managed to hold on to one another till gradually the pressure slackened, and bruised, panting, their clothes torn, they managed to break clear of the crowd at last.

Labouring for breath, the Comptroller turned to the other two. 'The old smugglers' route over the Nor' Loch,' he gasped, '– that is the only possible way out of the city for him tonight. Make for that while I rally the men.'

Setting a bos'n's whistle to his lips he blew shrilly on it, and shouting to Gilmour over the sound of the blast, Sandy made for the nearest alley leading from the Grassmarket up to the High Street. Gilmour caught up with him in a few strides, racing neck and neck with him to enter the narrow upward slope of Castle Wynd. From the High Street at its farther end, and down through the huddle of buildings be-hind the High Street's northern façade, it would take them only a few minutes to reach the Nor' Loch – the lake that formed the city's northern boundary – but Sandy had no breath left to explain this to Gilmour. Hoping the other would continue to trust his plotting of the route he ran rapidly on.

The narrow length of Castle Wynd gave way to the wide sweep of the High Street. Ahead of them as they raced across it, a shot rang out somewhere among the houses clinging to the slope that ran down to the Nor' Loch, and plunging into the maze of wynds and lanes that twisted between these houses, Sandy led on unerringly in the direction of its sound.

The Comptroller and his men were following not far behind them now, he realized, for every few seconds he could hear that piping blast on the bos'n's whistle. The alley-way ahead of them ended in a dim glimmer of water, and pointing, he gasped out, 'The Nor' Loch, sir!' But Gilmour had already quickened his stride at the sight of the water, and shooting past Sandy, he burst out of the alley ahead of him.

'There they are!'

Breaking out of the alley a few seconds later, Sandy heard his hoarse shout and saw him pointing as he ran along the edge of the loch. A hundred yards away a boat was pulling out from the shore, and just over half that distance from Gilmour a man was running along the bank, his hand extended and pointing to the boat.

The man in the boat was bending low to the oars, and as he straightened up for the backward pull, the running man's hand puffed fire. The shot roared out over the loch and the oarsman slumped across the thwart.

Momentarily Sandy checked his dash after Gilmour, then ran furiously on again as the man who had fired plunged into the water and began wading towards the boat. Gilmour was shouting, 'St Clair – come back! You cannot escape now!' but St Clair continued wading towards the boat.

He reached it, standing waist-deep in water, and grasped the thwart to heave himself aboard. In the same instant, the man lying against the thwart jerked suddenly upright. His arm came flashing up above St Clair and the knife in his hand described a brief, glittering arc in the air as he brought it driving down into St Clair's back.

Locked to the boat and to one another they hung rigid for a long moment, then slowly St Clair sank back into the water and Robertson, as slowly, keeled over against the thwart.

Sandy became aware of voices and the soft thudding of feet over the grass of the lochside, and turning, he saw the scattered forms of the Customs men racing towards them. He looked at Gilmour, but Gilmour did not speak until the first of the men reached him. Then all he said was,

'Bring a light. I want to see his face.'

Sometime in the course of his flight from St Clair, Robertson had shed his woman's disguise. He lay now dressed in his seaman's rig, blood congealing round the bullet wound in his neck, a drop of loch-water coursing down the scar on his cheek, and by the light of the torch that had been brought, Gilmour looked long at his face.

'Well?' the Comptroller addressed him at last. 'Are you satisfied now, Mr Gilmour?'

Gilmour glanced up from his kneeling position. 'Aye, I am satisfied,' he answered soberly. 'I have seen the face of the enemy at last.'

'And what d'ye think of it?' the Comptroller asked curiously.

'I find it strange that a man with such a capacity for hating, such uncommon cunning and such tenacity of purpose, should look so – so ordinary,' Gilmour told him. 'I find it hard to believe now that this ordinary little man is the faceless monster that has haunted my thoughts all these past weeks.'

'And this one?' The Comptroller stretched out a foot to prod contemptuously at the body of St Clair stretched out on the grass beside that of Robertson. 'What is your epitaph on him?'

'He was a talented man – but he met the kind of death he deserved,' Gilmour answered briefly, and bent to unfasten the flap of the pouch at Robertson's belt. The seal on the papers inside the pouch was already broken, and glancing quickly through their contents he exclaimed,

'This is it – St Clair's last dispatch!'

Rising to his feet he flicked the papers over in front of the Comptroller. 'Look, it is all there, the plan of campaign, the finances, the lists of supporters' names – even suggested supply lines for the commissariat!'

'St Clair was thorough,' the Comptroller said grimly, 'and a campaign as efficiently organized as this would have been a very different thing from the muddle of the Jacobites' last attempt at rebellion. You have kept your promise well to poor Symonds, Mr Gilmour.'

Gilmour thrust the papers into his pocket. 'I must post to London immediately with these,' he said, and the Comptroller nodded.

'You can be out of Leith in the *Princess Carolina* in an hour if you hurry,' he said. 'I will give you a man to row you over the Nor' Loch and guide you by the quickest route to the docks from its farther shore.'

'And you will take care of matters here?' Gilmour nodded to the bodies of Robertson and St Clair, and the Comptroller answered, 'Leave all that to me and get on your way. The *Carolina*'s Commander is standing ready for you.'

He held out his hand. Gilmour shook it warmly and then turned to Sandy. 'There is just one thing more,' he began, and Sandy said eagerly,

'Yes, sir?'

'I want you, if you will, to give this to Mistress Isobel.' Gilmour drew his signet ring from his finger as he spoke and held it out to Sandy. 'And tell her that I hope soon to replace it with a better, when I return. Will you do that for me, Sandy?'

'Yes, of course, sir, but –' Sandy paused for a moment, then taking his courage in both hands went on boldly, 'But what about me, Mr Gilmour? Have you no word for me?'

'*I* have.' It was the Comptroller who answered for Gilmour, meeting his glance above Sandy's head. 'I want to see you at eight o'clock tomorrow morning, clean and smart, in Mr Wishart's office. I have an engagement with that gentleman to discuss how your legal training can be used to forward the plan Mr Gilmour has left for you to enter his branch of the Customs Service.'

'Sir – I – I do not know how to thank you!' Sandy looked from one to the other, not knowing to whom he should speak first, and with a laugh Gilmour told him,

'Save your thanks, Sandy. You have shown you are well worth a place in the Service. Now help me to push out that boat.'

'Gladly, sir!' Rushing to the water's edge, Sandy steadied the boat while the oarsman and Gilmour climbed aboard. Gilmour's hand rested in a firm, friendly gesture on his shoulder in passing, and as Sandy pushed the boat out, he turned to call,

'I will expect your help on my next case when I return, Sandy.'

'I will be ready for you, sir!' Sandy called his reply over the widening stretch of water, and stood watching the boat vanish into the dimness of the loch's farther shore before he turned to face the city again.

Somewhere in that dark huddle of buildings, he thought, looking up to the High Street, Mistress Isobel would be waiting in the hope of some such token as he carried. And Mr Wishart would be waiting – most impatiently too – to hear the outcome of the night's work!

The thought of Mr Wishart's impatience recalled vividly the morning he had looked from the deed-room window and sighed to loose the law's shackles for a wider, freer life. With wonder then, he thought how marvellously his wish had been gratified, and smiling, he moved to take his rightful place alongside the other Customs men of the Lothian run.